ALSO BY THEA GUANZON

THE HURRICANE WARS SERIES

The Hurricane Wars

A Monsoon Rising

Star Wars: From a Certain Point of View: Return of the Jedi

Tusk Love

Tusk Love

THEA GUANZON

RANDOM HOUSE WORLDS
NEW YORK

Random House Worlds
An imprint of Random House
A division of Penguin Random House LLC
1745 Broadway, New York, NY 10019
randomhousebooks.com
penguinrandomhouse.com

LIBRARY OF CONGRESS CATALOGING-IN-PUBLICATION DATA
Names: Guanzon, Thea, author.
Title: Tusk love / Thea Guanzon.
Description: First edition. | New York: Random House Worlds, 2025.
Identifiers: LCCN 2025008578 (print) | LCCN 2025008579 (ebook) |
ISBN 9780593874264 (hardcover; acid-free paper) |
ISBN 9780593874271 (ebook)
Subjects: LCGFT: Romance fiction. | Fantasy fiction. | Novels.
Classification: LCC PR9550.9.G763 T87 2025 (print) |
LCC PR9550.9.G763 (ebook) | DDC [Fic]—dc23
LC record available at https://lccn.loc.gov/2025008578
LC ebook record available at https://lccn.loc.gov/2025008579

International edition ISBN 978-0-593-98489-5

Printed in the United States of America on acid-free paper

2 4 6 8 9 7 5 3 1

BOOK TEAM: Production editor: Jocelyn Kiker • Managing editor:
Susan Seeman • Production manager: Erin Korenko • Copy editor:
Laura Dragonette • Proofreaders: Debbie Anderson, Emily Cutler,
Julia Henderson

Book design by Alexis Flynn

Adobe Stock illustrations: analgin12 (Guinevere chapter illustration),
paprika (Oskar chapter illustration)

The authorized representative in the EU for product safety and
compliance is Penguin Random House Ireland, Morrison Chambers,
32 Nassau Street, Dublin D02 YH68, Ireland. https://eu-contact.penguin.ie

For Torrey, the good ship Guinskar's strongest soldier,
and Chloe, Ph.D. in Orc Studies

Tusk Love

CHAPTER ONE

Guinevere

The bandits had fallen upon them in the middle of the night, and all the guards were dead.

Guinevere crouched inside the wagon, watching through a hole in the side of the canvas bonnet as the bandits picked through the ruined camp. For some reason, this was the only thought running through her mind—that all the guards were dead. She had not learned any of their names since setting out from Rexxentrum, and now she never would.

There were five of them, which was the most her parents could afford to hire. She'd seen each guard fall to the onslaught of blades and arrows through the same canvas-edged hole, her screams stifled into the mound of her palm. According to her parents, it wasn't proper to converse with the hired help, which was why she hadn't. But she should have known the names of the men who'd died for her.

Didn't they deserve that much, at least?

No point wondering what corpses deserve. The voice in her head was the guttural hiss of newly lit coals crackling to life. Guinevere fought it as hard as she could, but it was like trying to hold back a sneeze. Her eyes watering, she left her bedroll and slowly retreated deeper into the wagon.

"Check inside!" someone barked, most likely the gigantic orc who had led the charge into the clearing and lopped one guard's head clean off his shoulders with an equally gigantic greataxe. "Let's see what we have!"

Guinevere scooted backward over the wooden boards until she could go no farther. She heard the panicked lowing of Bart and Wart and the restless stomping of their hooves on the forest floor as the bandits approached. Her parents' oxen were tethered to the trees beside the wagon, and she hoped with all her heart that the bandits would leave the poor beasts alone. Most likely, though, Bart and Wart were as doomed as she was.

You aren't doomed. Teinidh of the Wailing Embers raked her fiery claws through the scorched recesses of Guinevere's soul. *You have me. Set me free. Let me burn.*

"No," Guinevere whispered. She reached back, her hand resting on the lid of the pearwood trunk that had been so carefully transported over the Amber Road the last few days, along with the supplies for the journey and the wares that her parents would sell once she met them at the port city of Nicodranas.

Fire was uncontrollable; if Teinidh was unleashed, everything would be destroyed. The trunk—its contents—were too precious to risk.

Guinevere tried to calm herself with a series of slow, deep breaths. It was heightened emotion that called the wildfire spirit forth. If she could just tamp down on the fear . . .

The faint moonlight streaming into the wagon was blocked out by a host of figures peering inside. While the leader was an orc— Guinevere spied his hulking frame in the distance, trampling over the campfire that the guards had made to ward off the autumn chill—the rest of the bandits were human, garbed in pilfered, mismatched armor.

One was wearing a helmet, still wet with blood, that Guinevere recognized as having belonged to her guard. She gave an involuntary shudder, and the slight movement drew the men's attention.

"Well, well." One bandit squinted at the flowing, lavishly embroidered hem of Guinevere's white silk nightgown. "If it isn't a *lady,* done up so fine."

"Let's see if she's got any jewelry on her," another bandit eagerly suggested.

She let the men drag her out of the wagon. There were six of them, and their rough hands bruised her arms while she shook like a leaf and tried not to look at the dead guards strewn about the clearing. Teinidh scrabbled at the walls of her mind, insistent, hungry for the kill.

Now, now, now! Until there are only cinders, until the wind scatters them to Tal'Dorei and beyond.

No. Guinevere squeezed her eyes shut. *Please.* She didn't want to destroy the trunk, didn't want to hurt Bart and Wart, didn't want her parents to blame her for making things worse. *I must be braver. I will be braver.*

Yet fear surged within her like the inferno that she was trying so hard to suppress.

The bandits hauled her farther away from the wagon and closer to their leader but stopped when the one wearing the bloodstained helmet noticed the thin silver chain around her neck, glowing in the moonlight.

"Bet this is real silver," he mused as he and the other men surrounded her, flashing identical avaricious grins.

"What's the holdup, Symes?" the orc standing in the remains of the campfire demanded. "Bring her to me!"

"In just a minute, Lashak." Symes's grimy fingers brushed against Guinevere's neck as he gripped the chain. She bit her tongue so as not to cry out in fright. "Want to see what pretty trinket milady brought us."

He gave a none-too-gentle tug, freeing the rest of the necklace from where it had slipped beneath her nightgown's bodice. The bandits had clearly been expecting a valuable gem of some sort; they blinked in consternation at what was dangling from Symes's fist on the fine loops of metal.

It was a tiny sparrow skull, set in a bed of white-speckled brown feathers. Soil from the fire-razed forest where she'd been born had been packed into a hole drilled in the skull's top, from which sprouted a lacy green fern, lashed securely to its miniature container by intricate silver knots.

"Doesn't look like an aristocrat's pendant to me," remarked another bandit, scratching his bearded chin. "Looks more like one of 'em wild mage totems . . ."

They were going to figure out what she was, perhaps as soon as they drew their next breaths. And when they did, they would kill her, because she was too dangerous to keep alive. "*Sometimes I think she's better off dead,*" her father had said once, when he didn't realize Guinevere was within earshot.

Better off dead—but she didn't *want* to die—

Panic combined with Guinevere's fear, swirling and igniting, higher and higher. The dam burst. The bones and feathers of her totem shook. The ashen soil within fed her, fed the power she hadn't asked for, her eyes flashing as the connection to another plane was wrenched open.

The connection that had been forged the day she emerged into the world, red-cheeked and squalling and covered in her mother's water, while the woods her parents were traveling through disintegrated into ash all around them.

Now, twenty years later, in another forest halfway across the continent of Wildemount, Teinidh appeared beside Guinevere, blazing and statuesque, her humanoid body made of intertwined burning branches, eyes like molten craters and hair a crown of flames.

The bandits' jaws dropped, and they hastily began backing away. It was the last thing the six of them did in this life, other than scream as the wildfire spirit swept through their circle in a vicious red-gold blaze. The putrid, sickly sweet odor of charred flesh filled the night air.

By the time it was over, Guinevere swayed unsteadily in the middle of a ring of smoldering bodies blackened beyond recognition. Teinidh was gone, but the conflagration remained. Leaves and underbrush caught on fire, and flames swiftly licked their way toward the surrounding trees.

The bandit leader had been too far away to get caught up in Teinidh's attack. He was *still* far away, rooted to the spot, gawking at Guinevere. She turned and fled—not to safety, but to her parents' flailing oxen. The act of summoning Teinidh had sapped her of strength, but she picked up one of the dead guards' swords and, with what little might she still possessed, brought it down over the ropes that tied Bart and Wart to the already smoking tree trunks.

The two oxen bolted as soon as they were free, no thought left to them but to escape the inferno. As they vanished into the darkness, Guinevere stumbled back to the wagon—the fire hadn't reached it yet; she had to save the trunk—

A meaty fist tangled in her long, loose hair, spinning her around with enough force that she was vaguely surprised her neck didn't snap. With all his subordinates dead, Lashak roared in fury, raising his free hand to strike her. Guinevere's meager courage vanished, and she closed her eyes again, bracing herself for the blow.

But it never came.

When she dared to look, an arrow was sticking out of the bandit leader's spade-sized palm.

The orc seemed as startled as she was. For what felt like ages, the two of them could only stare at the projectile, which had sliced clean through Lashak's hand.

The spell was broken when a deep, resonant, and thoroughly *bored* voice drifted into their ears over the sputter of burning leaves: "Why don't you pick on someone your own size?"

Lashak shoved Guinevere away. She fell to the ground just as a tall, broad-shouldered figure strode into the clearing, and she surveyed him from her half-crumpled position through eyes that were beginning to sting from the acrid smoke.

He wore a travel-stained brown tunic, frayed breeches, and scuffed boots. Moonlight danced through waves of thick jet-black hair, some of which had been gathered into a disheveled topknot while the rest flowed free. A few strands tumbled down from a widow's peak to frame chiseled features put together with rugged elegance, overlaid with skin the dark gray-green of oakmoss. Firelight cast a burnished gloss over sweeping black brows, deep-set eyes the color of molten gold, and the white tusks that bracketed the stern line of his mouth. They weren't as large as Lashak's—not as large as they would have been on a full-blooded orc—but they were sharp.

The new arrival's bow was slung over his back, and he approached Lashak with a curved sword in each gauntleted hand. Despite his humble attire, there was a calm assurance radiating from him that dulled Guinevere's fear. That made her think that maybe, just maybe, she was saved.

Then Lashak snapped off the arrowhead, pulled the rest of the arrow out of his hand, and tossed it aside without even the slightest hint of pain. All seven feet of him faced his opponent fully; he drew his greataxe, which was several times the size of the other man's swords put together, and Guinevere realized with a sickening clench in the pit of her stomach that she wasn't saved at all.

"Someone my own size?" Lashak echoed with a sneer. "Would that be you, then, half-breed?"

The stranger rolled his eyes. "That kind of talk may have been acceptable in whatever provincial backwater you crawled out from, but we're a little more sophisticated here in the Dwendalian Empire."

Guinevere blinked at him. How was he so supremely unrattled? *He isn't even wearing armor.*

Letting out a battle cry that shattered the air, Lashak charged. And, without flinching, the stranger met him halfway.

Guinevere had grown up in a nice stone house in the Shimmer Ward district of Rexxentrum. Her parents were untitled, but they'd spared no expense to raise their only child like a proper lady, commissioning the finest gowns and hiring the best tutors—even long after the money had started running out. Deeply conscious of their sacrifices and desperate to shield herself from their criticisms, Guinevere had applied herself to her lessons with vigor, had never gone anywhere she wasn't supposed to, had made friends only with those of her station or higher, and had never intentionally broken a single rule. The only quirk she permitted herself was clinging to the totem crafted for her by the old hermit of Cyrengreen, and even then Guinevere had carefully replaced the rustic twine with the silver chain five years ago, to make it more fashionable.

Yes, she had lived an orderly, sheltered existence. And now she was down on her knees in the dirt, in her nightgown and her satin slippers, surrounded by dead bodies and a fire she'd caused, witnessing raw violence for the first time in her life.

Initially, she could make neither heads nor tails of the fight. The two foes each did their utmost to kill the other in a frightening blur of limbs and metal, etched in the pulsing scarlet of the ever-growing flames. But the longer she watched, the more the cycle of slashing and dodging and parrying made sense—like some particularly fiendish, complicated waltz—and it dawned on Guinevere that, while Lashak had the advantage in terms of size and strength, the stranger was faster and more agile.

And he was smarter, too. After crossing his swords over his head to block a ringing blow from Lashak's greataxe, he darted out of reach, then made as though to leap to the right. Lashak swung at where he assumed the stranger would land, but it turned out the latter had merely feinted—for he nimbly corrected his course and went *left,* then *behind* his opponent. The curved edges of his swords carved a path from Lashak's shoulder blade to his hip.

The bandit leader collapsed, howling. The stranger loomed over him, a sinister moonlit silhouette with bloodied swords and an impassive expression. His eyes snapped to Guinevere, and they were pools of liquid amber in the glow of the fire . . .

The fire!

She was on her feet before she knew it, the grievously wounded Lashak and the coolly triumphant stranger forgotten. The wagon's canvas bonnet was already ablaze, but she dove inside without a second thought. Gagging on thick clouds of smoke, the agonizing heat a miasma against her skin, she grabbed the satchel that contained the most valuable wares with one hand and the handle of the pearwood trunk with the other, and she shuffled backward out of the burning vehicle on her knees and elbows, slowed down by her dear burdens.

She shrieked as a pair of large hands clamped around her ankles in a viselike grip and yanked her the rest of the way out of the wagon.

No sooner had the stranger deposited her onto solid ground than he told her to run. She complied expediently enough, but she'd barely taken two lumbering steps before he tried to tug the satchel and the trunk out of her hands.

She held on tighter.

"Leave these," he instructed tersely.

Too rattled to speak, Guinevere settled for simply shaking her head.

He looked at her like she had *two* heads.

A fiery branch came crashing down, feeding the conflagration and dissolving into it. The flames rose higher. There was no more time to argue. The stranger wrenched the trunk from Guinevere's grasp and tucked it under his left arm, then he scooped her up, satchel and all, and effortlessly slung her over his right shoulder.

It all happened so fast. She was so shocked that she could do nothing more than cling to the satchel like her life depended on it—could do nothing more than stare at Lashak's prone, twitching form as the stranger set a breakneck pace through the woods, leaving the campsite behind to be swallowed up by smoky veils of red and gold.

CHAPTER TWO

Guinevere

This is so undignified, Guinevere thought as the half-orc warrior carried her through the dark forest like a sack of potatoes.

His steps over the grass were swift and sure. He shouldered his way through the undergrowth as though it weren't there at all. Soon he had put so much distance between them and the fire that she could hardly see it anymore. Not once was there any indication that he was in danger of dropping her or the trunk.

She couldn't help but be awed by his unflagging strength. He slowed his pace only when it began to rain—and she had never been so relieved to feel water on her skin. The fire would be put out. She would not be responsible for destroying an entire forest. And she still had some of the precious wares and the infinitely more precious trunk.

All things considered, it was an extraordinary stroke of good fortune.

THIRTY MINUTES LATER, GUINEVERE WAS utterly convinced that she'd betrayed her country in a previous life and the gods were punishing her in this one.

The rain came down in droves. She was cold and wet, her satin slippers covered in mud. The stranger had set her down once it became clear that the inferno was no longer a concern, and they'd been walking for what felt like an eternity in total silence.

She would have attempted to strike up a conversation—would have thanked him for saving her from the bandits, at the very least—but her teeth were chattering too much. Even if they hadn't been, she lost her nerve every time she glanced at his imposing figure. He veritably towered over her.

"There's a cave up ahead," he suddenly announced, raising his voice to be heard amidst the deluge.

He led her to a small hollow cut in the base of a moss-covered rocky outcrop. Once they were inside, he dropped the trunk, and she immediately sat on it, out of some foolish notion to not dirty her white nightgown any further. She rubbed her freezing hands together for warmth, grateful to be out of the rain.

The stranger peered down at her, his shoulders hunched. He couldn't straighten up fully without banging his head on the cave ceiling. Most of his features were shrouded in darkness, but she had the distinct impression that he was scowling at her.

At a loss for what to say, Guinevere resorted to pleasantries. Her tutors had assured her that discussing the weather always proved reliable in smoothing over any awkwardness.

"It truly is Fessuran, is it not, sir?" she said lightly, finding her voice at last. "Why, I don't believe there's been a shower as brisk as this all year—"

"What the hells are you talking about?" the stranger growled.

"The weather," she persisted, a little helplessly. "The amount of rain and the evening chill, they are very much indicative of the autumn month of Fessuran . . ."

She trailed off when he knelt down and rifled through her satchel.

He appeared to have no difficulty making out its contents in the oppressive gloom of the cave.

A flash of lightning briefly illuminated the stunned disbelief on his face when his gaze swiveled back to her.

"Jewelry." He sounded slightly strangled. "Goblets. Figurines."

Guinevere had no idea why he was reciting the contents of the satchel. "Pardon?"

"I thought there were supplies in here. I thought that was why you didn't want to leave it behind."

"Oh, no, not at all," she said, pleased that they were clarifying a minor misunderstanding between them. "I mean, I definitely couldn't leave the satchel behind, but those aren't supplies. That is inventory."

"Inventory," he repeated in a near whisper.

"Yes. Goods to sell. My parents are merchants, you see, and I'm to meet them at—"

The stranger shot to his feet. There was a sickening crack as the top of his head slammed against the cavern ceiling. He swore loudly, rubbing his scalp.

Guinevere was torn between chiding him for using such language in her presence and checking to make sure that he wasn't bleeding. Before she could do either, he spoke again, this time at a volume that bounced off the rocks.

"You almost burned to a crisp for a handful of brooches?" he bellowed. "I nearly died to save some shitty cups?"

She frowned. "Our merchandise is of superb quality. We do not sell rubbish."

He stared at her for several long moments. Whatever he saw made the fight drain out of him. He lifted his hands in a gesture that called to mind surrender. "You don't travel much, do you?"

"Not as often as I would like," she prevaricated. She'd been born in Cyrengreen and she'd spent the first three years of her life with the merchant caravans, but then her parents had installed her at the house in Rexxentrum, and she hadn't ventured beyond the Shimmer Ward since. However, there was a part of her that didn't want her rescuer to think she was *completely* naïve.

He sighed. "I left my supplies at my own camp when I heard the commotion coming from yours. It's probably all ashes now."

Her heart stopped. He'd lost all his supplies—*she'd burned them down*. Guilt and horror clawed at her, so intense that at first she thought Teinidh was trying to fight her way out again.

But the stranger must not have seen Guinevere unleash the wildfire spirit, or else he would never have bothered to save her, and he wouldn't let himself be stuck in a cave with her now. He would not have wanted to be further exposed to the disaster-in-waiting that she was.

"We need to make a fire," he announced. "A smaller one. To warm up."

She swallowed. "With what kindling?" Miraculously, her voice quavered only slightly.

It wasn't lying, she assured herself. It wasn't even lying by omission. She couldn't control Teinidh's comings and goings.

The stranger gave her another disconcerting stare and then, without saying a word, pointed to the pearwood trunk she was sitting on.

A lady never lost her composure, but panic heightened Guinevere's voice to a fever pitch. "Absolutely not! It's *priceless*!"

She clapped her hands over her mouth. She'd said too much. It sank in how very alone they were in the cave and how she knew next to nothing about this man, not even his name.

A muscle twitched in his chiseled jaw. "I'm nothing like the scum who killed your guards and looted your camp," he said icily, "but I have better things to do with my time than try to convince you of that. Don't worry, miss, I'll take my leave of you as soon as the weather clears."

He stomped over to the entrance of the cave and took up an unmoving position there, his arms crossed and his back turned to her. His posture was rigid with an alertness that made it clear he really was waiting for the rain to stop and would walk off into the night once it did.

Guinevere felt terrible. After he so gallantly saved her life, she'd repaid him by casting aspersions on his character—and based on what? His gruff demeanor, his ragged attire? What did *those* matter when he'd faced down a giant like Lashak even though he hadn't needed to?

She thought about the guards again. They could all have fled and saved themselves when the bandits attacked, but they'd stayed to protect her instead. And she hadn't even bothered to learn their names.

You must always be careful around the have-nots, Guinevere, her father often warned her. *They turn to crime at the drop of a hat. Do not let compassion blind you. A person born in misery perpetuates that misery everywhere they go. There's no overcoming ill breeding.*

She had never vocally disagreed with her father on that account, else he turn the subject to her own failings. But there was no denying that, right now, she felt like the ill-bred one.

Taking a deep breath, she went to her rescuer's side. His profile was like granite against the backdrop of shadow-clad bushes and shimmering rain.

"Sir," she squeaked out, "it wasn't my intention to offend. I was jumpy from the scare I had, but I know you're not like those ruffians." He made no response, and her nerve almost deserted her. But she persevered, because a lady knew when to apologize. "I'm so very sorry. I'm grateful to you for saving me, I promise. I beg your forgiveness for my—my unpleasant disposition. Please don't go. I couldn't bear it if you had to endure the night without shelter on my account."

His honeyed gaze flicked to her, contemplative, measuring. She held her breath.

Then—he grunted. As far as male expressions of sentiment went, it was aloof but conciliatory.

She relaxed. "I'm Guinevere." She offered it shyly, a hatchet to be buried.

Silence.

Complete and utter silence.

He leaned against the cavern wall and said nothing at all.

"This," Guinevere declared a little too stiffly, her cheeks flaming, "is the part where you tell me *your* name."

The stranger took his sweet time studying her, as though she were a puzzle he couldn't figure out. She lifted her chin, forcing herself not to flinch at his scrutiny. The corner of his mouth twitched like he was reluctantly amused by her defiance, one sharp, slender tusk gleaming in the moonlight.

"Oskar," he finally said.

It was the last word he spoke to her for the rest of the evening.

CHAPTER THREE

Oskar

He woke up at the crack of dawn, as was his wont, peeling himself away from the muddy soil at the entrance of the cave with a groan.

As he retrieved his bow and arrows, Oskar glanced over his shoulder, his lips twisting in derision at the sight of the still form curled up by the pearwood trunk. If he knew anything about the upper crust, it would be hours yet before Miss Guinevere bothered to rise.

Although it was understandable that she needed her rest, after what she'd gone through . . .

His sneer faded. It had been an automatic reaction, borne of his general contempt for all the fancy lords and ladies who treated those of his ilk as though they were dirt. He'd assumed Guinevere was no different when she acted like he was going to steal the damn trunk, but then she'd apologized—so timidly yet earnestly—after he'd said those harsh words to her.

Oskar conceded that he could probably be nicer.

He made his way through the morning mist, retracing his steps to the ashen remains of his former campsite. He was pleasantly surprised to find that at least one of his packs had survived the fire. Not the one with the food and waterskins, of course, because that would have been *too* lucky, but his clothes were safe, as was the letter from his mother's clan in Boroftkrah.

Driven by the compulsion to assure himself that it really was in one piece, he carefully took the worn paper out of its envelope and read what he had already committed to memory: a few terse lines in a clumsy scrawl, footnoted by a red wax seal engraved with a snarling panther that was the emblem of Clan Stormfang.

We grieve to hear of Idun's passing. Her son is welcome at our hearth. Come soon. This seal grants you safe passage through the Wildlands.

His mother had been a woman of few words, and it seemed her relatives were no different. But he knew that they were sincere. He was their last link to Idun—and they his.

With a muttered curse, Oskar pinched the bridge of his nose, staving off the sting of oncoming tears. The searing pain of his mother's death had mostly receded to a dull ache over the last few months, but it occasionally snuck up on him, and it always felt like he was realizing for the first time that he would never see her again.

His shoulders squared, and he walled his grief away—slowly, methodically, with the discipline of one who woke at first light every morning.

Oskar had gone straight to his shift at the blacksmith's after burying his mother, else the unreasonable man cut him loose. He didn't have the luxury to mourn. Not then, and certainly not now.

There was a problem that he needed to deal with.

THE PROBLEM WAS STILL ASLEEP when Oskar returned with breakfast, the sun high in the sky.

Indeed, Guinevere did not wake until the rabbit was crisp and golden on the spit that Oskar had rigged up over a fire constructed with dry leaves from the cave floor, branches relatively dry despite last night's rain, his tinderbox, and a whole lot of prayer.

Head bent over the task of turning the spit, he heard rather than saw her daintily step out of the cave, only the most fragile twigs snapping beneath her ridiculously impractical satin slippers.

"Good morning," she called out, in that polite, melodious voice of hers that was as pure as a glass bell. "Something smells positively delicious—*in the name of the six approved gods!*"

Oskar looked up.

He hadn't let Guinevere's physical attributes sink in the previous evening, as preoccupied as he'd been with keeping her alive. But he was paying attention now. She was a short woman, with clear skin as lustrous as copper. Her thick hair wasn't merely blond; it was so pale as to be almost the color of moonlight, stylishly chopped strands of it covering most of her forehead while the rest spilled down to her waist in a silvery cascade. Her eyes were too big for her heart-shaped face, their crystalline color an arresting shade of violet.

She was beautiful, in that otherworldly, untouchable kind of way that sent musicians and poets into paroxysms of delight. Which made what Oskar saw from the neck down even more jarring.

In all honesty, what *couldn't* he see? Not even the mud and soot staining her long-sleeved, ankle-length nightgown could detract from the fact that it was still somewhat damp and far too thin, clinging to every curve of her lush body.

The combination of ethereal beauty and earthy sensuality was too much for Oskar. It was like someone had conked him over the head with an anvil. Thus, it took him an embarrassingly long while to realize that Guinevere was staring at the skinned, dressed carcass on the spit with alarm.

"What *is* that?" she whispered.

He followed her line of sight. It was several beats before he could remember what the animal was called.

"Rabbit," he grunted.

He doused the fire and helped himself, giving the meat scarce opportunity to cool before slicing into it with his dagger. The gamy flesh burnt his tongue, but chewing it gave him something to do that wasn't ogling his accidental companion.

Guinevere sat across from him—decorously, her knees tucked together and her legs to the side. She looked like she was about to faint, and it prickled his curiosity. "Haven't you ever had rabbit before?"

"I—I have," she stammered. "Stews, terrines . . ."

In porcelain dishes, he silently filled in, *with jeweled forks, on linen-clothed tables decorated with fresh flowers. Maybe the butter's carved into the shape of a swan—or is that too gauche?* At any rate, Miss Guinevere had certainly never eaten freshly slaughtered rabbit from a crude spit while sitting on the forest floor with a blacksmith's apprentice who was actually little more than a glorified chimney sweep.

Oskar's thoughts came racing in fast and soured his mood, which had not been that cheery to begin with. He hacked off a generous portion of the roast, telling himself that he wasn't selecting the tenderest part of the animal on purpose, and handed it to her with an air of challenge. She glanced around surreptitiously, and he knew, he just *knew,* that if she asked him where he'd washed his hands before eating, he was going to snap at her . . .

Guinevere straightened her spine and took the chunk of rabbit saddle from him. Her expression couldn't have been more determined if she were marching into battle, and he suddenly felt more like laughing than snapping.

"Thank you, Oskar."

She said it so prettily. Pretty, too, was the way she ate—in small bites, like a proper lady at a fancy banquet, rather than the bedraggled survivor of a bandit raid gnawing game off a stick on the forest floor. Her bow-shaped lips pursed delicately around each tiny morsel of flesh, her pink tongue darting out to lick glistening juices from her fingertips.

Oskar stared and stared, then cursed himself and scowled.

CHAPTER FOUR

Guinevere

The rabbit was lean and somewhat tough, but Guinevere was too famished to care. She asked for more, which Oskar obligingly gave.

Once the edge had been taken off her hunger at some point around her third helping, the awfulness of her situation began to set in. She was three weeks away from Nicodranas, without her guards, without a wagon, without the oxen. Her parents were going to wring her neck.

Such a disappointment, Guinevere, she imagined her mother saying. *I knew you couldn't handle something even as simple as this.*

I can't believe you lost Bart and Wart, her father would moan. *They were like the children I never had.*

And the horrible thing was that it wasn't even the bandits' fault that the oxen and the wagon were gone. Guinevere had been the one to manifest Teinidh, because she'd been so afraid that she'd failed to keep a level head.

We should never have listened to that batty old hermit, lamented the imaginary version of her mother. *I should have tossed that terrible amulet straightaway!* The imaginary version of her father nodded along, although with less rancor because he wasn't the one who'd had to pop out a baby in the middle of an inferno.

"Where is it that you're supposed to meet your parents?" Oskar asked abruptly. Guinevere told him, and he arched a brow. "The Menagerie Coast is a long walk from here."

"I'd not planned on walking." Misery leached into her every word. "I had an escort, as well as a conveyance."

Gods, this predicament was dire. She had to keep it together, though. It would be most improper to fall to pieces with Oskar sitting across from her. He was so impassive and stern . . . and last night he'd dispatched that giant orc without breaking a sweat, and he'd carried her and the trunk effortlessly through the woods . . . and he'd even rustled up some breakfast . . .

An idea struck.

"Oskar," she said, with a slow-blossoming hope, "I don't suppose that *you* could escort me?" His features hardened, but in this instance, desperation overcame her natural timidity. "Once we reach Nicodranas, Father will see to it that you're adequately compensated for your trouble—"

"I cannot accompany you south," he interrupted. "I'm headed north. To Boroftkrah."

"Oh. I see."

It could not be overstated how hard Guinevere struggled not to burst into tears in front of a man she'd met only the previous night. But despair rose from the bottom of her stomach and filled her chest and tangled in her throat. What was she going to do? She didn't even know the way out of these woods. Her eyes grew moist and, mortified, she tried to rein it in, her bottom lip quivering.

Oskar's sharp jaw clenched. "However, I will take you to Druvenlode." He couldn't *quite* conceal his annoyance at this disruption in his schedule, which made matters worse. "It's the nearest settlement. If we start walking now, we can get there before dusk—damn it, Guinevere, stop crying."

"Druvenlode is still south, though!" she wailed, wringing her hands. "I'll be t-taking you out of your w-way!"

"It's no trouble," he said curtly. "I live there, and I need to restock what was destroyed in the blaze."

At this blunt reminder that the supplies for his own journey had also gone up in flames, thanks to her, Guinevere cried even harder. Memories of last night's events swept through her like a wave, jumbled yet relentless, dragging her into a deep and tumultuous ocean of belated terror that was no place for a girl who could call the wildfire.

A heavy hand fell on the round of her shoulder. Oskar was crouched beside her, doling out awkward pats as she sobbed. He was so strong and broad, her unlikely rescuer, and she was overcome by a fierce longing to throw herself into his arms, to draw comfort from his warmth. But years of etiquette lessons and cutting corrections stopped her. They'd only just met. He was neither a relative nor her betrothed. She was wearing a nightgown, for crying out loud. It wasn't proper. There were rules. Those bandits certainly hadn't lived by the rules, and Guinevere wasn't going to let them drag her down with them.

So she just stayed still and kept weeping.

"You're safe now. That's what matters." Oskar's tone was surly and ill at ease, but the words . . . somehow, the words were what she needed to hear. She clutched at them like they were lifelines. "It was unfair, what happened, but you made it through admirably. None of it was your fault. You're all right now. You survived."

Not your fault.

She had never heard that before.

Guinevere got her last few tears out of the way, then smiled at Oskar softly. He tensed and withdrew from her, shooting to his feet.

"Let's get going," he muttered.

He lent her a tunic from his surviving pack. It was most scandalous to wear a strange man's clothes, but anything was better than her muddy, too-thin nightgown. She retreated into the privacy of the cave to change, discarding the ruined white garment with a sigh of relief.

Oskar's tunic was spun from coarse, sandstone-hued hemp. It was the roughest fabric that Guinevere had ever felt against her skin. The hem fell almost to her knees, and the cuffs dangled so far past her wrists that she had to roll the sleeves up to her elbows, but the tunic was clean and dry and did not smell overly much of smoke. It was a vast improvement.

She slung the satchel over one shoulder and dragged the trunk out of the cave by its ornate handle. She was almost brought up short by the sight of Oskar slouched carelessly against a tree while he waited for her. He was tall and imposing in the dappled morning light, his skin a sylvan commingling of golden sunbeams and oakmoss shadows, the threadbare tunic clinging to his solid chest. His wavy hair was a black halo around his terse face and was pulled back enough for her to glimpse the points of his ears. His strong jaw protruded slightly, making space for those white tusks that sliced upward like crescents.

He looked dangerous. Like he belonged to this wilderness that had bested her. And yet the thrill that fluttered through the pit of her stomach laid no claim to any part of the inhospitable territory that was fear.

What was it, then?

Before Guinevere could examine her odd reaction to him, Oskar's tawny gaze fell on the trunk, and a long-suffering expression darkened his features. He went over to her and tucked it under his arm the way he had last night.

"I can haul it along," Guinevere protested, not wanting him to expend any more effort on her account.

He cast a dismissive glance over her petite frame. "Trust me, it'll be faster this way."

He stomped off, leaving her no choice but to follow.

They hiked west for several minutes, over gnarled roots and black earth, through bramble and birdsong, stewing in that awkward what-did-I-do-wrong-*now* silence that Guinevere was quickly coming to associate with her rescuer. Eventually the dense curtain of red-and-brown trees parted, revealing the Amber Road—the Dwendalian Empire's main thoroughfare, a wide and dusty path that snaked all the way from Rexxentrum to the Wuyun Gates.

It was a clear day. Beneath a deep blue sky, Guinevere spotted the towering, autumn-rusted peaks of the Silberquel Ridge in the distance; chiseled into its base was the collection of streets and rooftops that made up the mining city of Druvenlode. The Amber Road veered left of the Silberquel, spilling on into forever. Something about all the open space gave off a sense of endless possibility, and the back of Guinevere's neck prickled with excitement despite herself.

She was on an *adventure*. She would go to interesting places and meet interesting people. All she had to do was follow the road, and it would lead her to new experiences beyond her staid, elegant life in the Shimmer Ward . . .

"Quit dawdling!" Oskar called without looking back. He was several feet ahead of her.

Guinevere stuck her tongue out at him in an uncharacteristic burst of churlish mutiny, then hurried to match his pace.

CHAPTER FIVE

Oskar

"You're from Rexxentrum, aren't you?"

Oskar had not meant to strike up a conversation. He took after his mother in that he could happily go days without speaking to other people, least of all silly high-society ladies traipsing about in his tunic—practically swimming in it, all rumpled and slim-legged and wide-eyed, stirring in him a strange protectiveness that set off alarm bells in his head. The less he interacted with Guinevere, the better.

And yet his question stretched between them as they walked side by side on the Amber Road.

"I am," she admitted. "How did you know?"

"It's obvious." She had the shine of the capital about her. And he could leave it at that—he really *should* leave it at that.

"And how does the rest of Wildemount compare so far?" he persisted. Damn it. "Ruffians notwithstanding."

He expected her to complain about the bad roads, the poor fare, and the lack of amenities in the small villages on the wayside. The life of a traveler was hard compared to what she was used to, and he wouldn't hold it against her. Probably.

"It's certainly no spa day at the Silvered Sunset Oasis," Guinevere mused, "but, before the bandits came, I was rather enjoying it, actually." Her softly rounded cheeks flushed at the dubious glance Oskar tossed her way. "Camping in the forest, the open space, no lessons, going *everywhere* . . . It's all so new to me. After my parents moved me to Rexxentrum, I wasn't allowed to set foot outside the walls of the Shimmer Ward."

"No hobnobbing with the commoners?" Oskar drawled with a sardonic smile. The palpable guilt in her lack of response spiked his temper a little, and he changed the subject. "Where did your parents move you from?" *Incidentally, why do I even care?*

Guinevere's lilac eyes strayed to her muddy shoes. "Around." Her lithe copper-skinned fingers traced the silver chain where it dangled from her neck and disappeared into the collar of her tunic. His tunic. "They ply their trade everywhere, with the caravans. I was born in . . . in those woods south of Deastok."

"Cyrengreen," Oskar said meditatively. Even just uttering the name sparked something in his veins—an uneasiness. A certain resonating wildness. "I've been there a few times. Not at all like other forests in Wildemount. Creepier."

She didn't say anything. He should take a cue from her and shut up now.

"What sort of lessons?" Oskar prodded. In the name of all the hells—why was he keeping this chatter going? It was her fault. All those tentative, glass bell–punctuated pauses, the melancholy expression on that beautiful face. He wanted to unwrap the enigmatic layers until he got to the very heart of her.

"Er, needlework, music, etiquette, some painting, a bit of household maths . . ." Her blush deepened. "Nothing that would be useful out here, I'm sure."

Oskar now had enough information to form a picture of Guinevere's parents. It was far from flattering but woefully standard everywhere in the Dwendalian Empire. The merchant class in these modern times, despite attaining a level of wealth that few could even dream of, still keenly felt the sting of their inglorious beginnings, their egos dragged down by the yoke of the label *new rich* that trailed after them from one gilded drawing room to the next. So they raised their sons and daughters as aristocrats in the hopes of establishing what they thought a dynasty should be.

It was a load of nonsense.

Oskar brooded quietly for so long—for so many steps on the tree-lined, sweeping dirt road—that Guinevere turned the conversational tables on him. "Oskar? Why are you going to Boroftkrah?"

"To visit my mother's clan."

"How wonderful!" she chirped. Social graces, so fine and merry, wrapped around him like a serpent's coils, constricting his chest. "Does your mother live in Druvenlode as well? Will you introduce me? I should surely love to thank her for raising a chivalrous son who lent me aid when I needed it most."

He couldn't bear to say it. Not again. He'd already told the black-smith, the neighbors, the debt collectors, the undertaker. If he had to say out loud one more time that Idun was gone, it would be in a roar. His fury would swallow the world.

"You should concentrate on your supplies checklist instead." He changed the subject with a mild but implacable tone. He gestured at the satchel. "It should be easy enough to barter those trinkets of yours for rations—"

"But—"

"A medicine bag—"

"I can't just—"

"A length of rope—what is it with people never thinking they'll need rope—"

"The goods aren't mine to do with as I please!" Guinevere burst out. "I told you, they're for my parents to sell! I already left so much inventory behind with the wagon. The losses will be staggering. My father . . ." She fell silent, her shoulders slumped as though even this fleeting defiance had exhausted her.

Oskar was reminded, absurdly, of a hedgehog. Tiny and balled up in self-defense, with the odd pinprick of spine here and there. He scoffed. "Be that as it may, your folks aren't going to prioritize a bag of hairpins over their daughter's well-being."

She hesitated, her small fists clenching at her sides. As though she were unsure of her place in the hearts of those who were supposed to love her.

In that moment, Oskar saw red. No child raised by a caring parent would react the way she had. "Guinevere, you will barter as many goods as you must for the supplies that you need," he ordered. "If your father raises a stink about it, you have my permission to—to thump him."

"*Thump him?*" she repeated, scandalized beyond measure. He was glad that he hadn't gone with his original choice of words, which had been *beat him to a pulp*. She looked ready to faint. "Well, I never!"

"You can ever," he retorted.

Her mouth opened and closed like a fish out of water. Then she startled him by walking briskly ahead, leaving him in the dust.

He suppressed a reluctant grin. The hedgehog had claws, after all.

CHAPTER SIX

Guinevere

Druvenlode had been constructed in response to the rich Silberquel mines; it hugged their entrances in a rough crescent, a gray city carved into the surrounding rock, honeycombed by splotches of yawning darkness that led to the vast tunnels snaking beneath the ridge. Oil lanterns burned valiantly through the steam and coal dust that thickened the purple-hued drape of twilight, and horse-drawn carts laden with silver ore rattled the winding streets. Throngs of people went about their business loudly and at a frantic pace, in a hurry to wrap up the day's tasks and go home.

Guinevere couldn't help but gawk everywhere she turned. It was all so different from the neatness and carefully ordered elegance of the Shimmer Ward. She craned her neck for a better view of every food stall that she and Oskar passed, perusing their offerings of ham sandwiches and buttered waffles and meat skewers and cups of peas in cream. She wandered closer to inspect each billowing forge and sunken quarry. She cooed at every horse trotting by.

Oskar eventually clamped a hand around her upper arm. "Stop walking in circles," he muttered, tugging her deeper into the bowels of the city.

Soon they entered what Guinevere's tutors would have delicately called "a rough neighborhood." There were fewer lanterns, golden light so wan that it looked almost sickly as it fell on decidedly shabbier buildings and piles of refuse. The constant hammering from the nearby mines seemed louder—or perhaps there was less activity to drown it out. The people in this area of Druvenlode weren't shopping or working; they slunk into alleyways, huddled in groups on street corners passing around flasks, watched from glassless windows.

They watched *her.*

Oskar had thrown a cloak over Guinevere once the evening chill began to set in over the Amber Road. Now she clutched it tightly around herself, conscious of her bare legs beneath. The stares aimed her way ranged from perplexed to calculating, and it was all she could do to hold her head high and ignore them.

"Oskar," she whispered, "where are we going?"

He stiffened at the nervous tremor in her voice. "My house. It's fine, no one will bother you as long as you're with me."

"Why are we going to your house?"

"To eat and rest," he said shortly. "It's too late to shop, so we'll do that tomorrow morning."

"*Oskar.*" She was so shocked that she forgot her manners enough to pinch his arm. "I'm sorry, but I can't stay at your house."

He blinked. "Why not?"

"It's not proper!"

A man ambling past them in the opposite direction chose that moment to spit out his chewing tobacco. The wet black glob landed at Guinevere's feet, and she nearly twisted her ankle to avoid stepping on it.

Oskar shot her a wry glance. "As you can see, propriety is not foremost on the mind here in the Dustbellows."

"Well, it's foremost on *my* mind," she replied with a sniff. "Unless ... does your mother live with you?" It would be better than nothing, as far as chaperones went.

He hesitated a beat too long before shaking his head.

"Then—I really can't," Guinevere insisted. "Please take me to an inn. You may fetch me there in the morning."

They'd already spent one night together with nobody else around, back in the cave, and she'd traveled the whole day with him, wearing his clothes. She didn't know why she'd selected now, of all times, to cling this stubbornly to the rules of her world.

Perhaps because this town was so foreign. She felt unmoored. She would have taken any anchor.

"You don't have a coin to your name," Oskar reminded her. "How are you going to pay for a room?"

"I'll barter, as you've said." Guinevere sounded more confident than she actually felt. But she figured that she could reimburse her parents with the generous allowance that she was soon to receive. She just had to make it to Nicodranas with the trunk. The rest would come later.

Oskar blew out an exasperated puff of breath. "All right." He turned around, back the way they came, taking her with him. "We'll find somewhere for you in the Silverstreet district."

"It's a nicer part of town?"

He rolled his eyes. "Folks here in the Dustbellows—their bark is worse than their bite. But Silverstreet is less likely to offend milady's sensibilities."

THE SILVERSTREET INNKEEPER BEHIND THE reception desk threw back his head and let out guffaw after roaring guffaw. Guinevere had never felt more humiliated in her entire life.

He was big-boned and middle-aged, with a rotund belly that shook like pudding from the sheer force of his humor. She lifted her chin defiantly, knuckles clenched to white around the golden comb that she'd offered in payment for a room.

"Lass," he said, wiping tears of mirth from his eyes, "what am I supposed to do with a comb?" He ran a hand over his shiny scalp. "I'm as bald as a badger's arse over here."

Guinevere flinched at the crude idiom. "I also have some cups—" she started to plead, but he waved her away impatiently.

"I only take coin, even from pretty faces such as yourself. Off with you if you don't have any."

Defeated and more than mildly vexed, Guinevere marched back to Oskar, who was leaning against the stone mantelpiece with his arms crossed, the pearwood trunk safely shoved behind him. At first, he'd observed her pitiful attempt at negotiation with bemused interest, but at some point he'd devoted himself to casting a baleful glare around the room at large.

She looked around, puzzled. Only then did it sink in that the crowded lobby had grown somewhat quieter since she and Oskar arrived. The patrons who weren't openly staring at her were sneaking covert glances as they ate supper and played cards and puffed on pipes and nursed tankards of ale.

As soon as each one of them noticed the dour and hulking specter beside her, though, they couldn't return to what they were doing fast enough.

Once the inn had resumed its previous level of noise and activity, Oskar turned his full attention to Guinevere. "I thought you'd be better at bargaining," he remarked. "Being a merchant's daughter and all."

"Oh, stop it," she groused. "Now what am I going to do?"

He drew the hood of the cloak over her head with stern finality. Then he nodded to himself, as though satisfied, before answering her question. "Short of sleeping on the street, I'm afraid you'll have to take me up on my offer."

Guinevere was frustrated, embarrassed, and exhausted, and her feet hurt something awful. She couldn't think clearly enough to guard her next words. "The gentlemanly thing to do would be to put me up at this inn for the night."

All trace of amusement fled from Oskar's demeanor. "I'm not a gentleman."

"It's not much for a room, only a gold piece," she said wildly. Rules, she had to follow the rules; if it ever came to light that she'd slept in a strange man's house, her parents would die of shame, and Lord Wensleydale would—

She realized too late that her desperation had made her sound petulant. And that she'd made a terrible mistake.

Oskar's golden eyes had turned hard and sharp. No longer soft honey, but unforgiving, crystalline topaz. His oakmoss-hued features shuttered, and the craggy lines of his powerful shoulders went tense.

"I can't afford it, Guinevere."

A blunt statement of a simple fact, given in a cold voice stiff with desolate pride.

And how could it be that someone's pride could humble her like this? She hadn't been thinking. She was used to having money. Business had started going bad only two years ago, and her parents had shielded her from the worst of it. To her, a gold piece was nothing. She had not stopped to consider how that wouldn't be the case for everyone else.

Flooded with shame, Guinevere hung her head. "I'm so s—"

Before she could finish apologizing, Oskar grabbed the trunk. He tucked it under his arm again, the same way he'd been carrying it around all day. For *her*, even though she didn't deserve it.

"Let's go," he said crisply. "I'm tired."

She trailed behind him, out of the inn and down Druvenlode's stone-paved labyrinth of dark streets. The Silberquel mines did not cease their operations at night; the cacophony of hundreds of rumbling trolleys and pickaxes was a ceaseless aural wallpaper. Every once in a while, the shadowy mountains groaned as though in protest.

Oskar kept his distance from Guinevere. He wore night like a cloak around him, the pulsing glow from the streetlamps flickering over the plane of his broad back. They had reentered the Dustbellows by the time she mustered what little courage she had and bridged the space between them, her hand reaching out in front of her, fingers latching into the folds of his sleeve. She couldn't bring herself to say anything, her throat clogged with apologies that would never be enough, so she just held on and refused to let go.

He didn't look back or slow his pace, but at least he didn't shrug off her grip. That was something. Perhaps it was even enough.

I will stop being spoiled, Guinevere vowed fiercely to herself. *I will learn people's names. I will eat rabbit and be thankful.*

I will be better.

CHAPTER SEVEN

Oskar

His house was one of fifty carved into a singular massive slab of the Silberquel, grouped in vertical layers that were connected, tenement style, by a crude staircase that had also been chiseled out of the rock.

It was very near the mines. Oskar hadn't realized just *how* near until he set out on the Amber Road and found sleep almost impossible in the silence of the forest, with no constant hammering of pickaxes or churning of stone in the background.

The one-room affair that he called home was located on the ground floor of the tenement. He fit a key he hadn't expected to use again anytime soon into the lock on the creaky wooden door, and then he was leading Guinevere inside, setting matches to the tallow candles in the tin holders on the lone table.

As the stale air filled with the sour smell of burning animal fat and the interior was cast in a sickly yellow glow, Oskar tried not to think about how it would appear through Guinevere's eyes. He wouldn't give her the satisfaction. It had suited him and his mother well enough. There were two pallet beds, each one partitioned off with makeshift curtains for the sake of privacy. The stone floor had seen better days, but it had always been meticulously swept clean of the soot from the forges that tended to drift in through the window. He'd emptied out the cupboards before he left, but, prior to that, there had always been at least a wedge of cheese and some onions, and even as a boy he'd gladly helped his mother out by warming these over the bakestone in the shabby but well-maintained hearth.

It wasn't a palace, but neither was it total squalor. He could be proud of the life his mother had eked out for him. And if Miss Guinevere said *anything* about it—

Her stomach grumbled. She clapped her hands over the offending body part and stared up at him with a stricken expression on her face, her eyes so wide that a flicker of reluctant mirth tugged at him.

"Make yourself comfortable," he told her. "I'll go find us something to eat."

Oskar went to the house directly above his, calling in the favor the inhabitants owed him for fixing their rickety wooden shutters a week ago, and he came back down with a warmed loaf of bread made from black ale and rye seed, as well as a jug of sour wine.

His little guest had set the table while he was gone, using some of the much-vaunted merchandise from her satchel. The tallow candles and the house's grand collection of two chipped earthenware plates and a plethora of mismatched utensils had been carefully arranged on top of a red silk cloth trimmed in gold brocade, joined by two engraved silver cups. There were linen napkins on top of the plates, emerald green and folded into the shape of four-leaf clovers.

Guinevere beamed at him from across her handiwork, her violet eyes sparkling. Her hair was spun starlight even in the dull glow of the cheap candles. Her smile shone, and not just because her teeth were small and straight and perfectly white against her copper skin; there was an incandescent happiness to it. The simple pride in a job well done.

Oskar was severely unamused by the way his breath caught in his chest. He stomped forward and plunked their meager repast on the table. The irony of all the accoutrements costing more than the meal thousands of times over was not lost on him.

"Let me serve you!" Guinevere chirped after they'd sat down.

He leaned back in his chair, arms crossed, and watched as she poured the vinegary swill into the silver cups. Then she took a knife and valiantly sawed at the hard loaf, her brow wrinkled in concentration. Crumbs spattered all over the silk tablecloth, and he waited for her to complain.

But she didn't. "I was ever so surprised that I still remember how to fold the napkins like this," she said gaily. "Mother prefers the royal drape, but I think the clover pleat is much more charming."

Oskar had no idea what in all the hells she was talking about. "It's very nice," he mumbled.

He hadn't thought it possible for her smile to grow even more radiant, but now it fair outshone Catha when the brighter of Exandria's two moons was hanging full. She really was too pretty for her own good. He scowled at her, and it felt like self-defense.

Guinevere plunked generous wedges of bread onto both their plates. Then she broke a piece off her crudely chopped portion, popped it into her mouth, and chewed.

And chewed, and chewed.

Oskar took pity on her. "You have to dip it into the wine," he explained. "To soften it."

She blinked but didn't say anything. Of course she wouldn't. In her world, it wasn't proper to talk when one's mouth was full.

"You can spit it out and try again," Oskar said gallantly, pushing her cup of wine closer to her elbow. "It's poor manners, but you won't hear a peep from me."

Guinevere shook her head frantically, cheeks bulging, jaw working in overtime. It was so . . . *adorable*. Damn it.

"Cat got your tongue?" He couldn't resist teasing her. "Or is the bread really that good?" She shot him a pleading look that lightened his heart. "Must be the pinch of sawdust. It's my neighbor's ancient family recipe."

Guinevere squeaked. Chewed with more vigor. And, at last, managed to choke down the bread. "Oskar!" She fought back a mortified laugh. "You're—you're the worst!"

"I try." He felt it then, the crinkling at the corners of his eyes that indicated he was in danger of flashing her a smile of his own.

Oskar of Clan Stormfang did *not* smile. He hurried through the rest of his meal, then excused himself to draw water for a bath that Guinevere would probably appreciate. In all honesty, though, it was more an excuse to do something *but* stay at that cozy table, enjoying himself for the first time since his mother died. With a girl who would be out of his life forever by tomorrow afternoon.

For Oskar, the odd feeling started when Guinevere emerged from the tiny washroom smelling like tangerines and sugar cubes, spiked with a hint of magnolia. He recognized the scent instantly: a perfumed oil that his mother had brought over from Boroftkrah in her girlhood and had used only once or twice since. Distilled from a flower called the Snow Queen's Tears, which bloomed only on the Rime Plains and only during the short-lived months of the northern summer, it was the most luxurious item in the house, and Idun had wanted to make it last. Oskar had lifted the flask to his nose several times over the years, savoring the delicate fragrance, and he could just imagine Guinevere dribbling it into the bathwater he'd heated for her, blissfully ignorant of its sentimental value, taking it as her due because of *course* a bath had to have perfumed oil mixed in.

But it wasn't that she'd used it—he didn't begrudge her that. It was that his mother would never use it again.

The familiar ache behind his eyes twitched to life while he performed his own ablutions. When he left the washroom, it was with a clogged throat at the sight of Guinevere drying her hair by the fireplace. He'd lent her another tunic, and she was on her knees on the floor, running a comb through snarls of liquid silver. She flashed him a gentle smile, lit softly by golden flames, and a different kind of ache gathered in his chest.

"Oskar," she said, and it was strange how such a low, sweet voice could ask a question that sent the world crashing down all around him, "there's two of everything in the house . . . Your mother must have lived with you until recently. Didn't she?"

"Until recently. Not anymore," he replied, his tone laced with terse, dark warning.

Guinevere unfortunately didn't pick up on it. "Where is she now, then?" she asked brightly.

Oskar hung his wet towel over the rack beside the hearth with a viciousness that sent water droplets flying. There was no running from it anymore. He had to say it. Say it again.

"She's in the paupers' cemetery west of the Dustbellows. It was a mining accident. A tunnel collapsed." He'd hoped he could get through it calmly, but it wasn't long before his every word quivered with anger and resentment. It wasn't Guinevere's fault, but he resented her anyway, in that aimless manner of fire with nowhere to spread but everywhere. "The other miners dug her out and brought her to the healing house. She hung on until I got there. Long enough to make her last request—that I visit her clan in Boroftkrah."

I always wanted to take you, Idun had labored to whisper, her face graying against the pillow, the light leaving her eyes. *But there was never any time. There was always too much work to do. Promise me you'll go, even just once. Let them see you, this good thing that came out of my life. Let them know that I was happy—that someone loved me, so far from home.*

Oskar thought that Guinevere might have dropped the comb at some point, but he couldn't be sure because her petite form was suddenly blurry in his vision. Hells. This was the absolute last thing he needed right now, to be weeping like a child in front of this hoity-toity stranger from the capital. He retreated to the corner of the house that held his bed, tugging the curtains shut around it and sitting heavily on the edge of the mattress. He took one deep, heaving breath after another, willing the tears not to come.

He lost this battle quite dramatically. There was a rustling of cheap fabric as the bed curtains were drawn aside, and then Guinevere was sitting next to him.

"I'm sorry," she murmured. "I shouldn't have pried. Oh, Oskar, I can't even imagine . . . I'm so sorry."

And she wrapped her slim arms around his neck in the most gentle embrace he had ever known, and he was doomed. A sound caught halfway between a groan and a sob rattled out of his throat, and tears were pouring down his cheeks, clumsy and bitter, yet oddly freeing. How could he not have cried—*truly* cried—for Idun until now? It was exactly as terrible as he feared it would be, this ransacking of his defenses, but somehow it also *wasn't*. Guinevere dulled the sting with her warmth and her softness, with the surprisingly fierce way she held him, as though she were keeping the pieces of him together, tiny thing that she was.

They sank down until she was flat on her back and his face was hidden in the crook of her neck. She was all fragrant locks and soft skin scrubbed clean, smelling like flowers and citrus, like a fleeting dream of summer on the tundra. He fucking *inhaled* her. She was a lifeline in the sea of his grief, her burnished fingers tentatively carding through his hair in soothing strokes.

And what was grief, but a memory of love? He'd run from that horrible last day for so long that he'd forgotten all the good ones that came before.

Oskar wept into Guinevere's neck until exhaustion finally claimed him. And when the darkness fell, it fell like the funeral shroud over his mother's form, and it felt like goodbye, and also like grace.

CHAPTER EIGHT

Guinevere

She hadn't planned on sleeping in Oskar's bed. She'd waited until he stilled, his breath evening out, and then she'd tried to wriggle out from under him.

But he'd grabbed her at the last minute, with an insensate rumble of protest. He'd pulled her back against him, her spine tucked into the curve of his strong body, his arms clasped firmly around her waist.

It had been so very comfortable. She couldn't have moved if she'd tried. So she'd drifted off . . .

Guinevere woke first. The once roaring fire had subsided to faint embers, and the house's dingy interior was streaked with waxen rays of daylight that served to bring its shabbiness into sharper relief. The mattress was thin and scratchy, its springs digging into her hip and elbow.

Yet she'd never slept so well, or felt so drowsily content. It had to do with the man in the bed with her, her battle-hardened savior with a heart of gold, a man who had loved his mother. How could she have ever considered him terrifying?

The impropriety of their current position was not lost on Guinevere. But somehow she was in no hurry to extricate herself from it. She felt protective. She felt protected.

She reveled in it.

However, there was quite a lot to do today.

At some point during the night, Guinevere had resolved to be a useful and capable person who wouldn't inconvenience Oskar any more than she already had. To her mind, this involved preparing for her great journey while he slept in, so that they could part ways on the most amicable of terms. She would take his advice and barter and set off for Nicodranas in suitable condition, and he could continue on to Boroftkrah with a clear conscience.

It was a fine plan, yet she was loath to leave the circle of his arms in that snug little bed. Her parents hadn't hugged her much while she was growing up, afraid of the wildfire she couldn't control, but it was so nice to be held—especially by someone handsome and warm and strong and kind—and she shamefully wanted it to last as long as possible.

Eventually, though, she managed to scrounge up the will to clamber out of bed. Oskar didn't stop her this time, so deep asleep was he. Guinevere pulled on yesterday's borrowed cloak over the tunic he'd lent her after her bath, then allowed herself a moment to cringe as she stepped into her dirt-encrusted satin slippers. Finding a good pair of walking boots was definitely on the agenda today.

Guinevere beat the breadcrumbs off the tablecloth and the napkins, then rinsed the leftover wine out of the silver cups. She carefully packed everything back into the satchel and slung it over her shoulder, sparing one last glance at Oskar's slumbering form before she left the house. He hadn't moved at all, still curled up on his side, unruly locks of dark hair tumbling across his brow. His chiseled features were much softer in his repose.

He looked almost boyish. The sight caught at Guinevere's heart, but she very determinedly turned and left before she could linger on it.

THE DUSTBELLOWS WERE FAR GRIMIER in the bright morning sun than the previous evening's shadows had led Guinevere to believe. But what was it that Oskar had said about the folks here? *Their bark is worse than their bite.* So she held her head high as she marched away from the tenements at a briskly resolute pace . . . one that faltered a few seconds later when she realized that she had absolutely no idea where she was going.

But a little thing like that wouldn't stop someone who was useful and capable. A red-haired elf darted out of the alley Guinevere was passing by, and, drawing on her newfound sense of resourcefulness, she reached out and tugged at his patched green sleeve.

"Excuse me, please?"

The elf stopped in his tracks, gawking first at her hand on his arm and then at her face. He looked rather like a pirate, with a brass skull and crossbones dangling from his pointy right ear. His features were gaunt and pale beneath a mass of scar tissue. And he was holding, Guinevere belatedly noticed, a *knife.*

It was dripping with blood.

You are not going to faint, Guinevere told herself firmly. "Kind sir," she said, gingerly letting go of his sleeve, "might you be able to point me to the shops? For I have recently arrived in Druvenlode, you see, and I don't quite know my way around just yet."

"The . . . shops?" The elf's brow wrinkled, but he quickly appeared to arrive at some sort of conclusion after perusing her bedraggled appearance and the satchel slung over her shoulder. "There's not a fence alive operating these hours, girl."

Guinevere frantically racked her brain for a memory of Oskar mentioning a fence for her list of supplies. Even if he had, she certainly wasn't going to carry one all the way to Nicodranas. "I do not believe that I require any fences. Just rope, rations . . ."

As she rattled off what she needed, the elf looked more and more lost. A second, even more piratical figure staggered out of the alley— a stocky human with a hook where his left hand should have been. There was a jagged red gash in his side.

"Jimmybutcher, you decaying ratbag!" he roared through crooked yellow teeth, the stench of liquor on his breath nearly knocking Guinevere over. "I'll kill you for this! I'll make you regret you were ever born, you perfidious sack of shit!"

"Oh, you're a *butcher.*" Guinevere exhaled in relief at the elf. "That explains the knife."

The hook-handed man's beady gaze swiveled to her. "What?"

"What?" the elf asked her at the same time.

"I apologize for believing you to be a dangerous criminal at first, Mr. Jimmybutcher," Guinevere said sincerely. "I see now that you are merely carrying around the tool of your profession." She diplomatically omitted mention of the fact that he'd clearly stabbed his acquaintance with it. It had most likely been an accident, if they were both in their cups.

The hook-handed man's mouth had dropped open, but now it was working again. He spoke, quivering with indignation. "We call him that because he's a lowlife murd—"

Jimmybutcher elbowed him in his wound. "The lady wants to know where the shops are, Warwick," he said loudly, over the other man's yelps of pain.

Guinevere watched, aghast, as more blood trickled down Warwick's tunic. "Oh, you really shouldn't have done that!"

"Shouldn't I have?" Jimmybutcher countered mildly. "Let's escort the lady to the shops, Warwick. She's new to the Dustbellows."

"And she's *alone?*" Warwick's eyes nearly bugged out of his head even as he pressed his remaining hand over his side to staunch the bleeding.

"My thoughts exactly," said Jimmybutcher. "Come along, miss."

"Shouldn't Mr. Warwick consult a healer first—"

"What for?" Warwick demanded. "Think I'm soft, do you?"

Guinevere wordlessly shook her head.

The two men positioned themselves on either side of her, with Jimmybutcher walking slightly ahead. Guinevere was happy to follow along; despite their hardened appearances, they were very nice people, indeed, to take the time out of their drunken carousing to help her. She kept a watchful eye on Warwick at first, anxious that he would keel over from his injury at any moment, but he seemed none the worse for wear, and after a while she turned her attention to their surroundings.

"It must be a busy day," she remarked to her companions. "Everyone seems to be in quite the rush."

"That they are," Jimmybutcher agreed as the residents of the Dustbellows scurried past them, giving the trio a wide berth.

"Some are running back the way they came," Guinevere mused. "I wonder why."

"They probably forgot something at home," said Warwick. He looked askance at a man pulling a cart, and the latter burst into tears and fled, leaving the cart behind.

How very strange, Guinevere thought.

The shops they took her to were a vast cluster of stalls in the middle of a bustling public square bordered by huge warehouses on all sides. "Much cheaper goods here than any you'll find on Silverstreet," Jimmybutcher boasted. "Comparable quality, too."

Guinevere approached a stall selling boots with something like trepidation. The peddler eyed her skeptically, but she squared her shoulders and . . .

And it was as though an age-old instinct kicked in. She'd never gone to market before, but her early years on the traveling caravans, the years thereafter listening to her parents' discussions when they were home—it was to her great surprise that she found she'd stored some of that away.

Guinevere fished a plain gold ring out of her satchel and held it up for the peddler's perusal. "I believe this more than entitles me to a pair of your finest boots," she said. "Genuine leather, of course. And I'll take five sets of extra laces, too."

GUINEVERE HAGGLED SEAMLESSLY FROM ONE stall to the next. She assigned Jimmybutcher to carry her bags while the satchel grew lighter and lighter, although not alarmingly so. It helped that her parents dealt in luxury merchandise that might never pass through the likes of the Dustbellows again. Unlike the innkeeper, the peddlers weren't ignorant of their value, and she managed to wrangle concession after concession from them.

Soon she had a whole new wardrobe, the much-fabled length of rope, a bedroll, a waterskin, a map of Wildemount, some grooming supplies, and a medicine bag. This last one was bartered off a peddler who threw in bandages and salve for the bleeding Warwick, who accepted Guinevere's gifts and patched himself up, then insisted on helping with her bags as well.

At the southwestern edge of the square was a stall selling potions. Guinevere lingered here, inspecting the cunningly shaped glass vials filled with liquids in all manner of colors and consistencies. Nestled in their midst was an elderly infernal with curling gray horns and spectacles, her muscular arms folded over the wooden countertop while she waited for Guinevere to make her selections. Behind her was a cauldron filled with a simmering yellow liquid, which she absentmindedly stirred with her maroon tail. The motions released fume after fume of an overwhelming icy fragrance into the air, underpinned with the sugared melon scent of buttercups.

The infernal, sensing a potential sale on the horizon, spoke in silvery tones. "A draft to disguise the self, dearie. Fool your friends, walk wherever you please."

"It smells very refreshing," Guinevere said politely.

"I add a touch more peppermint than most alchemists," the infernal confided. "Helps mask the taste of adder tongue. Shall I prepare a vial for you?"

Guinevere couldn't think of a single situation where she or Oskar would need to drink chopped-up adder tongues. Also, it didn't seem very sanitary to mix a potion with one's tail. Right as she was about to move on, however, the infernal suddenly leaned forward.

Bespectacled eyes locked on to Guinevere's, slightly misty with the beginnings of cataracts but still piercing, still all-knowing. Flames danced in their depths, like candles in the fog. Infernals were children of the hellfire, and a slow wash of dread crept over Guinevere as

Teinidh began to stir inside her in response. Like called to like, after all. She had the uneasy sensation that the infernal could make out her totem, hidden though it was by the cloak.

Then the old peddler looked away. "Stay safe out there, my duck" was all she said.

CHAPTER NINE

Guinevere

As the sun reached its noontime zenith and people began slinking out of the warehouses and taverns for lunch, Guinevere gradually became aware that she was drawing quite the crowd. They followed her from one stall to the next, whispering excitedly among themselves. She supposed that it was to be expected, as she was a new face in the Dustbellows, but after a while she realized that the attention was evenly divided between her and her two companions.

"You and the Butcher are errand boys now, Warwick?" someone called out while Guinevere was purchasing foodstuff.

Warwick brandished his hook hand at the speaker. "You shut your trap or I'll gut you, and no mistake!"

The crowd tittered uneasily. It was made up mostly of people who were as rough-looking as Jimmybutcher and Warwick. Guinevere could tell that the peddlers were getting nervous—and so was she, come to think of it, but she tried not to let it show.

"Where's the girl from, Jimmybutcher?" someone else asked.

"How should I know?" The elf's drawl belied the tension that rippled fleetingly through his lanky frame. "Don't come any closer. Give her space."

The question was harmless enough, though, so Guinevere tossed a polite smile over her shoulder, in the general direction it had come from. "I'm from Rexxentrum, good sirs and madams."

The crowd immediately devolved into angry muttering. Shaking her head in bewilderment, Guinevere drifted to the next stall and requested several packets of jerky and dried fruit from the peddler, a smooth-faced boy around her age.

He shot her a bashful grin. "I'll give you the lot in exchange for a lock of your pretty hair, miss."

"My hair?" Guinevere blinked, surprised. "I'm, ah—"

"Insolent scoundrel!" Warwick banged his hook against the countertop. "Apologize to the lady!"

Before the poor boy could reply, a new voice belligerently rose up from the sea of spectators. "What *I* want to know is why our gang leaders are playing bag boys for some rich capital nob!"

Gang leaders?

Guinevere whirled around in dismay. Jimmybutcher and Warwick were lumbering toward the crowd, baring their teeth. The effect would have been more threatening if they hadn't been loaded down with shopping bags, which was probably the reason only a few people inched away.

"Don't you go telling me what I should and shouldn't do!" roared Warwick. "She might be a nob, but she's under *my* protection!"

"Mine, too," Jimmybutcher said quickly.

Warwick scoffed. "What do you know about protecting anyone? Your knife's still wet from when you stabbed me—"

"*He stabbed you?*" several voices chorused.

And, just like that, the crowd separated into two distinct groups, and weapons were drawn.

Every peddler in the vicinity dove for cover behind their stalls while their customers ran away. The air crackled with malevolence, knives and clubs and dwarven-made axes gleaming in the sunlight.

Guinevere would normally have run away as well. It was the sensible course of action. Yet she understood that this was all her fault, and she had to put a stop to it.

Quickly, before she could change her mind, she wedged herself between the two armed factions. "There's no need for this," she quavered. "I'm sure we can discuss it like reasonable—"

"*Guinevere!*"

Her name rang through the marketplace like a clap of thunder. And then people started—

—*flying?*

She stood on tiptoe for a better look, to make sense of why the world was suddenly all grunts and yelps and bodies being flung off their feet.

It was Oskar, shouldering his way through the throng, shoving people aside like they were mere gnats, not caring one whit about the weapons they wielded. His narrowed eyes gleamed like fiery suns in miniature, his sleep-tousled hair all wild black waves. He reminded Guinevere of a lion, padding toward her with lethal grace. Her stomach went . . . *swimmy*.

The crowd had made themselves scarce by the time he reached her. He shot a dark glare at Jimmybutcher and Warwick. "Get lost," he snapped.

"She with you, Oskar?" Jimmybutcher asked.

Oskar's hands clenched into fists. "That's not getting lost."

"Yes, yes, I'm with him!" Guinevere hastily piped up. She laid an entreating hand on Oskar's arm. "These nice men were just helping me with my bags—"

"*These nice men,*" Oskar said witheringly, "are two of Druvenlode's most notorious criminals."

"They are *not*," Guinevere protested, aghast. Then she glanced at Warwick's shoddily bandaged stab wound. "They are only in high spirits from the drink, and their friends—"

"Their *gang members*—"

"—are a little rambunctious," she continued stubbornly, but at this point Jimmybutcher and Warwick had dropped her bags on the ground and were slowly backing away. Oskar was practically vibrating.

"Now, now, Oskar." Jimmybutcher held up his hands, a placating lilt to his wry tone. "We didn't mean your lady any harm. She wanted to know where the market was, and we thought it'd be best to escort her."

"I *will* say that she trusted us a little too quickly. You have to look after her, Oskar," Warwick pronounced, the most sober that Guinevere had heard him during their brief acquaintance. He sounded almost fatherly. "No telling what sort of trouble she'll get into out here."

"I might already have an inkling," Oskar groused.

Jimmybutcher's elfin features twisted in something like sympathy. "Good luck, Oskar."

After Jimmybutcher and Warwick had disappeared, Oskar picked up all of Guinevere's bags and set off. She followed him back to the tenements, earnestly pleading her case the whole time. *He* was the one who'd said that Dustbellows folks' bark was worse than their bite, and in any case, Jimmybutcher and Warwick hadn't hurt her at all; in fact, they'd been kind enough to guide her to the marketplace after she'd stumbled upon them outside an alley . . .

Oskar didn't say a word until his front door had slammed shut behind them. He set her bags down and gave her a hard stare. The urge to press her lips to the aggravated wrinkle between his brows crept up on her like a fever, and she, too, fell silent. Lost at sea.

"Guinevere," Oskar gritted out as though each syllable were being dragged forth by wild horses, "I will take you to Nicodranas. Start packing. We leave within the hour."

CHAPTER TEN

Oskar

Of the six approved gods, Oskar trusted least in the Matron of Ravens, whose province was death and fate. The existence of a goddess for whom everything was set in stone periodically annoyed him like an itch he couldn't scratch. Out here in the mountains, down in the dark of the mines, people made their own destiny.

And yet . . .

Perhaps *some* things were inevitable. Maybe he'd always known what he was going to do from the moment he first saw Guinevere in the light of the inferno.

But that didn't mean he had to be *happy* about it.

"You cannot escort me all the way to the Menagerie Coast," Guinevere was protesting as Oskar divided up the stash of rations and supplies between their two rucksacks, hers glossy and brand-new. "You have to go to Boroftkrah. It was your mother's wish . . ."

"It can wait," Oskar said shortly. "My mother's shade will bean me over the head if I let a girl like you walk the Amber Road alone."

"Whatever do you mean, *a girl like me?*" cried Guinevere.

"Someone who gets in the middle of a fight between two rival gangs." Gods, just remembering it was enough to make him break out into a cold sweat. She was a danger to herself. "Stop arguing, princess. It's done."

She blushed violently. Then she asked, with the absentmindedness of an afterthought, "How did you know I was in the marketplace?"

"People told me they'd seen you there." With the Butcher and Phineas "Disembowelment" Warwick. Shit. Oskar was *not* about to recount how he'd torn out of his house when he woke up to find that she wasn't in his bed. How he'd gone around describing her to various passersby like a lunatic and nearly laid out the hapless street sweep who'd spotted a silver-haired girl haggling at the marketplace in the company of two lowlifes who had a body count in the triple digits between them.

He surveyed what it was, exactly, that she'd haggled for: far too much, and they would need to leave some of it behind, but it was incredible, really, what a few useless trinkets could get you, just because they were made of precious metals . . .

Inspiration struck.

"Do you know how to ride?" Oskar asked Guinevere.

THE STABLE MASTER ON THE outskirts of Druvenlode drove a hard bargain in spite of Oskar's best glowering. In the end, he could be persuaded to part with only two horses—a dappled gray-and-white draft mare named Pudding and a jet-black stallion called Vindicator.

The exchange had required nearly all the contents of Guinevere's satchel. Oskar could see how hard she was biting her lip not to complain, and he silently vowed that *he* would thump her father if the merchant said anything once they met him at Nicodranas.

But, in any case, Guinevere was rather quick to cheer up once Oskar began tying all their luggage to Pudding, the pearwood trunk included. She kept up a steady stream of chatter while he worked.

"This is brilliant, Oskar. I was so tired of walking. And the horses look very sweet, don't they? I wonder if they will turn out to be more intrepid adventurers than myself thus far . . ."

On and on she went. And, to his shock, it didn't bother him all that much. Hells, he was even listening to some of it.

He gave the trunk strapped to Pudding's back a good nudge, satisfied when it didn't budge, secure in its moorings. Guinevere had insisted that they cart the cumbersome thing all the way, rather than stuff its contents into the rucksacks. It was the shape that made it unwieldly; for a wooden box, it was light enough that he would have thought it empty if he hadn't heard something inside clinking on occasion.

His mind was still on the trunk as he helped Guinevere up Vindicator's back. "What *have* you got in there, anyway?" he asked, jerking his head in the direction of what was apparently Pudding's most valuable burden.

Guinevere peered down at him as she petted the black stallion's mane. "My dowry," she replied, with a smile that trembled for a fleeting moment before smoothing into its usual perfection. "I'm going to Nicodranas to get married."

CHAPTER ELEVEN

Guinevere

Vindicator was a stallion of the highest caliber, handsome and well formed, with an expression that was remarkably aloof for a horse. He trotted proudly over the Amber Road like a shiny streak of midnight, his great hooves striking the ignoble dirt with the arresting rhythm of thunderclouds.

Riding sidesaddle on such a fine mount, in her new dress, her new boots dangling together gaily, Guinevere felt like the princess that Oskar had so wryly called her hours ago. Of course, the dress was a square-necked, puff-sleeved affair that called to mind *tavern wench* rather than *princess,* and her mother would have conniptions when Guinevere arrived in Nicodranas like this, but it was clean and serviceable, and she'd learned not to take that for granted after having traipsed through the woods and the streets of Druvenlode in a nightgown.

If she had *one* problem with Vindicator, it was that he was given to high spirits, with a tendency to rear. She never would have been able to control him on her own, not with the sum total of her previous experience being the gentle ponies of the Shimmer Ward's stables.

But Oskar kept him well in hand, with firm tugs to the reins and calmly muttered assurances. Guinevere was pressed up against him in the nest of the leather saddle, her torso bracketed by his relaxed arms in what could almost be an embrace. It was scandalous, but she found that she didn't much care about that. It was as though the open road and the clear blue sky and the lack of people for miles around stripped away all her inhibitions. She didn't feel like herself.

What *did* bother her was how conscious she was of Oskar's big, warm body so close to hers. The brick wall of his wide chest that she was jostled against on occasion. The spurs of his lean hips. His rock-hard thighs, and the smell of him, all soap and sweat, leather and forest.

She could also have done without his many questions regarding her betrothed. He hadn't started asking them until they'd left the mining town far in the dust, and now they mingled with birdsong and rustling wind and the thunder of Vindicator's hooves—and Pudding's more amiable gait, the mare shuffling along close behind.

"What's their name, Guinevere?"

"His. Fitzalbert, Lord Wensleydale."

Oskar made a disparaging noise in the back of his throat. "How did you meet him?"

"I haven't yet," she admitted. "My parents brokered the match a few days after they arrived in Nicodranas on business. He is from a fine old Dwendalian family, but he has an estate on the Menagerie Coast as well."

Was it her imagination, or did Oskar's fists tighten on the reins?

"You're marrying someone you don't even *know*?" he growled.

She shrugged. Honestly, the topic was putting her in a bit of a mood. "It is my duty to marry well. Father writes that Lord Wensleydale is not too old and has all his teeth."

"Ah, yes, the two primary considerations in a spouse. Aside from the title, of course."

She turned her head to blink up at him. He was staring into the distance with stormy golden eyes, a muscle working in his sharp jaw.

"I don't want to talk about Lord Wensleydale," she said.

"Fine." Oskar didn't miss a beat. "What are you bringing him? What dowry could be worthy of such a toothy paragon of an appropriately aged man?"

"I don't know what exactly is in the trunk," Guinevere retorted hotly, "and I don't know why you're being so cross with me all of a sudden. How old are *you*?"

"Twenty-three," he snapped.

"Well, that makes you only three years older than I am, so do not act like you know so much more about the world—"

As though echoing the contention between his riders, Vindicator chose that moment to rear again. Guinevere's world tilted, and she was sent flying backward into Oskar. Instinctively, she looped her arms around his waist—and kept them there as he steadied their mount. He spoke to the stallion softly, his chest rumbling against her cheek, his voice flowing through her like wine.

Even when Vindicator had settled into a trot once more, she didn't let go. She would, if Oskar told her to, but he didn't. Her hands drifted up, her fingertips digging into the taut muscles of his back, learning their shape and the way they rolled. What a revelation, to touch a man like this, here where no one was around to tell her it was wrong.

But he was clearly not done interrogating her. "How can you lug that trunk across the Empire and have no clue what's inside?"

"It's jewels, I think," said Guinevere. "I hear them rattling around like stones on occasion. My parents say it's some kind of great treasure, at any rate. The trunk's been in my bedroom since forever. It's locked, and only Father has the key."

Over the last two years, she had wondered why her parents did not simply sell the trunk's contents. If it was as valuable as they claimed, it could surely have been the antidote to all their financial woes. Whatever it was, it was certainly valuable enough to entice Lord Wensleydale into marrying a merchant's daughter.

Oskar was grumbling to himself, a stream of cantankerous words that Guinevere could barely make out despite their proximity. His obvious unhappiness at the prospect of her wedding a stranger was a balm to her soul—at least *someone* was enraged on her behalf. She couldn't be, because that wouldn't be dutiful; that simply wasn't done. Everyone understood that marriage at high enough levels was just like any other business transaction.

She sighed, gripped by a melancholy sculpted from autumn air. She shifted against him until her head was tucked neatly under his chin. She hadn't really meant to, but it felt so nice that she didn't bother moving anymore. And it wasn't long before Oskar's grumbling faded away.

CHAPTER TWELVE

Oskar

Simply put, Oskar was in the hells.

Guinevere's bottom had been nestled snugly in the cradle of his thighs for the entire ride. It was a very soft, curvy, *betrothed* bottom. Every movement drove him half-mad, had him gritting his teeth.

The end result was that he spent the whole day at war with his erection. He lobbed cannonballs of shame at it, struck it down with arrows of guilt, employed evasive tactics of thinking about anything—*anything*—else, but it kept trying to spring back up after each ignominious retreat.

By the time they set up camp for the night, he was in a bad enough mood to ride all the way to the Menagerie Coast instead and punch her father. What kind of man bartered his daughter off just for the sake of having a title in the family?

But maybe he was overreacting. Maybe this Lord Wensleydale was actually a decent fellow and Guinevere would be happy with him. She was definitely happy with his wealth and his social status—after all, she wasn't uttering a word of complaint about her fate.

And, anyway, it had nothing to *do* with Oskar. He was just her escort. After he dropped her off at Nicodranas, their paths would never cross again.

So why was it that, as he lay in his bedroll and gazed up at the two moons and the glimmering stars, he had the sudden urge to wring this faceless aristocrat's inbred neck?

Lying beside him, Guinevere was also having a hard time falling asleep. She tossed and turned in her bedroll, the only thing separating her from the hard ground. He worried that she'd be black-and-blue come morning. But it wasn't his place to worry, was it?

"Oskar." Her glass-bell voice spun through the night in a silver thread. "How did you come to know Mr. Jimmybutcher and Mr. Warwick?"

To say that Oskar's first instinct was to snap "*None of your business*" would have been a lie. He *wished* it was his first instinct. It should have been. But Guinevere sounded so genuinely interested, in that polite and careful way of hers. He remembered her holding him in the night, murmuring words of comfort, her arms catching his bitter tears. Would she receive his past just as softly, he wondered, and why did he want to find out so bad?

What was it about this girl?

"Warwick and the Butcher used to run in the same gang," said Oskar. "It split last year when a brawl broke out during their secretariat elections. But, when I was fifteen, I . . . I worked with them."

To Guinevere's credit, she didn't fall into a dead faint or anything like that. She waited, silently, patiently, and Oskar's next words came easier.

"It was a lean year. The seam Ma worked was starting to dry up. At the same time, I'd outgrown all my clothes. To buy fabric for new ones, she sold something of hers. Something precious. I was friendly with the gang back then, and we had the bright idea to steal it back."

"And were you—er—successful?"

"Yes." He'd put the night watchman in a headlock and punched through the shop window with his bare fist, forever earning him Warwick's and Jimmybutcher's respect. The three of them had scampered off, out of Silverstreet, back into the seedy safety of the Dustbellows, the starlight pounding at their heels, and Oskar had been riding high on the rage and recklessness of youth. "But when she found out, my mother was . . . disappointed." That slow shake of Idun's head, the way her strong shoulders had slumped—all somehow worse than anger would have been. "She told me that what I stole had been bought fair and square. She couldn't bring it back to the shop, because I'd end up in prison, but she said—"

And here the words hitched in his throat; here the stinging behind his eyes started up again. He blinked furiously, willing himself to get through this with at least *some* of his dignity intact. "She said that life could get hard and mean, but *I* didn't have to be." He'd forgotten that over the last few months; he'd lost it when she died. How bittersweet to remember it now, beneath a roof of moonlight. "The very next morning, I went around town looking to learn an honest trade. Smithing seemed as good as any. I wasn't that invested, but Ma looked so proud when she saw me off on the first day of my apprenticeship."

It wasn't the most graceful way to end a story. It was awkward and abrupt. But it was all there was.

"Your mother was absolutely wonderful," Guinevere said with a sigh. "I'm happy that you had someone like her."

And that—helped, somewhat. It felt . . . good, and right, for Idun to be acknowledged in this way. It wasn't that strange, after all, to lie next to someone in the dark and tell them things he'd never told anyone else. Maybe he'd been waiting all this time to say these words out loud.

"What was it?" Guinevere asked, soft and bright and curious. "The item that you, ah, liberated?"

Oskar *did* hesitate then. He didn't want her to feel bad. That in itself was a shock—that he cared as much as he did. But he'd come too far to lie to her now.

"It was the flask of perfumed oil," Oskar admitted. "The one that smells like tangerines. Ma brought that with her from Boroftkrah."

Guinevere bolted upright. Catha and Ruidus cast the panic on her face in sharp silver relief. "*Oskar!*" she wailed. "You should have—oh, gods, I am mortified." She wrung her dainty hands together, her plush bottom lip quivering. "I am so terribly sorry, I wasn't thinking—I—how can you even *stand* to look at me—"

Honestly, looking at her was no great hardship. Oskar was seized by the inexplicable urge to chuckle. She was so . . . adorably proper. And properly adorable. "It was just gathering dust on the shelf. Ma would have wanted you to use it," he said, and it was the truth.

"*Oskar,*" Guinevere said again, plaintively, her features crumpling.

He reached out and caught her by the arm, gently guiding her back into her bedroll. She didn't resist, but she was practically shaking with fretful energy, and so he didn't move his hand away, his loose grip as consoling as he could make it. Inwardly, he searched for a way to take her mind off her distress.

"Let me tell you about Boroftkrah," he heard himself say. And maybe it was as much for his sake as hers. Maybe this way Idun of Clan Stormfang could be kept alive, in a fashion.

Guinevere gave a hesitant nod.

"Boroftkrah lies on the Rime Plains. It's separated from the Dwendalian Empire by the icy Dunrock Mountains. There are no houses, just a collection of animal-skin tents, fenced in by wooden pikes. The snow falls nearly all year round." He was speaking in his mother's cadence, memory handed down from one generation to the next. "That entire region is called the Greying Wildlands. A harsh land of frost and alps and taiga. Legend has it that there's a curse over the entire thing, originating from deep within the ash forest, which contains the ruins of Molaesmyr."

"The kingdom of the northern elves," Guinevere breathed. "I've read about that. It was destroyed a long time ago, in some kind of cataclysm. The survivors fled west, into the Empire." She paused, a tentative little shadow next to him in the dark. "What prompted your mother to come here?"

"The way she explained it, there was a restlessness in her," said Oskar. "She wanted to see what else was out there, beyond her clan's hearth. What else she could be." Somehow, it was easier to tell these stories to someone who had already heard the worst of the lot. "Life on the tundra was hard . . . but life in Druvenlode wasn't much easier. I've often wondered if she regretted it."

"Of course she didn't," Guinevere said quickly. "If she stayed in the Wildlands, she never would have had you."

The sweetness pierced him, as true as any arrow. His breath hitched. Something inside him caved in.

"You're not going to make me cry again, Guinevere," he said gruffly. "Don't even think about it."

She stifled a laugh. "I should very much like to see the elven ruins," she murmured. "And Boroftkrah, and the Frigid Depths . . . I should like to climb the Dunrock, even—just to see if I can. It all sounds very beautiful."

Oskar snorted. "Beautiful?"

"In a terrifying way. All that ice and snow, at the end of the world."

He was about to reply that he didn't understand how something could be terrible and beautiful at the same time, when he realized that he *did* understand. He'd seen it. Guinevere bathed in firelight, her eyes blazing, men reduced to ashes, the forest burning down.

"Tell Lord Wimpledale to take you there one day," he muttered.

"Wensleydale."

"Whatever."

THE NEXT DAY, GUINEVERE ANNOUNCED that she would ride astride rather than sidesaddle.

"My lower back hurts," she bashfully admitted, and Oskar had to gnaw on the inside of his cheek to refrain from pointing out that a change in position would hardly help someone who wasn't used to spending long hours on a horse. She was still going to ache, and they should just call the whole journey off, and she should just *not get married*.

She had donned a pair of fawn-colored skintight breeches for the occasion. Oskar knew that they were fawn-colored and skintight because Guinevere hiked up her skirt as her thighs spread over Vindicator's back, revealing those breeches and the way they left very little to the imagination.

And Oskar's imagination was the problem. Not even an hour in, he was already wondering how Guinevere's slender, shapely legs would feel wrapped around his waist.

Adding to his dilemma was the fact that her new position ensured that her bottom was even *more* snugly nestled against him than it had been yesterday.

Two hours in, he leapt off the horse. "I prefer to walk," he grunted at his puzzled traveling companion. *I prefer to not have my cock rear up and send you running and screaming all the way back to the Shimmer Ward.*

Vindicator leaned in to take a bite out of Oskar's nose. Oskar deftly grabbed the stallion by the muzzle, redirecting his efforts to an apple he produced from his pocket.

"You're very good with him," Guinevere remarked. "Do you ride often?"

"The blacksmith regularly sent me on errands throughout the Empire. I'd take his horse, sometimes all the way to the Menagerie Coast to deliver letters." At her incredulous look, he sighed. "It was cheaper than the mail coach."

"You're well rid of him, then," Guinevere huffed. "But was working for the blacksmith how you learned archery and swordsmanship?"

"Swordsmanship, yes. In a fashion." He'd practiced with the blades on the days business was slow. He had an aptitude for it; his mother had liked to say that battle ran in his blood as it did in his long-lost father's. "Archery was more out of necessity. I've been hunting since I was a boy."

Idun's clan had hunted the Rime Plains for countless generations.

She was the one who'd taught him how to string a bow, how to skin a carcass. A story of subsistence.

"What about you?" Oskar asked Guinevere. "Any talents I should be aware of?"

"I'm . . . I'm fairly decent at embroidery," she said in a small, small voice. He glanced up at her, and the expression on her beautiful face was terrified. Of his judgment? In all fairness to her, he'd been judging her from the moment they met. A pang went through him.

"Good," he said. "You can teach me how to stitch my tunics. I tend to rip seams."

She exhaled with a tentative grin. "All right, Oskar."

LATE AFTERNOON ROLLED IN ON the crest of a glacial breeze that sent red leaves scattering across the Amber Road. Guinevere had gone mostly quiet after lunch, and now she was slouched in the saddle, stifling the occasional yawn.

Walking beside her, holding Vindicator's reins, Oskar was already planning where to camp for the night—there was a serviceable clearing just off the path another hour ahead, but if Guinevere could hang on for a couple more hours, they'd be nearer a water source—when the autumnal bushes on either side of them rustled.

Four figures sprang out. A diminutive purple gnome and a tuft-eared katari with sandy fur and a dark mane on the left, a towering white-scaled dragonblood and an orc with braided black hair on the right. Oskar would have thought them mere bandits, but they all wore the same type of light armor in uniform shades of brown and red, a spider emblem blazing on their leather breastplates.

And they had neatly outflanked him, Guinevere, and the horses.

This was when Vindicator proved he was worth his weight in fancy cups and gold figurines. As soon as the katari reached him, the stallion swung around, and his hind legs sent the leonine humanoid flying back into the bushes with a powerful kick to the chest.

Oskar drew his sword. In a blink, it clashed against the orc's cutlass.

Up close, he noted the willow-leaf shape of her emerald eyes and the porcelain smoothness of her seafoam skin. Not just an orc, then, but one with elven blood. An uniya. Her tusks flashed in the fading sunlight, and she broke their blade-lock, twirling away from him and then crashing back again, her movements as light as air.

Even as Oskar engaged her in fierce combat, part of his attention was always on Guinevere. She was clinging to Vindicator's neck for dear life; the stallion had grabbed the gnome's loose chain-mail collar between his teeth and was shaking him like a rag. Meanwhile, the dragonblood was charging at Pudding, who had stopped plodding along and was now blinking at her surroundings in abject confusion.

As their blades met again, Oskar parried, succeeding in knocking the cutlass out of the uniya's grasp. He slammed the hilt of his sword against the side of her head, and she fell to the ground, dazed. He turned to intercept the dragonblood.

"Bharash!" the gnome yelled. "Grab the trunk! *Quickly*—" His words devolved into a scream as Vindicator hurled him at his draconic comrade.

Unfortunately, Bharash was built like a small mountain. The gnome bounced harmlessly off his back—and was immediately set upon once more by Vindicator. Guinevere had taken the reins and urged the stallion forward, and he wasted no time in trampling the enemy that he'd been tossing about mere moments ago.

Bharash whirled around, saw Oskar coming, and opened his reptilian jaws, a bluish glow pooling at the back of his throat.

I did not sign up for this.

Oskar dove in the nick of time, dropping his sword in the process. A column of frost energy sailed over his head. He hurried to straighten up, spitting out dirt, fumbling to unsheathe his second blade—only for an enormous scaled fist to slam into his jaw.

By the All-Hammer's crusty underpants, I really did not sign up for this.

Sprawled flat on his back, his ears ringing, he distantly heard Guinevere screaming his name. Then the dragonblood was looming over him, blocking out the sun.

"Forget him!" the gnome was yelling again as he rolled around on the ground, incipient sparks of magic flaring from his purple fingers only to be instantly quenched by Vindicator's hooves. "Bharash, the trunk! *The girl!* Get—"

Oskar saw red. He couldn't care less about the stupid trunk, but they were taking Guinevere away over his dead body. He surged to his feet, lunging at Bharash. They grappled and swung at each other and, gods, Oskar was *not* going to be able to move after this . . . but he had no choice except to keep moving *now.* Guinevere was steering Vindicator toward him, leaving the now silent gnome in the dust, eerily still. But already the uniya was coming to, and there was a chance the katari would rejoin the fight at any second.

I can't win against these numbers, Oskar thought. *Not with a fucking dragonblood.*

He shoved Bharash away with one last burst of strength and slapped Pudding on the rear. The dappled mare took off with a startled whinny and surprising speed, vanishing into the tree line, luggage rattling, just as Vindicator and Guinevere sailed in front of him in a black-and-silver blur. Oskar leapt onto the stallion, one hand clamped around Guinevere's waist, the other reaching for his remaining sword—which he sank into Bharash's shoulder before the latter could give chase.

The dragonblood bellowed and fell back, Oskar's sword sticking out of him. Then came the flight into the forest, Vindicator streaking through shrubbery and low-hanging branches like an obsidian comet that destroyed everything in its path, Oskar trading his mouthful of dirt for a mouthful of Guinevere's pale hair as it flowed behind her, whipped about by the stallion's momentum. He heard raised voices, a roar that might have been the katari's, footsteps in hot pursuit. These faded into oblivion as Vindicator widened the distance, soon catching up to Pudding, but Oskar wasn't about to take any chances.

"Keep going," he told Guinevere. He mapped out the terrain in his head. "Until we get to Labenda."

Where the foliage was thickest. Where it was easy to disappear.

"I don't know where Labenda is!" Guinevere cried.

"Believe me," said Oskar, "you'll know."

CHAPTER THIRTEEN

Oskar

He had to hand it to her. She was a trooper. She rose to his challenge. To the challenge set by Vindicator's speed and spirit and by the rough, uneven forest floor with its myriad obstacles.

Eventually, the ground softened into bog. Stately oaks gave way to gnarled banyan trees, tangled so close together that sunlight became a distant dream, occasionally peeking in through sparse gaps. The horses slowed down, Pudding nickering anxiously as her heavy hooves navigated the shifting wetland.

Guinevere reached out to pat the mare. "You did such a good job," she cooed. "You protected our things valiantly! A queen among packhorses, indeed. And you!" She transferred her tender ministrations to Vindicator. "You're not just a stallion, are you? You're a destrier!"

"He had better be, for how much you bartered for him," said Oskar, more grumpily than he wanted. Hadn't *he* done a good job, too? Why wasn't she stroking *his* hair?

And perhaps because he lived to be contrary—or because Guinevere's praise encouraged him to show off—Vindicator reared again.

The ground wasn't conducive to it. The stallion stumbled, though mercifully did not fall. But Oskar and Guinevere did. They tumbled down into an elevated patch of mud and grass. He managed to slip his palm behind her head to cushion the impact, but the rest of his body landed right on top of hers as they hit the ground with a dull *thump*.

"Shit. Guinevere." His other hand drifted along the delicate contours of her body, gently squeezing, checking for anything broken. "Are you all right?"

She didn't say anything at first. She was staring up at him. There was an entire universe in her violet eyes.

"I'm fine," she said at last. "We're both fine. I didn't think we would be." She wasn't talking about their fall. "When those people attacked..."

"I would never have let them hurt you," Oskar growled.

But *he* might have hurt her, and he rolled off in a panicked bid to relieve her of his considerable weight as soon as possible.

Her soft palm came up to rest against his cheek in the slightest of nudges, and he found himself rolling *back* on top of her. It was supremely awkward. Leave it to Miss Guinevere to take the air out of his bellows. Her touch was as light as a butterfly's, but he would remember it forever.

"It's you I was worried about, Oskar." She confessed it like it hurt. "I don't know what I would have done if—if you'd died."

"There was no way I would have allowed myself to die," he said roughly. "Not when it meant leaving you there alone."

She smiled at him. She was the most beautiful thing he'd ever seen, lying in the mud, her silver hair as wild as a bird's nest. Her action drew his focus to her lips. Their dusky pink color, the winsome curve of them. The bow that gilded the upper; the pillowy lushness of the lower. How would it all feel?

"I'm sorry," she said. "I've not been much help to you. From now on, I'll..."

He was leaning in almost before he knew it. Her hand trembled against his cheek, and her eyelids fluttered tentatively shut. He took her chin between forefinger and thumb, carefully angling it so that she wouldn't be grazed by his tusks. Then he was closing his eyes, too, his heart pounding as his lips met hers . . .

Her mouth felt rather velvety. Like it was covered in short, sleek—hair?

Oskar's eyes flew open.

Pudding the mare had nosed between them, sniffing inquisitively, probably wondering why they hadn't stood up yet. Now she was also probably wondering why Oskar was kissing the side of her muzzle.

He sprang away, scrubbing his lips with the back of his hand. Guinevere got to her feet, blushing. She dusted off her dress, ran her fingers through her hair, absently petted Pudding. Looked everywhere but at Oskar.

It was the dose of reality he'd sorely needed. What had possessed him? Daughters of wealthy merchants betrothed to equally wealthy Dwendalian lords did *not* dally with former blacksmith's apprentices.

There was something about that line of thought that bothered him in a way separate from what had just happened, but he couldn't quite put his finger on it. So he did what was best for all parties concerned—he cleared his throat and changed the subject.

"They were after you and the trunk. Why?"

"I don't know."

It occurred to him that she might be lying. "What's inside, Guinevere?"

"I don't know." She wrung her hands. "I apologize for not knowing, but don't you think I would tell you, if I did?"

He shrugged. They'd only just met. He must never forget that. This was a hard conversation, but it was necessary. Still, he made an effort to gentle his tone. "If you're transporting something dangerous—or something that people like that would want . . ."

"Oskar." She finally met his gaze. "I swear by the Lawbearer, I have asked and asked over the years what's in there. My parents were never anything but vague. I fell out of the habit of prying, and the trunk became just another piece of furniture in my room. It had never occurred to me that it could be something people would—would kill for." Her voice wobbled slightly, yet her face revealed nothing but the raw, unvarnished truth. "And now I'm wondering again. But the answer is in Nicodranas."

"Well, it's too bad that you're not going there anymore, then," Oskar retorted. "I'm taking you back to the capital, where you belong."

Guinevere's mouth rounded in shock. After a beat, she lifted her chin, an uncharacteristically steely glint in her eyes. "I *have* to go to my parents. Alone, if I must."

"Don't be ridiculous," he snapped. "Those people were mercenaries. If they pick up your trail again, you won't stand a chance."

"It's a risk I'll have to take."

He swore, and she flinched but stood her ground, a stubborn set to her jaw. They regarded each other warily, from opposite sides of an impasse. Oskar felt a migraine coming on, although that might have been an aftereffect of Bharash's ringing punches to his skull.

It was a troublesome mess he'd gotten tangled up in, and no mistake. He'd lost both swords, and his body ached everywhere from the dragonblood's blows, even parts he hadn't known he possessed. The sensible thing to do would be to wash his hands of the whole affair— but he couldn't very well take his leave of the bullheaded, naïve miss. People helped one another, be it in the Dustbellows or on the Rime Plains or in these woodlands. His mother had taught him that. It would be an insult to her memory to let Guinevere fend for herself.

Grumbling under his breath, he stomped over to Pudding and retrieved a map from one of the packs, consulting it in the dim light. "If we can find the Bromkiln Byway, it will take us straight to Berleben, which is the nearest settlement. But that will have to wait until tomorrow morning. Right now, we need to set up a defensive perimeter and get some rest."

"A defensive perimeter?" Guinevere echoed, sounding lost.

Oskar shot her a wry glance. "This is the Labenda Swamp. You can't go ten feet without something trying to kill you."

He was half hoping that she'd lose her nerve, that she'd cry off and agree to let him take her back to Rexxentrum, now that he'd laid out for her how dangerous Wildemount was beyond the safety of city gates. But Guinevere had been surprising him ever since they met. She paled only slightly, then nodded.

A trooper, he thought again. A trooper who was going to ruin his life, if she didn't somehow cause the end of it.

CHAPTER FOURTEEN

Guinevere

The Labenda Swamp was humid even in the grip of a Fessuran night, but Guinevere wasn't sure if it was the swamp, per se, or what had almost happened earlier that was sending spirals of heat through her veins, keeping her awake.

Oskar's idea of establishing a defensive perimeter had mainly involved setting up their bedrolls on the highest and least wet piece of ground they could find—a small, mossy hill—and stationing Vindicator at the base of it. They hadn't lit a fire because it would only serve as a beacon to all sorts of unsavory characters, the mercenaries included. Supper had been cured meat and wedges of hard cheese, and then Oskar had told her to get some sleep because *she* was going to take second watch.

Guinevere didn't have the slightest notion what one did on any order of watch, but she'd gamely agreed. She was determined to pull her own weight.

However, sleep was turning out to be impossible.

It kept looping through her mind—not the attack on the Amber Road, but Oskar nearly kissing her afterward.

He *had* been about to kiss her, hadn't he? Guinevere was no stranger to the act. She'd kissed people before—girls in her dance classes, boys at Shimmer Ward parties. She knew what it meant when someone's eyes darkened, when their breathing quickened, when they leaned in.

But no one had ever looked as good in that state as Oskar. And she had never before wanted it to happen *this* badly.

How would that even work? Wouldn't those sharp tusks of his cut her?

Why was she so eager to find out?

She was fidgeting, flushed and uncomfortable in her own skin. But now that she had all the time in the world to reflect on the day's events, they caught up with her, and soon her dark little desires had given way to something infinitely more terrible, and then it *was* the attack on the Amber Road that was looping through her mind. All the fear of that afternoon's ambush—the terror that the adrenaline had held at bay—came rushing over her now, with all the force of a breaking dam.

Those mercenaries had popped out of nowhere. One of them had drawn a cutlass on Oskar; another had blown ice at him and walloped him. All while Guinevere had stood uselessly by.

What happened? she asked herself. *Why couldn't I . . . ?*

All her life, she had known one thing to be true: the wildfire spirit manifested when she was afraid. Watching Oskar fight for his life, she had felt terror clawing at her throat—but Teinidh hadn't come.

The one time Guinevere *had* tried to help, by taking Vindicator's reins . . . She felt sick to her stomach as she remembered the crunching of the gnome's bones beneath the stallion's hooves. Had she killed someone? Again?

What was in the pearwood trunk? How could her parents have left such a thing in her care?

She clapped a hand over her mouth, gnawing into her palm so she wouldn't scream. Her gaze darted to Oskar, sitting a few feet away with his back to her as he kept a watchful eye on their surroundings. From this angle, he looked like he was holding up the sky. Shielding her from the world's dangers despite how tired he must be.

She couldn't add to his stress. She continued biting down on her despair until at last her exhausted body gave out and she fell into a fitful sleep.

HER FATHER'S NAME WAS ILLIARD. From him she had inherited her head of silver hair. He kept his trimmed short, sideburns connecting it to a platinum mustache. In the firelight, his hair glinted nearly the same color as the dagger he held over her.

Guinevere was wailing. She couldn't move. She didn't like this strange stone room with its odd smells of herbs and offal. She didn't like the scrawny, unkempt figure peering impassively at her over her father's shoulder. She couldn't make out the rest of his features—they were muddled by the shadows, by the veil of memory. But even if they hadn't been, she would scarcely have noticed him. Most of her attention was on her father and the sheer desperation on his face.

"It's the only way, Master Illiard," murmured the figure. "Do it now, before Accanfal finds—"

And Illiard brought the blade down over his daughter, and Guinevere was screaming—

"Wake up. Guinevere, you have to wake up."

A deep, solemn voice pierced the fog in her head. Big hands settled on her shoulders, prompting her to sit up in her bedroll, guiding her out of the darkness. But she would never be free of it, not completely. She was still half-asleep when she opened her eyes, the tears that had been welling up behind them now free to spill down her cheeks.

The night was so vast and the banyans so overgrown that she could barely see Oskar crouched beside her. But she could touch him. Her fingers compulsively traced the ridges and hollows of his face before she snatched them back, the pad of her thumb brushing against the pearly smooth contour of one tusk as she did so.

"You need to go, Oskar," she told him, still wrapped up in her odd dream, hardly even aware of what she was saying. There was a name, but she lost it swiftly; it slipped from her grasp like a minnow escaping downstream, leaving uneasy ripples in its wake. "I can't . . . it's not safe to be with me. There's something—something in my blood—" Where had that come from? Was she talking about the wildfire spirit? She was trying to push him away, but he only held her tighter. Their faces were so close together that the tip of her nose nudged against his. He smelled like starlight and autumn wind.

"It was a bad dream," he said gently, as steady as a rock. "It's over now. You're all right."

"You need to go," she repeated. Yet she was clinging to him, one hand fisted in his tunic, the other buried in his soft, lovely hair. "Go to Boroftkrah. I've taken you out of your way for long enough. I'm spoiled, naïve, and troublesome. I'm sorry." Her lips shaped each failing against his jaw. "I'm not worth it. I want you to go."

She made to pull away. Made to release him. But he curved a muscular arm at the small of her back, keeping her pressed against him.

"You *are* a little spoiled," he admitted. But his tone was gravelly and warm. He tucked a lock of hair behind her ear. "You *are* incredibly naïve." His hand drifted lower, sword-calloused fingers wiping away her tears and sliding down the sensitive skin of her neck, along the silver chain. One of them rested in the indent between her collarbones, just above her totem. She shivered. "You *are* far too troublesome." The warm hand left her skin, and she nearly cried out in protest, but then it was back, this time tipping up her chin.

"You're all these things. But, Guinevere—" Her name hitched in his throat. Her name was a quiet rasp in this place of shadows and water. "You are also very kind and sweet, and much braver than you give yourself credit for. And you're so . . ." He paused, as though struggling to find the right words. "You're so *interested* in everything," he whispered at last. "In all that this world has to offer. Your heart is bigger than the Marrow Valley. I don't think I could leave you if I tried."

He sounded distressingly pained for someone listing all her good qualities. Tentative, in a bewildered sort of way. Yet there was nothing tentative about him when he brought his lips down to hers.

And, just like that, Guinevere had her answer to the question of whether his tusks would hurt her. They didn't. She knew now how their mouths would fit together: *Perfectly.*

CHAPTER FIFTEEN

Guinevere

It was too dark for her to see anything. All she could do was *feel.*

For such a curmudgeonly man, Oskar's lips were as soft as satin. He kissed her so tenderly at first, like one false move would mean the end of them both, and it was the balm her bruised heart sorely needed. Whatever parts of her had remained trapped in nightmare—he woke them up. He set them free, and then ablaze, with the sweet pressure of his warm mouth, with his hands all over her.

Guinevere felt like purring. Maybe she did. She made *a* sound, at any rate. One that must have beckoned and encouraged, for Oskar's kiss turned teasing. He nipped at her bottom lip with teeth somewhat sharper than a full-blooded human's—shocking, exquisite pinpricks of sensation. He licked at the seam of her mouth and rumbled in approval when she opened for him in obeisance to some primal instinct.

And then his tongue was inside and, *oh,* the glide of it. The taste of him, mingling with the salt of her tears.

He hauled her into his lap, deepening the kiss. She eagerly followed his lead, her skirt hiking up as her thighs wrapped around his hips. She'd peeled off the breeches before going to bed, and it was only the flimsy material of her drawers that separated her from the hard protrusion straining against his trousers. Guinevere knew what *that* was, and her head swam with the dizzying, exciting realization that she could be the cause of that in a man as fine as Oskar. There was a moment when she somehow managed to slide against him just right, and he growled low in his throat, and she moaned into his mouth. A scandalous sound. She didn't care. She moved, chasing the friction, her breath emerging in gasps that Oskar ruthlessly swallowed without fail. Heat unfurled through her in blazing tendrils, and she was melting all over him, aching, greedy for more.

"We should stop," he lifted his mouth from hers long enough to grunt.

"We should," she agreed.

She pulled him down to her and kissed him again.

He was more than just an escape from her dark dreams. He was freedom and adventure, the open road that would lead her to the ocean. She wished there were enough light to see his face, but there wasn't, so she learned him instead, there in the night, beneath the tangled trees. She learned the racing beat of his warrior's heart, the cleverness of his hot tongue, the hard length of him against her damp drawers. She learned the kissing rhythm that he liked, the coiling of his powerful muscles, the shakiness of his exhales.

She learned that his hand—the same hand that hunted, that brought down men twice his size—could move as carefully as a lone raindrop trickling down a windowpane. Down her face, down her neck, down to her left breast.

"Is this all right?" he asked against her lips. He sounded like he might die if she said no.

Guinevere didn't want to say no. But she couldn't say yes, either, because she'd forgotten how to talk. Counting on her actions to speak louder than words, she arched into his touch, letting her breast fill his palm.

Oskar squeezed and caressed. He broke the kiss and transferred his lips to her neck, nibbling, sucking. He thumbed at her through her bodice until the fabric felt agonizingly tight, stretched over the raised bead of her nipple. Not knowing which sensation to focus on, Guinevere reached for it all—rolling her hips so she could grind against his hardness, rolling her shoulders so she could rub against his palm. Baring her throat to his teeth, baring her jaw to the curve of one menacing tusk that was pressed to it like the flat of a blade.

And why was it that this looming danger didn't make her want to stop? Why was she tempted to go further, to see how much she could take?

There is a wilderness in me.

It was a scattered thought, pieced together amidst the haze of desire. Then Oskar's hips thrust up, his clothed erection nudging the bundle of nerves at the apex of her thighs, and she could no longer think at all. He was rumbling curses into her neck, and the flames were roaring through her. She was burning up, she was going to burst, surrounded by him . . .

In truth, when the howling started, Guinevere initially believed that the sounds were coming from her. That she was singing the loss of lifelong inhibitions to the mad, mad moons.

CHAPTER SIXTEEN

Oskar

The howls were a long way off, but they echoed through the swamp, popping Oskar's bubble of *soft* and *sweet* and *hiked-up skirt* and *Guinevere.*

He drew back, wrenching his mouth from the pulse point in her throat, and it immediately felt like a mistake. First of all, because he hadn't *wanted* to, and secondly—

Secondly, because looking at her, in the dim light of orcish vision, made every muscle in his body want to reach for her again.

Guinevere was a mess, pupils blown wide with arousal, lips wet and swollen from his kisses, nipples hard beneath her dress. The sight of those little peaks made Oskar's hands itch to be on them again.

It was the howling that restored his sanity. A low and predatory chorus that curled through the endless miles of bog along with the shadows of the deep, humid night, unsettling the horses. The source could not be determined, but everything that lurked within Labenda was some degree of harmful. The open swamp was certainly no place to be letting one's guard down.

No place to be fondling one's traveling companion.

"I have to return to my post." He uttered the words as though he were trying to convince himself. "You have to get off my lap."

Guinevere nodded mutely and complied. Her squirming rubbed her against his erection one last time, eliciting a frustrated, hitched moan that spilled from her kiss-stung lips like an obscene prayer. Oskar gritted his teeth so ferociously that he was mildly surprised he didn't crack his molars.

She scooted away from him and he stood up, and he felt the loss of her like a punch to the gut.

Last time I ever try to console a crying woman, he grumbled to himself as he walked back to his lookout point to resume a forgotten duty. Yet there was an ache in his heart that called that particular piece of bluster out for what it was.

THEY COULD BARELY MEET EACH other's eyes the next morning. Fortunately, there was too much to do to get embroiled in a difficult conversation about Things That Should Not Have Happened Last Night. They traveled on foot, carefully guiding the horses over the marshy ground with its myriad obstacles of large roots, quicksand, and fly-flecked animal carcasses. The mosquitoes descended upon them with a vengeance, clouds of black specks that buzzed in their ears and all over their exposed skin.

Guinevere managed to hold her peace far longer than Oskar thought she would. At the two-hour mark, she slapped at her nose. "Oh, this is utterly beastly!"

He fought back a snort. She turned to him, an unhappy expression on that ethereal, copper-skinned face. There was a tiny welt on the tip of her pert nose, the latest addition to her collection.

"How come they're not biting *you*?" she demanded.

"They're trying." But his skin was much tougher than hers. He surveyed the bumps all over her delicate face and the backs of her lovely hands, and he contemplated how long it would take to murder every mosquito in the swamp. "We'll get you some salve at Berleben."

"If we ever find it." She grimaced. "I apologize. I'm not being a very good adventurer, am I? You shall hear no more complaints from me henceforth—*what* have I stepped on?"

"Best not to think about it," Oskar quipped as the pungent odor of newly disturbed fecal matter permeated the air. At least she was breaking in her new boots.

As it turned out, though, *he* wasn't being a particularly competent adventurer, either. He was so distracted by her that he forgot a cardinal rule of traveling through the wilderness: when there was fresh shit, the one who shat wasn't far away.

The troll reared up from out of the murk. It was colossal. Bulbous. Its hair hung in mossy strings, and its body was a mass of pustules.

It had crashed through the undergrowth right in front of them, roaring, baring razor-sharp fangs, ready to attack. The horses screamed, and Guinevere screamed, and Oskar's hand was flying to his sword hilt before he remembered that *he didn't have a single damn sword left*—

Then Guinevere's scream tapered off into a series of violent coughs. And she started . . . spitting.

The troll froze. The horses froze. Oskar froze.

"I swallowed a mosquito!" Guinevere wailed, on the verge of tears. "Several mosquitoes! First the bandits and losing the wagon and the oxen, then nearly getting caught up in a gang fight, then the mercenaries, then the excrement, and now—now *you*!" Drawing herself up to her full height, looking every inch a vengeful, bedraggled queen, she pointed a shaking finger at the stunned troll. "You and the mosquitoes! By the six approved gods, I have had it! This truly is the last straw. My feet hurt, and my mouth tastes like bugs, and—actually, now that I think about it, *I forgot to pack a hairbrush!*"

Apparently, her right foot didn't hurt too much to prevent her from stomping it, sending up a spray of swamp water. The troll was used to its victims running away or fighting back . . . It was *not* used to a pint-sized lady from the Dwendalian capital throwing a tantrum with all the righteous ire of the upper class. It blinked its dull red eyes, clearly struggling to make sense of this unfathomable new situation.

Oskar loosed an arrow at its throat.

The troll staggered, its bellows shaking the treetops, the feathered shaft vibrating in its gullet. It frantically swiped one enormous, clawed hand toward Guinevere.

The vines stopped it. They erupted from out of the waterlogged ground in a swirling mass of thick green tendrils, anchoring the troll's arms in place, wrapping around its legs. It put up a struggle, but the vines only coiled tighter in response to its every spasm.

Oskar's next arrow sank deep into its chest. The vines fell away, and, with one final groan, the troll collapsed at Guinevere's feet. But Oskar didn't relax. Not yet. He knew magic when he saw it. He notched his bow again and swung around, taking aim at the spellcaster.

Or he *would* have, if he could *see* them.

The swamp was a muddle of earth colors in the wan morning light. It took far too long to spot the brown-cloaked shape lounging underneath the banyans. When his brain finally assembled the figure out of the bark and the roots, out of the moss and the rocks, it was all Oskar could do to not let out a wail of utmost despair.

Anything but this. Anything but one of . . . *them*.

There were various types of magic users throughout the world of Exandria. There were the relic smiths, who infused eldritch power into their wondrous mechanical creations; the divine healers, who sewed up skin and mended bone with the blessing of their gods; the fathombound, who sold their souls to dark, otherworldly beings; the arcanists, who stretched the limits of magic with their noses buried in books.

Then there were the wild mages, whose powers came from nature. Many of them disavowed violence and meat. They voluntarily withdrew from civilization to live as hermits, in harmony with the wilderness. People called them the wardens of the forest.

Oskar called them bloody treehuggers.

There was no mistaking them, really. They were generally unkempt and covered in grime, with a certain light in their eyes—not madness, but close to it. The glint of someone who had gone many moons without talking to another sentient being.

This particular warden was no different. He was of the feygiant race, which—well, if anyone had to be a warden, it might as well be the reclusive feygiants, who were rarely truly at home in the cities, anyway. His towering physique would have been imposing had his floppy ears and broad pink nose not contributed to an illusion of perpetual gangliness. Everything about him was hair, from the pale gray fur that covered every inch of his skin, to the golden beard that twitched with all manner of insects, to the tufts on his bare toes.

The feygiant didn't seem all that concerned about the arrow being pointed at him. His hazel eyes were trained over Oskar's shoulder. He was frowning at the sight of the dead troll.

"There was no need to spill blood," he chided Oskar in a raspy voice that sounded like some drowsy creature burrowing into a pile of leaves. "I could have calmed it."

"It was inches from her," Oskar said tersely. "I wasn't going to take any chances."

The feygiant's frown softened. "You guard her as I guard the forest. That, I can understand."

Guinevere turned a very fetching shade of pink. Judging from the heat suffusing his own cheeks, Oskar knew he was pink, too, although probably less fetching. He returned the arrow to its quiver and the bow to his back.

"We're looking for Berleben," he told the feygiant. "Could you point us to the road?"

But the other man had stopped paying attention to him. He was studying Guinevere with keen interest. "You have . . . something," he mused. "The troll stopped and listened to you. That usually doesn't happen, unless—"

"I'm sure I don't know what you mean, sir," Guinevere hastily interrupted. "I surprised it with my carrying on, that's all."

"No need for honorifics. My name is Elaras."

Guinevere flashed a shy smile and then very prettily introduced herself, Oskar, and the horses. Pudding and Vindicator were absolutely taken with Elaras, and he with them. They nuzzled at him, and he petted them and clutched both their reins in his hand, and even though Oskar had been the one to ask the question, he addressed his response to Guinevere. "You are quite a bit off course. The Bromkiln Byway is another two hours from here, as the crow flies. But I shall be honored to guide you."

"Oh, we couldn't possibly," she demurred. "It's so much trouble . . ."

"Not at all," replied Elaras. He cast a derogatory glance at Oskar. "At least this way, no more hapless beasts need perish."

He and Guinevere set off, chatting happily, the horses in tow. Oskar was left to trail after them, thinking dark thoughts about how much he hated treehuggers. But his sudden extraneity also gave him a chance to reflect on Guinevere's behavior.

The first time he saw her, she'd been on fire. The night of the bandit attack, her eyes flashing, her hair lifting in an unnatural wind, the spirit surging out of her form. He'd been awed by such raw magic, until she'd failed to call upon it when the bandit leader grabbed her, and Oskar had to step in.

Then he'd brought up making a fire, in the cave, and she'd said that they didn't have any kindling. As though she couldn't summon flames with a snap of her fingers.

To be fair, she probably couldn't—that much had become apparent as the days wore on, as he learned more about what kind of parents she had, as her wildfire hadn't blazed into existence during the mercenary attack. There was no room for magic lessons amidst all the napkin folding and the curtsying. Back in the cave, instinct had warned Oskar not to pressure her into talking about her wildfire spirit, and he was glad that he'd listened. The way she'd cut Elaras off just now, it was obvious that she wanted to keep her abilities a secret.

From everyone. Including Oskar.

He couldn't deny that it hurt a little. But she would tell him when she was ready . . . and if that day never came, what of it? She owed him nothing.

CHAPTER SEVENTEEN

Guinevere

Try as she might, Guinevere couldn't stay away from Oskar.

No matter how charming Elaras was, in his own rough, earthy manner—no matter how fascinating she found him, the first warden of the forest she'd ever met—her thoughts were never far from the scowling man drifting behind them like a particularly dour thundercloud. It wasn't long before she left Elaras to his own devices— not that he seemed to mind, as he was quite happy crooning at Pudding and Vindicator—and she doubled back to walk beside Oskar.

"I'm sorry," she said ruefully.

He blinked. "What for?"

"I complained again. Right after I promised I would stop."

Somehow, he looked even grumpier. "You're going through a situation that you were never expected to face. You're handling it much better than I would have, had our lives been reversed. From now on, Guinevere, quit apologizing for every little thing that's not your fault."

"I'm sorry," she said automatically. Then she realized that she'd apologized for always apologizing, and something in her went cold.

She knew why she did it, of course. She knew where that habit of hers came from. But for someone else to put it into words . . . it was embarrassing, and awful.

They eventually reached a clearing, where they stopped for lunch. Oskar attached the feed bags to the horses, then vanished into the undergrowth to hunt. Guinevere perched on an exposed tree root while Elaras leaned against its trunk, and the look that he subjected her to was so penetrating that she soon began to fidget. Even the caterpillars in his blond beard were staring at her.

But it eventually became clear that the feygiant's gaze was fixed somewhere south of her chin. With a start, she realized that her totem had spilled from her bodice at some point, and she hurried to tuck it back in, safely out of sight.

"Wait." Elaras held up a furry, long-fingered hand. "Watch."

Guinevere did as he instructed, quietly subsiding while the swamp burbled and thrilled around them. And, when it happened, it happened like spring sped up—the humid, greenish air took on a brighter tone, the weak sunlight fell in a cloud of gold upon the tiny bird skull dangling from her neck, and the little fern in its hollow rustled amidst a breeze that blew in from another world. The lacy fronds twitched and unfurled around a new stalk that sprouted from the plant's center, a stalk that swelled into a fresh green bud that then opened, ever so gently, into a miniature swirl of spiked magenta petals.

Guinevere let out a gasp. She cradled the pointed skull in one trembling palm, her fingertips carefully brushing against the thistle flower that now adorned it. Her veins thrummed with echoes of power. Everything about this moment was too big for her heart to hold.

"So much of magic like ours is this," said Elaras of the wilds. "The leap in the sparrow's pulse as it casts itself into the wind. The galloping of horses over an open plain. The sound grass makes when it grows. All you have to do is listen." He scratched his shoulder idly. "It's around us, the song of Exandria. All you have to do is embrace it."

Guinevere shuddered. "My magic is *not* like yours." To say it out loud for the first time—to admit to someone else that she had magic—it felt like sacrilege. It was an upset to the careful order of things. Her fingers curled a bit more tightly around her totem. The petals brushed against her skin, as soft as butterfly wings. "I cannot create anything. I can only destroy. If you knew what lives inside me—" The words caught in her throat.

If Oskar knew . . .

"I can hear her, somewhat," Elaras told her. "The embers. You have never really listened to her before, have you?" Taking her silence as confirmation, he suggested, "You should give it a try."

"I can't." Guinevere swallowed. "If she manifests, she'll hurt you."

An understanding smile broke out on the feygiant's cowlike face. "She won't manifest. It's a harmless little chat. And, in any case, I can take care of myself," he said soothingly. "Just listen to her. Shall I teach you?"

Guinevere knew that she really shouldn't. Not only could Oskar come back at any moment, but this thing that lived inside her was a sickness. It should not be encouraged.

That was what the rational part of Guinevere believed. The part that was a good daughter and a proper lady.

But there was another part as well. The part that belonged to the wilderness that she'd found last night, in Oskar's arms, her throat bared to Catha and Ruidus. Her stable, orderly, well-behaved future lay at the end of the Amber Road, but before she got there, she could be the girl who wanted to see the elven ruins, who wanted to summit the Dunrock. The girl who had ranted at a troll and lived to tell the tale.

If she didn't try now, could she really live the rest of her life not knowing?

Guinevere took a deep breath and nodded mutely at Elaras. It was a rush akin to stepping off a cliff. The warden taught her how to sit, back straight, arms folded, legs crossed over the grass. He bade her close her eyes, and she did, the darkness seeping in, the sounds of the swamp roaring to life in the absence of sight. He guided her through a slow and rhythmic breathing pattern, telling her to focus on the air collecting in her lungs and on the letting go of it. Over and over again.

"Find the connection, Guinevere." Elaras's voice was as deep as the moss. It beat on like a drum. "It's there inside you. Let it all unfold."

Guinevere tried. She really did. But something about sitting still and quiet made her uncomfortable. All her little doubts, every unpleasant thought and memory she'd ever had—they rose to the surface, unimpeded. She felt vulnerable, laid bare—and also like she was doing something wrong. Any moment now her parents would come charging in from the bushes and yell at her, because why wasn't she hiding her curse, why was she putting her family's future in jeopardy—

It was a child's fear and, thus, bigger than worlds. Guinevere gave a violent jerk, opening her eyes with a panicked exhale.

Elaras was frowning. But it wasn't directed at her. His hazel eyes were open, too, glazed over with a faint, eerie light. The air trembled, stirred by invisible currents of magic.

"Mr. Elaras?" Guinevere called out anxiously. "Are you quite all right—"

"Someone's looking for you," he cut across her, his tone hushed. He looked genuinely afraid for her, and a chill went down her spine. "I'm sensing . . . a heavy presence. How did you come to make such a powerful enemy?"

"I don't—I'm—" She tensed, remembering her dream. Her father holding the blade, the figure standing behind him. That hoarse command: "*Do it now.*" Her father'd had to do something, before someone . . .

There had been a name. She'd heard it as clear as crystal then, but now it hovered frustratingly out of her reach. Her gaze flickered to the pearwood trunk strapped to Pudding's back. Mercenaries always worked for someone else, didn't they? Was it the same powerful presence that the feygiant was picking up on?

Dear gods, what had her parents gotten her into?

When Guinevere looked at Elaras again, deep furrows were carved into his brow. After a while, he shook his head in annoyance, long ears twitching. "I lost the thread," he muttered. "You might be dealing with another magic user. Which makes it all the more imperative for you to learn how to wield *your* magic."

"But it's impossible!" Guinevere burst out. "I can't!"

"At this point," said Elaras, "I don't think it matters whether you *can*. The simple fact is that you *have to*. You must learn how to protect yourself. And the horses." He paused, then added begrudgingly, "And Oskar."

When he put it like that, of course Guinevere had no choice. She would do anything to keep her little party safe. She summoned some semblance of determination from deep within herself, and she closed her eyes once more and let Elaras guide her through the meditation process anew. This time, she tuned out all her niggling fears, and it was easier now that she had a purpose.

Oskar, Pudding, and Vindicator. She would protect them from . . . well, whoever it was.

The various noises of Labenda settled in around her. She opened her heart to it all, and it was impossible until it wasn't. Something clicked like one last puzzle piece sliding into place, the great chain of being turning over with the song of the seasons. She gripped her totem, her fingers curving through silver and around bone, the earth of her origins warm and soft. She found the pathway and she followed it down, into herself, into the ashes. And somewhere there at journey's end, Teinidh of the Wailing Embers turned to Guinevere and grinned a mouth of fiery coals, like she had been waiting.

Hello.

CHAPTER EIGHTEEN

Oskar

*W*hat, Oskar wondered as he returned to the clearing, *am I looking at?*

Guinevere and the treehugger were sitting cross-legged and facing each other, their eyes closed. She was clutching the little skull that she wore on a chain around her neck, and there was now a thistle flower sprouting out of it. The grass was moving, as were the shrubs and the banyan branches, but there was no wind. The horses pranced anxiously.

Not knowing what else to do, Oskar gave a discreet cough, tossing the catch bag full of catfish onto the ground. The plump, slow-moving creatures had been lurking in the shallows, easy to bring down with arrows that he'd used as makeshift spears.

Guinevere reacted like he'd speared *her*. She screamed and leapt to her feet, shoving the skull back beneath her bodice, her violet eyes wide with horror.

He frowned. "What—"

"Mr. Elaras thinks there's a heavy presence chasing us!" she all but yelled.

"I don't *think* it," said the feygiant, opening his own eyes. "I *feel* it, and thus I know it to be true. Which is why you must—"

"He sensed that there was something wrong, so he was trying to discern what it was." Guinevere turned to Elaras. "Isn't that so?"

She was a bad liar. Her silvery-blond hair was practically standing on end. Even with her back to him, Oskar had a pretty good idea of the sort of look she was giving Elaras at that moment—all trembly and beseeching. It came as no surprise that Elaras caved, nodding slowly.

"I suppose that that's all there was to it," he mumbled.

Master con artists, the two of you are not, Oskar thought dryly. In all likelihood, they had been doing some sort of magic-user thing that was far beyond his grasp. But Guinevere clearly didn't want him to know that *she* had magic, so he decided to let it go and focus on a far more worrying detail.

"Who's after us?" he asked Elaras.

"I don't know," said the warden of Labenda.

"What do they look like?"

"I've no clue."

"Are they after the trunk? Were they the ones who hired the mercenaries?"

Elaras blinked. "What mercenaries? And do you mean that trunk over there that Pudding's carrying?"

Oskar lost his patience. "Thanks for nothing."

"It's not as though my magic drew me a picture," Elaras huffed. "It doesn't work like that."

"Of course not. That would be *too* convenient." Oskar dropped a hand on Guinevere's shoulder, waiting until she had faced him again before he spoke anew. "It's safe to assume that this is the same person who hired those mercenaries. I think we should hole up somewhere—perhaps Zadash, which is teeming with the Crownsguard—and send word to your folks. Wait for them and Lord Walnutdock to come get you."

"*Wensleydale.* No." Guinevere's reply was shaky, yet it came without hesitation. "There's a ball to be held in my honor. The invitations have already been sent out. I need to get to Nicodranas as soon as possible."

"Guinevere—"

"And I'll do it with or without you."

Oskar was getting heartily sick of these revelations that Guinevere kept casually tossing out. First she was betrothed, and now—"You're willing to risk life and limb just so you can attend a damn ball?"

"It's not a damn ball, it's *my* ball," she retorted. "It's very important. One doesn't simply reschedule a ball!" She drew a quick breath before retreating into that prim composure of hers that he normally found charming against his will, but now it set his teeth on edge. "However, I am not willing to risk *your* life and limb, so I believe that it would be for the best if we part ways."

"Fat chance." He released her shoulder, all the better to clench his hand into a fist at his side. "I already said that I wasn't going to leave you."

And he wasn't going to glare at her any longer, either. It was sort of . . . ripping at something within his chest, to treat her this harshly.

He settled for glaring at Elaras instead. The feygiant had looked away to give them privacy while they argued; he was contemplating a wall of vines as though he longed to disappear into them.

In all honesty, becoming one with the undergrowth didn't seem like such a bad idea at this point. Mysterious luggage, killer mercenaries, a sinister magical presence . . . Oskar couldn't *believe* that he'd gotten into this mess.

But he'd be damned if he didn't see Guinevere through it.

"I'll prepare our lunch," he told her, nodding at the bag of catfish. To Elaras, he said, "I found a huge shelf of hen of the woods for you. I'll fry them up with some of our onions."

Elaras blinked. "Thank you. That's very kind."

Oskar rolled his eyes. "You don't have to sound *so* surprised."

THEY FOUND THE BROMKILN BYWAY without further incident. It was a road that cut through the otherwise interminable murk of Labenda, spilling from the mists in a well-trodden ribbon. Elaras moseyed back into the undergrowth after wishing them good fortune in the journeys to come, and the party—such as it was—continued on to Berleben, reaching it in the late evening.

"Oh, it's positively quaint!" Guinevere declared in a tone of hushed awe. "How charming."

Oskar shot her a skeptical look. Berleben was a ramshackle city that seemed one mild earthquake away from collapsing into the swamp from which it had sprung. Several thatched stone buildings jostled for space atop wooden stilts and rickety platforms connected by fraying rope bridges, but the entire eastern side of the city was a mess of hovels lying dolefully slumped in several inches of brown water. In the long shadows of the banyans, the districts were illuminated— a generous term—by feeble torches that flickered over the ambling silhouettes of Berleben's inhabitants, bringing into soft relief their swamp-colored clothes and catching in their eyes like lanterns.

Unlike the Silverstreet innkeeper back in Druvenlode, the one manning the Drowned Nest was amenable to bargaining. This probably had more to do with Berleben's remoteness than with any discernible powers of persuasion on Oskar's part, but the desired result was achieved: one room, in exchange for him chopping the firewood that had piled up on account of the innkeeper's bad back.

Well, it was *almost* the desired result.

"What do you *mean* there's only one bed?" Oskar snapped.

"I meant exactly what I said," the elderly innkeeper snapped right back. "All the rooms with double beds are booked. Take it or leave it."

"Like I have a choice." A resigned Oskar grabbed the key and led Guinevere to the room at the end of the hallway, where they dropped their bags and he tried not to stare at the too-small bed before ushering her back out and plunking some coins down on the innkeeper's counter for her supper.

"Where are you going?" Guinevere asked him.

"To chop some damn wood." He had to get started on it now if they were to have any hope of leaving the next day.

The girl he'd met in the clearing off the Amber Road would have quailed at his surliness. *This* Guinevere took it in stride and bestowed upon him the warmest, most beatific smile that he'd ever seen.

"For you I shall negotiate a meal fit for a king," she promised.

"Bread and ale is fine. Don't use any more of your trinkets."

She ignored this and waved him off.

THE INNKEEPER HADN'T BEEN EXAGGERATING; there was a veritable mountain of logs out back, all needing to be split and stored before Labenda's damp leached into them.

Working by torchlight, Oskar soon lost himself in the mundane task of swinging an axe down on one doomed log after another. There was refuge in the mindless physicality of it. He didn't have to think about pretty women with fiancés, or spider-emblemed mercenaries, or secrets lurking inside a pearwood trunk. And perhaps he'd end the night so exhausted that he'd fall asleep immediately, without thinking about who was in the room with him and how sweet her kisses had been.

He chopped wood until his muscles burned and his stomach growled, and then he pushed a little past that. It was bitter work for so little in exchange, but nothing he wasn't used to. Only when his head started to swim did he make his way back into the inn, planning to grab a bite and pass out on the floor of his and Guinevere's rented room, in that order. The hour was late, and he was expecting her to have already retired. She *should* have already retired, because there was another long day of travel ahead of them tomorrow.

Thus, Oskar was justifiably annoyed to find Guinevere still in the lobby of the Drowned Nest, surrounded by other patrons. The evening's festivities were in full swing; a burly dwarf was playing her lute in the corner, and the ale was flowing. Some of it was flowing *into* Guinevere. Prim, innocent Guinevere, chugging a tankard like a seasoned sailor while her audience cheered.

"Oskar!" She lurched to her feet when she saw him. Her eyes were shining, and she looked so happy that he almost couldn't breathe.

Then she stepped closer, flinging her arms wide open, and he said, "Don't," because he was sweaty and dirty, but she hugged him anyway. He automatically looped his arms around her waist. The inn's patrons hooted, but they might as well have been wallpaper. For him, there was only Guinevere, soft and warm in his embrace.

She gave a sigh of contentment, snuggling against his chest. "You stink."

"So do you, princess," he mumbled into her silver hair. She smelled like a distillery. "How much have you had?"

"Enough" was her mysterious reply. "I said I'd never had any, so the nice innkeeper offered it on the house. I like ale so much better than wine, Oskar!"

"Clearly." Oskar glared at the innkeeper, who at least had the decency to duck his head, abashed.

"This is a decent establishment, son," said the innkeeper. "No harm was going to come to her under my watch."

"Yes, don't be mad at him," Guinevere implored, tapping a finger gently against his right tusk. Oskar turned his head to look from the innkeeper to her, a motion that settled his jaw firmly in the curve of her palm. "I was bored, and you were gone a while."

What was it about her touch that could instantly soothe his temper? Oskar sure as hells didn't know. He calmed down, mad about calming down, and attempted to lead her to their room. "We need to get you into bed."

She shook her head fiercely, rooting herself to the spot with surprising strength for someone so short. "Not until you've eaten first."

He knew better than to argue with somebody who was in their cups. And, besides, he was famished, and she could probably stand to get some water and bread into her to cancel out all the ale.

With a hand on the small of her back, Oskar returned Guinevere to her table. The people already occupying it took one look at his expression and fled to other, less life-threatening seating arrangements. Guinevere didn't notice until she was sitting beside Oskar on the bench; only then did she peer around owlishly. "Where have my new friends gone?"

"You just met them," he said. "They're not your friends."

"They *are*!" She wagged a finger at his face. "There's Nulf, who owns the mill. Artin, who grows mushrooms. Orkelm, who has a tendre for Kali—that's the musician over there in the corner—but he's sort of in between jobs right now and can't offer for her hand..."

As a serving girl brought food and beverage to their table—as Oskar dug in—Guinevere continued rattling off the names, occupations, and hopes and dreams of what seemed like every customer in the Drowned Nest. Oskar was actually paying attention, gods help him. He couldn't contribute to the conversation at the pace he was eating, but he listened to her every word.

When she finally ran out of people to tell him about, she beamed at him and asked how he liked the meal. He grunted to show his appreciation. A hunk of roast pork seasoned with coriander, beef and carrots in a flaky pie, some buttered potatoes, slices of freshly baked bread to be dipped in a generous bowl of the pork drippings... It was the most luxurious supper he'd had in ages. Perhaps in his whole life.

"I explained to the innkeeper that he'd already gotten quite the bargain, you doing the work of ten men for a measly room with only one bed," Guinevere said proudly. "I did not have to give him a single thing from my satchel. I am very good at negotiating, aren't I, Oskar?" He nodded, his mouth full, and she proceeded to chatter at him about how the old man was thinking of selling the Drowned Nest and retiring to Zadash, where his son lived. "I suppose Zadash is our next stop, isn't it? It's apparently a rather grim city. My friend Lunete fell into the sewers once. Oh, I have not told you about Lunete; she lived next door to me in the Shimmer Ward before she married..."

Guinevere was slurring her words and inching closer to him, and before Oskar was even fully aware of it, she was in his lap. She wrapped her arms around his neck and went on talking, and she was very, *very* drunk, and he finally stopped eating so he could feed her and give her water, which was easier to do with her in his lap. Hence, why he hadn't removed her from it. Obviously.

"You," he said, "are going to have a devil of a headache tomorrow morning."

She gave him a wounded look as she chewed her potatoes. Her eyes were glassy in the firelight, as dark as a deep ocean. And damn his ego, but there was something to be said about the most beautiful woman in the whole swamp gazing only at him. His chest puffed up at all the envious glances being leveled his way.

But it was only a dream. He was delivering her to her betrothed. The Amber Road didn't stretch on forever, and these days couldn't last.

It wasn't long before Guinevere started yawning. Oskar swept her into his arms, tucking one behind her back and the other behind her knees, and he stood up and carried her to their quarters. She made no protest; instead, she sleepily cuddled closer while her slim legs dangled gaily in the air.

"You shouldn't be so trusting of everyone you meet," he muttered. "You barely know anything about the world."

"I know that you're the strongest, bravest, most handsome man I've ever met!" She yelled it to the rest of the inn, which exploded in good-natured cheers of assent before Oskar kicked the bedroom door shut.

He helped her clean her teeth and take off her boots. He didn't want to undress her—she would probably keel over from the impropriety of it—so he put her to bed still wearing her travel-stained clothes.

"I'm going to wash up now," he told her gravely. "Behave."

She giggled, wrinkling her nose at him. Her long hair was spread over the pillows in a moonlit cascade, and some odd compulsion made him tuck a few wayward strands behind the shell of her ear.

He finished washing and changing behind the privacy screen to find that she had dozed off, splayed out like a starfish, her mouth slightly open. Oskar bent down to carefully liberate one of the pillows. He was almost, *almost* successful in this endeavor—but, at the last possible second, Guinevere woke up. Those incredible eyes fluttered open and those slim hands were fisting in his shirtfront and she was tugging him down to her, upsetting his balance. He barely managed to avoid crushing her, catching his weight on his elbows, caging her in between the mattress and his body.

"I like kissing you, Oskar," she confessed shyly, biting her lush bottom lip. "Shall we do it again?"

Would that it were that easy.

"We can't," he rasped. "You're drunk."

She pouted. "But do you *want* to?"

The noble thing to do would be to tell her that it didn't matter what he wanted. Even if she were sober, she was still promised to someone else. But Oskar wasn't very noble, and he couldn't bear to bring up Lord Wattledump or whatever the fuck his name was. Not when Guinevere was all giggly and tipsy in the lamplight, and looking only at him.

He pressed a kiss to her smooth brow. "Go to sleep, Gwen."

"You're a meanie," she said without rancor, her eyes at half-mast.

"I really am," he ruefully agreed. "You shouldn't forget that."

She drifted off without another word, her breathing evening out, and only then did he move, easing one pillow out from under her and reluctantly clambering off the bed to sleep on the floor.

CHAPTER NINETEEN

Guinevere

*T*his, Guinevere told Teinidh the next day, *is all your fault.*

A laugh like the sputtering of a dying fire was the elemental's only response.

Guinevere was the sole diner in the lobby of the inn at this early hour, which meant that no one was around to witness her shame as she abandoned her manners to rest her elbows on the table while she spooned a bit of coddled egg into her mouth. Her head throbbed something fierce. It was a punishment.

Last night, Teinidh had spurred her into trying ale for the first time. Guinevere had regarded the frothy tankards being passed around with curiosity, and the wildfire spirit had leapt on that like a . . . well, like a moth to a flame.

It's not ladylike to drink ale, Guinevere had protested.

Neither is it ladylike to rub yourself all over strange men in the swamp, Teinidh had retorted.

Oskar is not *a stranger—*

But he isn't your betrothed, is he? Drink the ale, little girl. You want to, so just do it. I won't shut up otherwise.

Guinevere was quickly coming to the conclusion that, more than being dangerous, Teinidh was downright *annoying.* She regretted taking Elaras's advice and opening the connection. She regretted it with every inch of her aching head and dry-as-sawdust mouth.

But she would doubtless be in direr straits were it not for the hot bath that she'd gratefully sunk into when she woke up. Oskar had apparently arranged it for her before he headed out to resume his wood-chopping. And, in fact, once she'd broken her fast and helped herself to the mushroom coffee that was a Berleben specialty, Guinevere felt very nearly like her old self again.

Planning to keep Oskar company while he worked, she skipped out the back door of the Drowned Nest and into the murky sunshine. Almost immediately, however, she realized that she'd made a terrible mistake.

First of all, the moment she saw him, every utterly humiliating thing that she'd done the night before came crashing back to her with the intensity of a thousand flares from a thousand suns apiece.

Second of all, he was shirtless.

After all these days on the road with a rather inordinate amount of hugging on horseback, Guinevere was no stranger to the feel of Oskar's body. She knew that he was rock solid and well formed underneath his simple tunics. But nothing could have prepared her for the actual sight.

For the sweat-damp waves of his midnight-black hair curling against his broad oakmoss shoulders, and the beads of moisture that trickled tantalizingly into the divot between his sharp collarbones. For the wide expanse of his chest, the sculpted plane of his abdomen . . . the spurs of his lean hips, peeking out from dark trousers that hung far too low to be decent. For those *arms,* bare and gleaming in the daylight, the cords in them rippling with each swing of the axe.

Dear gods, his muscles had muscles. Guinevere felt faint.

Inside her, Teinidh cocked her head in interest. Licked her lips like a cat with a fiery tongue.

Oskar didn't notice Guinevere standing there for several long moments, which was just as well, because it gave her time to collect herself. Unfortunately, she didn't do a very good job of it, because—

—when he caught sight of her and straightened up, lowering the axe, his golden eyes crinkling at the corners as his lips curved into a lopsided little grin—

—she all but fell to pieces at his feet.

Twenty years of existence, and how could she never have known about someone like him?

"Good morning, sleeping beauty," he drawled. "How's your head?"

"Oh, Oskar," she said plaintively, because it was all she could think to say.

His grin widened. The years fell away from his face. Oh, to have him like this forever—boyish, rumpled, lighthearted. And shirtless. Mustn't forget shirtless.

"And what have we learned?" he asked.

"That ale is devil's water," she murmured.

"Good." He nodded toward the inn. "I'm almost done. Go back inside and rest while you can. There's around two days' worth of travel between us and the next city."

"What if . . . what if the mercenaries attack again?" Even just saying it made her look around, half afraid that her words would conjure them.

"Ambushing someone in Labenda would be like setting fire to yourself to kill a vampire," said Oskar. "I don't think we have anything to worry about until we're back on the Amber Road. And even then, I'll be ready for them."

He was one man against several. It was ridiculous to feel assuaged. And yet, somehow, she was. Somehow, she understood, deep in the marrow of her bones, that Oskar would never let anything happen to her.

He cast an assessing look at the bits of sky visible through the gaps in the trees, gauging the time, and went back to chopping. His brawny arms swung, and the axe sang, and one chunk of wood after another split on the stump as effortlessly as though he were merely sinking a knife through butter.

Guinevere castigated herself for being the worst kind of voyeur as she just stood there, watching his shoulders roll like mountains and the sweat glisten on his forest skin. But it was physically impossible for her to turn away.

At least—until Teinidh started *purring.*

Guinevere wished she could reach inside and put her hand over the wildfire spirit's eyes. Given the impossibility of that, she settled for retreating into the Drowned Nest with acerbic haste.

So possessive, Teinidh chided her. *Not very sisterly of you to stop me from appreciating a handsome man.*

I'm fairly certain no sister of mine would have singed off Mother's eyebrows. Guinevere still remembered being locked in her room for three days thanks to that fiasco.

She was shouting and shaking you because you refused to give up your totem. You didn't understand why she hated you so much. Teinidh shrugged lazily. *I was protecting us the only way I knew how.*

THE REST OF THE JOURNEY through Labenda was uneventful. Guinevere supposed that it might have to do with the fact that they were on the Byway, which was riddled with the tracks of horses and carts. The swamp's fauna would have learned to steer clear. She sometimes got the impression that they were being watched, but Oskar seemed unconcerned when she brought it up.

"Probably just that treehugger making sure I don't litter in his precious swamp."

"Treehugger?" She relaxed against him, rocked gently by Vindicator's steady pace. "Oh, you mean Elaras. He was nice, wasn't he?"

Oskar made a noncommittal rumble in the back of his throat. Guinevere wondered if he was uncomfortable with her basically using him as an armchair; she attempted to straighten up in the saddle, but he curved an arm in front of her stomach in response, keeping her there. She subsided with a happy little sigh.

"Oskar," she said, "about last night—thank you. For taking care of me. And for not . . . you know."

She hadn't been lying when she said she liked kissing him, but she didn't know how she would have felt doing it with her mind all muddled from the ale. This thing between them—it was so new. Completely uncharted territory, as terrifying sometimes as it was exhilarating.

"No need to thank me." His tone sounded vaguely bleak. "You deserve to be treated right. No one should be taking liberties. Not even Lord Whistledong."

She didn't bother to correct him. Her mood had once again soured at the reminder that she had a betrothed waiting for her on the Menagerie Coast.

BY MIDMORNING OF THE NEXT day, the swamp had blurred back into temperate red-gold forest, and Guinevere was in dire need of a bath.

She'd slathered herself in salve the previous afternoon. Oskar had kept his promise and bought a small round tin of the stuff before they set off from Berleben, and it *was* effective—in both soothing her existing bites and staving off new ones. She swore that she'd seen more than a few of the tiny insects shrivel and fall to the ground the instant they came into contact with her skin. Whichever enterprising Berleben native had invented the salve was a mad genius.

There was a major drawback, however: It smelled absolutely horrid, a cloying blend of incense and bitter herbs and musk. It was a thick, oily, yellowish concoction that trapped her sweat . . . and there had been a *lot* of sweating in the oppressive humidity of Labenda.

The end result was that she currently felt about as attractive as the troll Oskar had killed. She smelled much worse, too.

Oskar was no help at all. After Guinevere instructed him to not hold her so closely while they were riding because she stank, he teased her mercilessly, leaning in whenever she least expected it, burying his nose in her neck and taking deep breaths, smirking every time she squealed and pushed him away. She was becoming quite cross with him, although she had to admit that his cavalier attitude got her to see the humor of the situation. Got her to laugh at herself when she would have normally wanted to die from embarrassment.

They were almost to the Amber Road, by his estimate, when she heard the not-so-distant roar of water. She cast him a beseeching look, and he wordlessly steered Vindicator off the Byway and into the forest, Pudding trotting close behind. A few more minutes, and then Guinevere was letting out a gasp of delight as the undergrowth gave way to a glade so beautiful that it might as well have been enchanted. Here the river that snaked through the woods coursed over shale terraces in curtains of white froth and spilled into a lake the bright blue color of melted fine-grade turquoise. The water's glassy surface scintillated with diamond pinpricks of reflected sunlight, bordered by the garnets and topazes of Fessuran. It was a surfeit of jeweled radiance, rendered further dreamlike by the lilt of birdsong that thrummed through the clearing and mingled with the rush of the cascade to form a wistful lullaby.

Oskar helped Guinevere dismount, and he set the horses to grazing while she ducked behind some bushes and stripped off her clothes, carefully tucking away her totem amidst them. Even though she was outdoors, there was no room for hesitation—not when she thought about getting clean the way a starving man thought about eating. And, for her, there was no lovelier feeling in the world than slipping into that cold, fresh water, letting it whisk away the sweat and the dirt. She might have moaned a little.

Guinevere splashed about happily for a while. But a fair bit of the salve still clung to her skin, and she swam over to the far shore where Oskar was standing with his back to her, arms crossed and feet slightly apart.

"Oskar," she said sweetly.

He grunted.

"Could you hand me the soap? It's in my pack."

He didn't move. "You should have brought it with you."

"I forgot. *Please?*"

He huffed out an exasperated breath, then went over to Pudding and rifled through one of the rucksacks dangling down the mare's dappled side. When he returned to Guinevere, it was with soap in hand and topaz eyes looking everywhere but at the water . . . eyes that he squeezed shut, with all his might, when he crouched down and held the soap out to her.

Guinevere would have liked to blame Teinidh entirely for the wicked impulse that surged through her just then. But it was more accurate to say that she was the one who came up with the idea and Teinidh pounced on it and crooned in delight, and the flames of mischief built and built until they roared like the terraced waterfalls behind her.

She would never have done this to anyone in the Shimmer Ward. She would never have done this, period. Out here in the open wild, though, where the sky was endless and the trees were vast and the air was clear—well, there was no better place to not be herself.

Or perhaps to truly be yourself, Teinidh hummed. *Or ourself.*

What do you mean by that?

The wildfire spirit didn't respond, so Guinevere forgot all about her. She wrapped her eager fingers around Oskar's wrist and tugged him into the lake.

CHAPTER TWENTY

Oskar

One minute he was balanced precariously on grass-bordered shale; the next, the world was tilting at a sharp angle and he was coughing up water.

Why, that little—

Oskar righted himself, sputtering. Guinevere giggled as she treaded water by his side, wet and naked, so gloriously naked beneath the neck-deep, rippling turquoise surface. He desperately glued his eyes to her face, refusing to let them travel any lower.

She blatantly found his predicament hilarious, and a man's pride could take only so much. It was pettiness that spurred him into peeling off his wet tunic and tossing it onto the banks. Followed by his boots, his trousers, his underwear.

Her laughter died at some point during all this. She was studying him with eyes so big and violet beneath heaps of wet silver-blond hair. Unlike him, she wasn't doing a great job of keeping her gaze at a decorous level. He remembered how responsive she'd been when he kissed her in the swamp, and if the blood in his veins hadn't already been rushing south at the mere fact that she wasn't wearing any clothes, it was certainly doing so now. With haste.

She finally looked at his face long enough to see the menace there, and her lips quirked against another giggle as she started backing away.

Oskar followed, padding on the lake bed until it dipped far below his feet. "I can put up with a lot of things for you, Gwen," he said softly, "but I'm not putting up with *this*."

She burst out laughing. Again. Ah, but he sort of missed those first few hours when she'd been afraid of him. For her impudence, he sliced his arms through the water, sending a wave her way. It hit her and she shrieked, vengefully splashing him back before swimming toward the waterfalls, as quick as a fish.

The soap that had been pried from his grasp during his ignominious plunge into the lake now bobbed at the periphery of his vision, a pink slab, roughly flower-shaped. He retrieved it before giving chase to Guinevere—a chase that did not last long, for she reached the lowermost fall, which was as good as a dead end. She stopped swimming and spun around, the turquoise currents shifting over her copper skin, and she faced him with a wide smile, breathless with mischief.

The lake had shallowed again. Oskar's bare feet touched lightly over smooth rock as he advanced on his quarry. He held up the soap with what he hoped was a threatening glint in his eye. "Time to finish what you started, princess."

"Have mercy," Guinevere not-so-earnestly implored him, almost doubled over from the force of the mirth that shook her slim shoulders.

The last of whatever annoyance Oskar might have felt due to his unexpected swim drained away. It had never stood a chance. Gone was the painfully timid lady he'd rescued from the bandits. In her place was a playful woodland nymph, her smooth brown skin glowing against the backdrop of layers of waterfalls, her eyes a deep, deep amethyst in this autumn light. This part of the lake came up a little past her waist, only sections of her pale, drenched hair covering her breasts.

She was temptation incarnate, so vibrant, so filled with joy at being alive. He couldn't look at her for long without a peculiar ache settling within his rib cage. But neither could he bring himself to look away.

"Let's get you cleaned up," he said, and he had to wonder at his own voice, that low, gravelly thing that was nearly inaudible beneath the rapids.

Guinevere hesitated only for a moment. Only long enough to swallow once, a graceful rippling amidst the water droplets that dotted her throat. Then she waded toward him slowly, the lake surface sloshing and the waterfalls cascading and the birds singing, and how could everything else be movement when Oskar's inner world had gone so still?

This is harmless, he fiercely but silently insisted as she came to a stop in front of him. The lies that people told themselves. His hands settled on her shoulders, carefully turning her around. He gathered her pale hair in his fist and worked the soap through it with as much gentleness as he could manage, rubbing it into her scalp and then combing the rose-scented lather through the silken strands. He tried not to glance down her front, at her now uncovered chest—gods knew that he tried—but he was so much taller than her, and it was impossible to not catch a glimpse here and there. Her breasts looked as magnificent as they'd felt in his hands, perky and full, with dusky pink nipples that begged to be taken into his mouth. He'd thought that he was safe with his lower half submerged in cool water, but a certain appendage refused to succumb to environmental awareness. It twitched and, much to his horror, it *rose,* and he took a small, panicked step back so that she wouldn't feel it against her buttocks.

"All right?" she hummed.

"Yes." He coughed. "It's slippery here, that's all."

"Be careful, Oskar."

"That's what I keep telling myself," he muttered.

He was relieved when the time came to splay her hair down her front again, hiding those maddeningly perfect breasts, but it was a relief that didn't last long. Because running the soap down her back, feeling all that slick skin, was both a gift and a slow torture, not helped in the least by her little shivers of delight and the contented sounds she made.

"Ooh, that feels so good," she breathed out as his thumbs traced the curve of her spine.

Gods help me. Oskar gritted his teeth. He was so hard that it hurt. *Give me strength.* He hurried through the rest of his task, scrubbing the lingering salve from her arms and neck, already pondering the logistics of retreating behind the nearby shrubbery to take himself in hand without her knowing. He knew that he would remember how her body felt beneath his fingers for the rest of his life. That tiny waist, those delicate elbows, those elegant shoulder blades, all that soft, soft skin—he would relive every bit of her in his dreams until his last breath.

But that was a concern for the future. For now, *right now,* every inch of him was clamoring for release. The sheer need fogged up his mind, leaving room for only the faintest glimmer of common sense: he had to stop touching her.

"All done," he announced, his arms falling away from her form.

There it was once more, Guinevere's hesitation. Oskar saw it in the way her shoulders tensed, coppery and dimpled against the falls. Some kind of decision seemed to unfold throughout her entire being, and finally that lovely spine straightened in determination.

Right before she backed into him, leaning all those soft curves against his frame.

"You missed a spot." She sounded bashful yet fierce at the same time. As though bashfulness waved a battle flag. She smelled like roses. "Could you wash my front, too, Oskar? Please?"

CHAPTER TWENTY-ONE

Guinevere

Elaras had told her to listen to the song of the universe, and so she had. She'd listened to the sound of water, roaring, rippling, splashing. She'd listened to the wind stir the burnished leaves and the birds warble their hymns of harvest's close. As Oskar's large hands moved so carefully over her, she'd listened to his breathing grow ragged against the back of her neck and his voice drop as low as night in her ear, and she'd understood that this was a melody as old as time.

Most of all, Guinevere had listened to herself. To her heart speeding up and her blood bringing a flush to the surface of her skin. To the throb of desire within her that unraveled throughout the secret parts of her body like hunger and like hope.

This had definitely not been what the warden of the forest had in mind, but she'd listened, and she'd made her decision. Because she wasn't about to go the rest of her life not knowing.

But now she was leaning back against Oskar and he wasn't doing *anything* and oh, dear stars above, what if she'd miscalculated? She'd miscalculated, and she was naked in a lake with a man. Her face started to flame from reasons that had naught to do with arousal, and she made to peel away from him and perhaps sink under the water and never emerge ever again—

He reached around her, parting her hair and pressing the soap into the valley between her breasts. It was an outcome brought about by her own making, her own wanting, but still she hadn't been prepared for the sensation. She would have given a jolt of surprise, but his arm slung across her torso held her still, trapping her against the wide wall of his bare chest.

In truth, there was very little by way of seduction in how Oskar washed her. He was efficient. He had a job to do, and he did it, and it wasn't long before her upper body was squeaky-clean and covered in pinkish suds. But he was peering over her shoulder while he worked, and the intensity of his golden gaze scorched her soul. Every time his rough palm grazed her breasts and her stomach, it added to the fire. And she could feel . . . *him*. His manhood, as the other girls back in Rexxentrum had laughingly called it in conversations held well away from their chaperones' ears.

Guinevere had never seen a manhood before. She desperately, voraciously wanted to see Oskar's. But that would mean turning around and no longer feeling it resting on her buttocks, hard and thick against the base of her spine—which was another kind of revelation, in its own way.

He must have noticed that she'd noticed. "This is the consequence of what you asked for," he said gruffly. "Just ignore it."

"What if I don't want to ignore it?" Heavens, she was shameless. This little adventure was making quite the strumpet out of her.

He scoffed. The soap traveled lower and paused, as though its wielder waited for confirmation that this was still permissible. Guinevere could only nod. Oskar's hand dipped into the water and pried her legs apart so he could scrub at the inside of her thighs, and once he did that, once he opened her up like that, something leaked out of the place that the Shimmer Ward ladies had also laughingly called their flowers—the dripping wetness of arousal, quickly whisked away by the lake's currents. The side of Oskar's hand brushed very near where it had come from, and Guinevere could no longer hold back what sounded almost like a sob.

She needed him. She needed, she wanted, she craved. Teinidh was swirling within the walls of Guinevere's heart in a dance of flame and darkness, and Oskar was . . .

Oskar had let go of the soap. His hands had latched on to her waist. "Hold your breath," he instructed. She did, and he guided her under the water, rinsing off the suds. And when she came back up, he was still her glorified backrest, only this time—

Only this time, he was kissing her neck. His right hand palmed her left breast, his other hand tracing heated patterns on the plane of her stomach. She eagerly surrendered to the delicious sensations, arching into his touch as he played with her nipple, lolling her head against his shoulder to give his lips unfettered access to her throat. At the corner of her eye, a flash of pink was being borne away by the turquoise waves, and she grinned despite herself. Despite what he was doing to her.

"That was, ah, my only bar of soap, Oskar," Guinevere admonished in between hitched breaths.

"I'll buy you another in Zadash," he rasped into her skin. The hand that was on her stomach drifted lower, into the soft curls that shielded her wetness. "I'll buy you anything you want, just, *gods,* Guinevere, let me in."

She parted her thighs, and his hand slid between them. He cupped her in his palm, which was warm despite the coolness of the water, and she whimpered and strained, torn between shock at a man's hand being *there* and the primal insistence that it wasn't enough. He needed to move his fingers. He needed to put them *in.* Hadn't he asked her to let him in?

So impatient. Teinidh's voice was wisps of smoke blowing over a high prairie. *Did you get that from me?*

It sounded like a taunt and a secret all at once.

Shut up, Guinevere seethed. She rolled her hips, rubbing herself all over Oskar's palm. Just once. Just to see what it felt like. She bit back a cry at the exquisite friction of it. He pinched her nipple lightly, and she jerked.

"I can cover you with one hand, princess." The words came out slightly strangled, yet still at that low, low pitch that echoed through her like a pulse. "Sure you'll be able to take me?"

"Oh!" Her eyes widened. "Don't say"—his fingers began stroking her under the water, and her thoughts scattered to the winds—"things like—like that," she finished weakly, panting.

"Things like what?" Deep voice like rough velvet, darkly amused. Hot fingers sliding and caressing between her legs, strumming at her breasts. "Like how soft you are? Like how I've wanted to do this from the moment you first looked at me with those sweet eyes? Like how I think about your tits all the damn time? I want to suck them until you *cry out,* Gwen. Do you think you'll ever let me?"

"I'm . . . I . . ."

She was blushing furiously, the ghostlike spray from the falls doing little to cool her heated face. She'd heard about love-talk, of course, but the ladies of Rexxentrum had said it mostly involved their partners telling them what fine women they were. Nothing this meltingly crude. Then again, nothing else in the world was like Oskar. He nuzzled at her jaw, the curve of one ivory tusk grazing the edge of her cheekbone, and under the water his fingers found it—what the other ladies called the *pearl,* less laughingly and more coyly, as though imparting a great secret. Guinevere's knees went weak, and she reached back to clutch at Oskar's nape for support, and he rumbled his approval while he slicked the calloused pad of one finger against that sensitive bundle of nerves.

"That's right, my lovely adventurer," he said. "Hold on to me while I'm making you come."

"You certainly think highly of yourself," she moaned into his shoulder, writhing against him. "I haven't come *yet.*"

He muffled a scrape of laughter against the side of her face. "Is that a challenge?" he asked, pressing a quick kiss to her temple.

And he sank a finger inside her.

It slid in easily at first, thanks to the water, thanks to her own frenzied wetness. But the moment it started to sting, she winced, and he went no further.

"Gods, you're tight," he gritted out, and something about those words made her clamp down on him, as though to prove it. "Fuck, Gwen. So tight, so beautiful—"

And then he was giving her these shallow, careful thrusts, the angle allowing him to rub against her swollen little bud as he did so, and she was looking at the waterfalls and thinking about flowers and pearls until he picked up the pace and she saw only stars and thought about nothing except chasing the pleasure, the pressure, rolling her hips against his marvelous hand, arching closer to his marvelous chest, dotting that stern, clean-shaven jaw with kisses, breathing in the scent of him.

Before long he added another finger, and she took it with a gasp, with his gravelly curse resounding in her ear. "I'm almost there," she *whined,* because there was no other word for it, for the spirals of aching need, for a life spent so long without loving touch. Her peak was so close she could nearly taste it, but what if it never happened, what if some vagary of fate were to snatch it back—

Guinevere panicked even as her world poised on the brink of sublime shattering. She thrashed in Oskar's embrace, clawing at his arms and nape, distressed noises spilling from her lips.

"It's all right." He slanted his mouth over hers in a soothing kiss, swallowing up her cries. "You'll get there. I'll take you. Just trust me."

And, wonder of wonders, she did—because his heart at her spine was strong and steady in its beating, because Oskar had never let her down. Not once since the night they met. She stopped fighting for it, she surrendered, and soon the tangled paths of pleasure that his clever fingers wove caught on fire, and Guinevere was crashing headlong into climax. Screaming with the waterfalls, her toes curling over the lake bed, her body seizing within the strong embrace that was the only thing keeping her from floating away.

Oskar didn't give her any chance to recover. While she was still reeling from sheer bliss, he eased his fingers out of her and grabbed her by the hips. "Sorry," he muttered, sounding barely tethered to the last thread of his sanity, "sorry, I have to—"

And he hunched over her, settling his chin in the crook where her shoulder met her neck, and his erection slid between her thighs, rubbing along her wetness, his hips snapping against her buttocks.

Oh, Guinevere thought hazily, *oh, my.*

Somehow she knew to shift her stance to give him easier access. Somehow she knew to rake her fingers down his scalp and encourage him with nonsensical, keening exclamations. Somehow she knew to arch so he could paw at her breasts while at the same time moving back against him, thrust for thrust, dragging herself all over the throbbing length and girth of him.

They rocked together in this strange and exhilarating imitation of sex, lake water sloshing all around them, and if the Shimmer Ward ladies and her parents could see her now—sheltered, prim, proper Guinevere, stark naked, used by a man in the great outdoors—a man mindlessly seeking his own pleasure, huffing and panting against her neck, his thick fingers rubbing her nipples raw—

Her second orgasm took her by surprise. It was hauled out of her on the crest of her aftershocks, and she cried out and fluttered, Oskar's name rolling off her tongue like a hymnal as she fell off the edge of the world once more.

And, this time, he joined her there. With one last squeeze to her left breast, with a few more haphazard thrusts and then a stilling of his hips, he spilled into the water between her legs. She saw it fleetingly— a burst of milky white—before the turquoise currents melted it away.

Oskar spun her around and kissed her. Guinevere sighed happily into his mouth, her fingers tracing the pointed shell of his ear. When they broke apart, the tension was gone from his usually stern features, and his topaz eyes were warm in the sunlight.

He ran a hand down her wet hair until his thumb caught in the hollow between her collarbones. "You're going to be the death of me, you know," he remarked.

It might not have been as refined and romantic as all the other love-talk she'd heard about, but Guinevere decided that it was quite perfect, actually. She wouldn't have it—or him—any other way.

CHAPTER TWENTY-TWO

Oskar

Now that they'd left the Labenda Swamp far behind, he really should have been more concerned about the mercenaries. There was every chance that, if the group hadn't picked up their trail already, they would at any moment stumble upon Oskar and Guinevere on the way to Zadash.

It was ill-advised to dawdle out here in the open. But that was just what Guinevere did—she burned away all of Oskar's common sense.

After they'd toweled off and changed into fresh clothes, Oskar built a fire to dry his sodden boots and garments. Then he stretched out on the red-gold grass, one arm behind his head, the other holding Guinevere close as she curled up next to him, pillowing her head on his chest. He stared up at an azure sky streaked with fluffy white clouds while the wind blew the scent of roses through the caverns of his heart.

"You're a virgin," he blurted out. There had been no mistaking that viselike grip on his fingers.

She nodded, nuzzling into his shirtfront.

"You're not saving it for Lord Wangledumb, are you?" He hated that he even asked. But there was a grasping, feverish sensation rising up from the pit of his stomach, scouring the back of his throat with the bitter, blood-red haze of a sudden possessiveness.

Guinevere traced patterns over his ribs, gentling his harsher nature as only she could. "There was a time when it didn't matter to me," she quietly admitted. "Or . . . I didn't *let* it matter. I set off on the Amber Road thinking only of my duty. But now that I—now that *you* have happened—" She burrowed against him like the hedgehog that he'd once compared her to in his own musings, a shy little thing digging into the safe haven of the earth. "No. I'm not saving it for him. I don't owe him anything yet. I don't even *know* him."

Then don't marry him, Oskar wanted to shout.

Instead, he tightened his hold on her. "You don't owe me anything, either," he heard himself say, and he meant it. Admittedly, there was a part of him that wanted to roll over and claim her, right here and now, but he wrestled with the impulse and won, and buried it deep. "This . . . can be anything you want it to be. It's all up to you. You have my word."

Guinevere lifted her head and peered at him with searching lilac eyes. "What do *you* want, Oskar?"

Ah, there was the rub. He wanted things he had no right to ask of her. *Gwen,* he imagined himself saying, *would you do me the very great honor of throwing your lot in with this penniless vagabond and living the rest of your life from hand to mouth? Will you abandon your wealthy fiancé to travel the northward Amber Road with me, riding every day until the horses inevitably collapse and we must cross the dust-covered miles on our aching feet and sleep on the ground and wake in the morning to do it all over again—all so that we may spend a few weeks or perhaps months freezing to death in the wastelands of my mother's home? And when I decide it's time to return to the embrace of the Empire, you will come with me, of course, and we will go back to Druvenlode, and those soft hands will work to the bone and those lady's lungs will darken with soot, and would you be so kind as to never regret it, please?*

He chuckled. It came out as bitter as the future he'd mapped in his head.

"At the moment," he drawled, "I just want to get you to the Menagerie Coast in one piece. On that note, we should probably pack up and leave before the mercenaries find us here. I don't even have my damn boots on."

THE HORSES TROTTED OUT OF the forest and onto the Amber Road in the early afternoon, and Guinevere was perfectly polite to Oskar as they rode on Vindicator's back the rest of the way to Zadash. She spoke when spoken to, was solicitous of his welfare, and was overall the epitome of a pleasant traveling companion.

So why did he feel like he was being punished?

It was the distance in her eyes in the few moments when she looked directly at him. It was how she no longer yakked his ear off about her life in Rexxentrum, or pointed out interestingly shaped clouds or peculiar trees. He hadn't realized how badly he'd miss that. He didn't know if she was mad at him or merely disappointed by his glib response to her sincere question, but he was resolute in his belief that he'd done the right thing.

There was no future for them, and he had better remember that the next time his cock tried to do the thinking for him. He could never in good conscience sleep with her. And, since it had already been established that he had no self-control where she was concerned, he needed to make it so that she didn't want to sleep with him, either.

Fuck, but doing the right thing was a pain in the ass.

The Amber Road was fairly crowded that day. Oskar, Guinevere, and their horses were joined by trade caravans, messengers, farmers and their grain carts, Crownsguard recruits on their way to their new posts, carriages of aristocrats and their servants, entire families piled into one wagon . . . Everyone wore the fatigue of days spent traveling, but it was softened by eagerness at the sight of their destination's most renowned landmark—the Tri-Spires—already visible on the horizon.

Zadash was one of the larger cities in the Dwendalian Empire, as much the commerce and entertainment hub of the Marrow Valley region as Rexxentrum was the glory of the Zemni Fields.

And all Oskar could think about was Guinevere's silly friend falling into its sewers, and how Guinevere's eyes had sparkled when she told him about that. She was probably never going to chatter at him about anything ever again. It was a depressing prospect.

The sun had begun to set when their motley procession of travelers reached the north-facing tip of the massive stonework triangle formed by the fifteen-foot-high city walls. One by one, each group drifted in through the entry gate, flanked by Crownsguard in vermillion-and-bronze armor keeping a silent watch. Oskar hopped off Vindicator's back, clutching his reins in one hand and Pudding's in the other, and he guided his party through the bustling streets.

Zadash was infamous for giving newcomers a subtle sense of vertigo. The city had blossomed around the Tri-Spires, a trio of venerable towers that loomed high over a sea of asymmetrical streets and arched interior walls and the buildings that had been crammed into every available inch on and between them. These were soaring buildings, layers of shops and dwellings and offices piled atop one another, slumped together and leaning toward the pavements.

Oskar barely spared a glance for the odd architecture, though. He was too busy scowling at everyone who was either calling out to Guinevere, trying to catch her attention, or just simply staring, dumbstruck, at the beautiful silver-haired lady on the magnificent black stallion.

Not that he could blame the poor sods. By now he was more or less resigned to the fact that Guinevere would cause a stir everywhere she went. At least she didn't seem too bothered by the scrutiny; she was looking around, drinking in this new place with her trademark wonder. A wonder that she was no longer sharing with him, and it cut like a knife.

Living conditions seemed to become more affluent the farther in from the entry gate they went. Upon reaching the Innerstead Sprawl, a central, circular district that was respectably middle-class, Oskar steered his party west, searching for the Song and Supper, a decent inn that boasted relatively cheap rates for Zadash. He'd been tipped off to its existence by one of the peddlers at Berleben's small marketplace, where he'd bought the salve.

Oskar stopped walking and absentmindedly patted Pudding's nose while he scanned the mess of buildings for the inn's signpost. It was a moment of stillness that allowed him to become aware of a weighty sensation on the back of his neck, which, the longer he assessed it, gained a prickly current.

He had the instincts of a lifelong hunter and tracker. In this case, the difference between a predator lurking in the undergrowth and a danger hidden in the crowds was minimal. He and Guinevere were being watched. And not only by the people gawking at her. This was a different kind of gaze—intent and calculating. He stopped looking for the inn and started looking for whoever *it* was, his eyes narrowing from one cluster of strangers to the next. There were some drunks slouched outside a tavern, a woman haggling with a fruit peddler while her children clutched at her skirts, a group of men loudly arguing over a broken cart . . .

"*Guinevere?*"

The cultured accent broke through the Sprawl's hubbub. A carnation-skinned infernal was swanning over, for there was no other way to describe how she walked, all fluttering arms, piles of jewelry clanking together with each light, skipping step.

"Lila!" Guinevere cried, and the absolutely hilarious thing was that she began swanning, too, her arms fluttering even more vivaciously as she squirmed in the saddle. Oskar had to hurry to help her dismount before she fell off. Once she was on solid ground, she gripped her cloak tighter around herself—to cover, he realized with a peculiar twist to his insides, her humble dress. She beamed at Lila, and they exchanged airy cheek kisses and then held each other's hands and emitted squeals of such high pitch that they surely should not have been audible to the humanoid ear.

"Fancy seeing you here!" Lila tossed back her horned head, a curtain of sapphire hair spilling down one silk-clad shoulder. "Foxhall is checking in on some investments and I thought I'd tag along— fascinating city, isn't it! Do you remember Lunete telling us about the time she fell into the sewers?" She and Guinevere giggled, then the infernal looked around expectantly. "I suppose your parents aren't too far off."

"They are, rather," said Guinevere. "I'm to meet them on the Menagerie Coast."

"How perfectly titillating. Where on earth is your chaperone, then? I should like to greet—" Lila's mouth snapped shut as it became clear that there was no mobcap-wearing spinster in the immediate vicinity. Her ruby eyes fell on Oskar, who had been standing there for the last few minutes with his presence going about as acknowledged as a potted plant.

Guinevere swallowed. "Oskar," she said in a quiet, stricken voice that gnawed at him, "permit me to make known to you Lila, Lady Foxhall. A neighbor of my family's, from Rexxentrum. Lila, this is Oskar, my . . ."

She trailed off, at a loss on how to describe him. Embarrassed to be seen with him, more like. Him and his threadbare clothes and his cheap boots.

"I'm the chaperone," Oskar said curtly.

Lila's features twitched. She sucked in a sudden breath, as though remembering something, and turned to Guinevere with none of the righteous condemnation that Oskar had expected. Instead, her expression was filled with pity.

"Chin up, my dear. Things will get better," Lila told Guinevere. "It's only a temporary slump, isn't it? I'll talk to my husband about opening some shares to your father on his next venture. Foxhall will give Master Illiard a friendly price, never fear. In the meantime, why don't you stay with us while you're in town? We have the most darling house in the Tri-Spire district, with a lovely view of the Constellation Bridge."

"Thank you." Guinevere's small hands balled into fists. "But Oskar and I are in no need of charity just yet. It was nice to see you, Lila. Please give my best regards to Lord Foxhall."

With that, she spun on her heel and walked away, leaving Oskar no choice but to follow with the horses while Lila blinked after them in confusion.

CHAPTER TWENTY-THREE

Oskar

"What was that about?" Oskar demanded once they were out of earshot. "What's in a slump?"

Guinevere's posture was ramrod straight, so incredibly tense. He'd seen more relaxed spears. She didn't say anything until they found the Song and Supper farther down the block and stopped beneath its awning. People hurried past on their way to a hundred somewhere elses, but the two of them stood unmoving, adjacent islands in a wave-tossed ocean, never more distant from each other than they were now.

Although . . . it was technically not *just* the two of them. Pudding was looking from Oskar to Guinevere and back again, bewildered in her usual way. As for Vindicator, he swung his great neck in yet another attempt to bite Oskar's face off, but Oskar impatiently shoved the stallion's head away as he awaited Guinevere's response.

"It started two years ago," she mumbled, her eyes downcast. "My parents came home for the winter quite worried because they hadn't made much during the caravan season. Nor were they able to recoup their losses in the next. Father eventually grew desperate enough to invest the bulk of our remaining funds in the maiden fleet of a new shipping company headquartered in Nicodranas." She gave a helpless shrug. "To be fair, it seemed a good idea at the time. The ships were to ply the route between Issylra and Wildemount, transporting high-quality products that neither continent would otherwise have much access to. Unfortunately, the entire fleet sank in a storm only four days after setting out from Issylra's coast."

Oskar didn't have a very high opinion of Guinevere's father, but the story still chilled him. To pin your last hopes on that one thing, only to have them dashed through no fault of your own . . . It was a familiar tale. So many of his neighbors in the Dustbellows had lived it.

"We sold off most of the furniture," Guinevere continued dully. "It was . . . difficult, watching the house grow emptier each day. Then the majority of the servants had to be laid off. But still there was money for my education, my training—because it's all up to me now, you see." She finally looked up at Oskar, and her gaze begged him to understand. "I am their only child. I have to marry well, to save my family. My parents hurried to Nicodranas on the off chance that they could get back at least a portion of the investment, but they were also on the lookout for a match for me. So when they wrote that Lord Wensleydale was interested, and to bring the trunk and whatever remaining wares we had, of course I went at once. It's the only way."

Right from the start, there had been some things about Guinevere's situation that didn't make a whole lot of sense. But they had floated around in Oskar's mind, random pieces that he didn't realize belonged to the same puzzle until it was all laid out like this. This was an answer to questions he should have asked, if only he hadn't been so distracted by her. By all the horrible, wonderful things that he felt for her.

For the daughter of a wealthy merchant, she had been traveling with no lady's companion and precious few guards. If the contents of the trunk were as valuable as they were purported to be, the woefully inadequate security measures had been shortsighted to the point of being idiotic. But now Oskar saw the choice for what it had been on her parents' end: desperation.

He had greatly misjudged Guinevere even back then. Like him— like his mother, like everyone he knew in Druvenlode—she'd been trying to survive with what she'd been given. And hadn't her will to survive surprised him every single day that they'd spent on the road?

The more he thought about it, the angrier he became. At himself, for how he'd treated her at the beginning of their acquaintance. At her parents, for placing the burden on her shoulders. If the contents of the trunk were so valuable that a lord had proposed marriage sight un-seen, they could have sold it for a fortune without ever needing to place their only child's fate in the hands of a stranger.

But Wensleydale was a *titled* stranger. And people could still be selfish and ambitious when they were desperate, perhaps even more so.

Oskar reached out and wiped a smudge of Amber Road dust from the sleeve of Guinevere's cloak. This, too, was consolation, the way he had learned it growing up.

"You're more than a pension fund, Gwen," he said heavily. "You are your own person, with your own dreams for the future. I hate that your folks don't understand that, but I wish *you* would."

Something terrified flashed in her eyes. "Isn't their comfort mine as well, though?"

No other words could have been as much of a death knell to what-ever it was he'd been hoping. He thought about how her first instinct upon seeing her Shimmer Ward neighbor had been to conceal the shabby dress that she'd enjoyed bargaining for. He thought about how reluctant she'd been to introduce the likes of him to Lady Foxhall. She belonged in her world, not his. Never his.

"Go inside." He jerked his head toward the inn's front door. "I'll stable the horses."

Guinevere wrung her hands. "I'm sor—"

"What did I say about apologizing for things that aren't your fault?" Oskar cut across her as blandly as he could. She had no idea what he was thinking, but he'd brusquely changed the subject, and so she'd realized that something was wrong and immediately assumed that she was to blame. Gods, he could *strangle* her parents.

She chewed on her bottom lip, then nodded and shuffled into the Song and Supper with a slumped, dejected sort of gait. His chest ached, but he determinedly turned his mind to practical matters and led Pudding and Vindicator to the stables behind the inn.

When he rejoined Guinevere, it was in a lobby whose glory days were long past. The paint was peeling from the walls, and there was a certain odor that permeated everything, musty and bordering on rank, as though a large rat had curled up and died in a forgotten corner long ago and the smell had never been aired out. But the tavern area was lively, with a ragtag group of musicians playing to a boisterous crowd. While Guinevere hung back by the chipped old wall, more than a few people noticed her and began to stare. Oskar glared at all of them as he drew the hood of her cloak over her face.

They went over to the innkeeper and negotiated for a room. The nightly rate was staggeringly cheap; as Oskar soon found out, however, that—as with all things—had its price.

"What in the hells happened to all the beds in Wildemount?" he thundered. "Are we in a shortage?"

The innkeeper scratched his head. "I don't know what to tell you, lad. It's peak travel season, isn't it, with the harvest at an end . . . You get the last available room, which has one bed, or I give you back your coin and you try to find somewhere else."

Oskar was incandescent with rage. He snatched the brass key from the innkeeper's hand and gave it to Guinevere. Loaded down with most of their luggage, he followed her as she made her way to the staircase that led to the second level, where the rooms were.

But there it was again—that prickly feeling. An intent gaze from the shadows. Oskar paused with one foot on the lowermost step, turning slightly to assess the crowd.

Through the haze of tobacco smoke, over a sea of chatter and clinking tankards, his eyes met emerald-green ones. The uniya mercenary from the Amber Road sat at a corner table, half-shrouded in darkness. She wore a red dress, and her black hair was loose and flowing rather than in braids; he wouldn't have recognized her, if not for those eyes that he'd first looked into while in the heat of battle. She smiled at him over the rim of her tankard before downing its contents.

"Oskar?" Guinevere called from several steps above him. "What's the matter?"

"Nothing." He continued walking up the stairs.

The other mercenaries were nowhere in sight, and he rather doubted that they would try anything funny within the walls of Zadash, where the Crownsguard were never far away. Still, once they got to their room, he told Guinevere to bolt the door after him and to not open it for anyone else.

"But where are you going?" she cried.

"I've heard there's a place nearby that does the best sandwiches in Wildemount," Oskar lied through his teeth. "So that's our supper settled. I'll go and buy them. You need to freshen up and rest."

"We can just eat here at the inn—"

Oskar shook his head. "These sandwiches apparently have to be tasted to be believed." He removed his hunting knife from his belt and gave it to her. "Just in case."

Wonderful, he groused to himself a minute later as he headed back down the stairs. *Now I have to go find a sandwich shop.*

First things first, though. As soon as Oskar had drifted back into the uniya's line of sight, she stood up and left. He followed her to an alley that the front of the inn overlooked and leaned against the wall, arms crossed, while she claimed the opposite wall and mimicked his pose.

"I'm Selene," she said. "It's nice to meet you under less . . . volatile circumstances."

Oskar grunted. From here, he had a good view of the Song and Supper. He watched it intently, ready to charge in if anyone even remotely suspicious entered or if there were signs of a scuffle.

"There's no need for that." The uniya had a rich, throaty voice, with a hint of a twang that had most definitely been picked up from the streets. "We wouldn't dare. Not here. You know as well as I do that the Crownsguard are always watching."

"Who's 'we'?" Oskar demanded. "Who are you working for?"

"Someone who wants the trunk and the girl. Who will pay hand-somely for both," Selene replied. "Handsomely enough that my men and I won't mind giving you a cut."

"Not interested."

"I haven't even told you how much—"

"It doesn't matter how much," said Oskar. "I'm not interested."

She told him anyway. She named an amount that made his eyes water. But he schooled his features into an impassive expression and sank into a stony silence.

The corner of Selene's tusked mouth twitched in annoyance. "You *do* know what's in the trunk, don't you?"

"Of course," Oskar said without missing a beat. He wasn't curious enough about the trunk's contents to give the mercenary the upper hand in this conversation. He was getting really good at this lying thing.

"Then you are aware of how valuable it is, and you realize that we will not stop until we acquire it. The spider's web snares all, from By-saes Tyl to the Wuyun Gates." Selene straightened as she warmed to her topic. "We know that your name is Oskar and that you killed the bandits who attacked the wagon. You left only Lashak alive, although barely. We have been on your trail since Druvenlode, and we will hound you all the way to the Menagerie Coast. It would be so much easier for you to just take the money and give us what we want."

"You mean that it would be so much easier for *you,*" Oskar countered. He was, in all honesty, a bit ticked off that she'd assumed such a crude attempt at intimidation would work on him. "Let's discuss what really happened, shall we? You were looking for a girl in a wagon that had set out from Rexxentrum. You found Lashak, probably in the same forest where I left him, and he gave you my description." *And he must have croaked before he could tell you that I wasn't the one who killed his men.* "The nearest settlement was Druvenlode, so you went there and asked around until you learned my name and confirmed that I was traveling with the girl. You then caught up with us, but we all know how that turned out." He shot Selene a look of cool triumph.

"You did not track us to Zadash. This is the next big city on the Amber Road—it's *common sense* that we would stop here. So spare me the bullshit. Maybe you thought it would work on me because you heard I'm just a laborer. But you're going to have to try much harder than that."

The uniya's emerald eyes flashed. He could see it on her face—she was deciding whether to strike now and remove him from the equation permanently. He cleared his throat, darting a meaningful glance beyond the alley. At the six members of the Crownsguard patrolling up and down the street.

Selene glowered at him. "You're making some very powerful enemies, Oskar."

He snorted. "You couldn't even defeat my *horse*."

And he shoved off from the wall and stalked away. If there was one thing he hated more than treehuggers, it was mercenaries. Give a bunch of people some matching armor and a random emblem to rally around, and they started thinking they were better than everyone else.

As luck would have it, there was a kiosk selling sandwiches not too far from the inn, manned by a disinterested-looking gnome. Oskar ordered the venison and crumbled cheese for Guinevere and the much cheaper salted pork and onion for himself.

"These are apparently the best sandwiches in Wildemount," he informed the proprietor while the latter hacked off slices of venison from the spit.

The gnome's bushy brows drew together in surprise. "Who in the Platinum Dragon's name told you *that*?"

Oskar smirked. "Just some guy."

CHAPTER TWENTY-FOUR

Guinevere

There was an awful, burning sensation in Guinevere's chest. Not the blaze of wildfire, but the sharp sting of ice. She drew the moldy curtains shut and stepped back from the room's lone window, through which she had watched Oskar disappear into an alley with the beautiful woman in the red dress.

Maybe I'm jumping to conclusions. Maybe she's just an old friend of his.

But that didn't clear up why he'd been so eager to stash Guinevere away behind a locked door . . . unless he didn't want his friend to get the wrong idea, which ripped open the possibility that he considered the seafoam-skinned brunette woman more than a friend.

Of course, there was another, perhaps more logical explanation. Oskar had needs, like any other man. That much had been made obvious by the waterfall terrace. But the fact of Guinevere's betrothal had prevented him from fulfilling them all the way with her, so he'd turned to one of Zadash's night doves as soon as he could.

Or maybe she wasn't a night dove—just a pretty lady who'd happened to catch his eye. Whatever the case, he'd lied to Guinevere about going to buy sandwiches and had gone off with *her* instead.

Doesn't that just grind your gears? crooned Teinidh, her flames licking at every jagged insecurity lodged in Guinevere's soul, trying to twist each one to fullest advantage. *Don't you just want to march out there and claim what's yours?*

You are a terrible influence, Guinevere informed her, managing a trace of haughtiness that was all she had to give before she slumped under the weight of crushing futility. The humble room's peeling walls felt as though they were closing in, the blazing hearth too bright. Oskar wasn't hers and would never be hers. Not only because she had to marry someone else, but also because of what was inside her.

Oskar was a good man, and every moment that Guinevere stayed with him was another moment he could perish in the uncontrollable wrath of wildfire, or at the hands of the mercenaries who wanted her and the trunk. She had been too incredibly selfish—too shamefully scared—to let him go.

That had to end today.

She had no right to be angry at him for lying to her. He'd made her his responsibility, but that didn't mean she was any less of a nuisance. He'd be better off turning around and heading for Boroftkrah, like he'd originally planned—like he'd promised his mother—and dallying with all the old friends and night doves he encountered along the way without having to worry about a useless, naïve girl who was hiding a horrible secret from him despite everything he'd already done for her.

It was past time for Guinevere to take matters into her own hands and do what was best for him.

For them both. Because every moment that she stayed with Oskar was another moment wherein it became more and more difficult for her not to imagine staying forever.

The innkeeper had proudly announced that, although the Song and Supper was an older establishment, they still provided little complementary luxuries such as enough writing materials to pen and post one letter (*"with our inn's seal!"*). Guinevere rummaged through the desk drawers, and soon enough she was scribbling a note to Oskar. Her tutors would have despaired at the inelegance of her hurried strokes, but what mattered to her was that she meant every word that she jotted down from the stream of scattered thoughts racing wildly through her mind.

Dearest Oskar,

I'm afraid that I haven't been very honest with you. Although, is it really lying if you don't reveal what wasn't asked in the first place? That's where the term "lying by omission" comes from, I suppose . . .

I'm making an absolute hash of this, aren't I? Let me start over. Dearest Oskar, there are things I should have told you right from the start. I didn't, because I was scared. Not to say that I've uncovered any hidden bastions of courage— I haven't—but I will tell you now because I owe you this.

You are already aware that I was born in Cyrengreen. What you don't know is that I was born during a forest fire. My parents were fleeing the blaze when Mother's water broke. She gave birth to me right then and there, and one of the spirits of the fire attached themself to my soul. This was all explained to my parents by the dwarven hermit of those woods, who chanced upon us and fought back the flames. Hammie nursed Mother back to health after her difficult labor, and he made my totem for me. He packed it with the scorched earth of Cyrengreen, reinforcing my connection to the wildfire spirit, because I was born too early and by all accounts shouldn't have survived. But, as long as I had the totem, he said, the spirit would lend me its strength and I would live.

Now that I think about it, Hammie was probably a wild mage like Elaras, wasn't he? Was he telling Mother and Father the truth about the totem, or was it just to prevent them from getting rid of it? They certainly tried to when I was older, but I was stubborn, Oskar. I clung to it. It was a part of me. This was the only instance when I was ever a disobedient child.

But I can't blame my parents for wanting to pretend that I'm normal. My wildfire spirit's name is Teinidh of the Wailing Embers. She manifests when I am angry or afraid. I cannot control her. I was the one who killed those bandits the night we met. The one who started the fire that you and I barely escaped.

I've been a danger to you all this time, but no more. You've told me to stop apologizing, but in this case it really is my fault, so I am sorry. You cannot know how sorry I am. But I hope that my departure will finally make things right. And, while I suspect that you'll be quite cross at first, eventually you'll see that this was for the best.

Thank you, Oskar, for everything. I wish you a safe and pleasant journey to your mother's homeland. I must be selfish one last time and request that you think of me on occasion, for I shall miss you very much.

Yours,
Guinevere

Inside the walls of Guinevere's heart, Teinidh was shaking her head. No one is going to read all of that.

He will. Guinevere could barely see the parchment through her tears. She placed the letter on the table and slung her rucksack onto her shoulders, then made her way to the pearwood trunk across the room. She would drag it along the ground by its handle all the way to Nicodranas if need be, although she hoped that Pudding would be nice enough to come with her.

There was little time to spare, but Guinevere found herself hesitating in front of the pearwood trunk. She studied the ornate fleur-de-lis carvings on its lacquered surface, as she had spent many hours doing in her childhood when the trunk was the everlasting mystery shoved to one corner of her room.

What do you remember from back then? she asked Teinidh. *Do you know what's in here?*

I see what you see, the wildfire spirit replied. I remember what you remember. I forget what you forget.

And do you dream what I dream? Guinevere thought about a firelit room that smelled like herbs and offal, and a dagger in her father's hands. It seemed important, somehow, that nightmare her stressed brain had produced amidst the mud and the banyans of Labenda.

We share everything, Teinidh said with a sniff. Except opinions, clearly. It is my opinion that you're overreacting. We don't have to leave.

Oskar is safer without us. Guinevere grabbed the trunk by its handle. And . . .

And she hadn't actually touched the trunk in a while. Oskar was always carrying it for her. She certainly hadn't touched it since Elaras taught her how to listen to the magic that was all around.

The minute her fingers closed around the handle, she heard it. A roaring like thunder, a rushing like blood. There was an almost mechanical rustle, as though she were listening to something man-made—as though the stars had been plucked from the heavens and wrestled into simpler forms. It was nothing like the wild, but it was magic all the same.

And buried underneath it was a more familiar song. The leap of the bird into the wind. The turn of the seasons. The ocean, vast and roiling, endless and primordial. The croaking of ravens . . .

Snap out of it.

You have to go.

Guinevere forced herself out of the waking dream of black feathers and howling wind. She hauled the trunk to the door with some difficulty and then threw open the bolt and exited the room.

She nearly walked into Oskar.

"I had no idea you'd be back so soon!" Guinevere cried, dropping the trunk's handle.

"It's not like I went to Tal'Dorei." Oskar was holding a brown bag from which wafted the mouthwatering aroma of roast meat. Had he been telling the truth about the sandwiches, after all? His topaz eyes narrowed as he took in the rucksack on her shoulders and the pearwood trunk at her feet. "Where do you think you're going?"

"Um—" A hundred lies quickly sprang to mind and just as quickly evaporated in the face of such damning evidence. She settled for wringing her hands together. She couldn't believe that her plan had failed as soon as she'd set it into motion.

I mean, I can believe it, Teinidh drawled. *Maybe if you'd written a shorter letter . . .*

Oskar strode forward, leaving Guinevere no choice but to back into the room. He nudged the trunk inside with his foot, and he closed the door behind him with a soft thud and bolted it with his gaze fixed on her. She hung her head and awaited his judgment, more pent-up tears stinging her throat.

"Are you hungry?" he asked. "Do you want to eat first before we fight?"

"Let us get the fighting over and done with," she said miserably.

"Suit yourself." He brushed past her on his way to the desk, where he carefully placed the brown bag. This was not her parents' rage. She hadn't known that it was possible for someone to move quietly while being angry, for someone to be mad at another person while still caring about whether they'd eaten.

Oskar noticed the letter and picked it up. Guinevere was seized by the urge to snatch it from him and rip it into a million pieces, but she made herself stay where she was, watching him read it from out of the corner of her eye, her pulse hammering a mile a minute. His sharp oakmoss features remained completely impassive; there wasn't even the slightest furrowing of his brow. There was no clue at all as to what he was thinking.

Not that she *needed* any clues. It was fairly obvious that he was disgusted with her. Who wouldn't be? He got to the end and lowered the parchment slightly, frowning—not at what she'd written, Guinevere realized, but at the damp spots that her tears had left.

Then he looked at her and she waited for him to send her away. To banish her from his life for good.

Oskar chucked the letter into the fire.

Guinevere's mouth dropped open as the flames surged to consume their newest bit of kindling. "What—"

"I already know about your magic." They were the last words she had ever expected to hear. "I saw you, that night. I heard the commotion from my campsite, and I went to investigate, and I got there as the bandits were dragging you out of the wagon. You handled them before I could intervene." His gaze turned contemplative. "I'd never seen anything like it before. The wildfire spirit—Teinidh, was it?—flowing out of you. Turning all those evil men to ash in a blink. Terrible and beautiful, all at once."

"You . . . you knew." Gracious, what was wrong with her? He'd already said that. But her brain couldn't come to terms with it. She had to repeat it, in her own voice, with the movements of her own lips and tongue, before she could accept a reality so different from what she had convinced herself would transpire. No shock, no horror, no revulsion. Just Oskar, calm and steady in the twilight. "You knew all this time. And you never—never said anything—"

He shrugged. "I assumed that, if someone as talkative as you wanted to discuss it, you would have. I had no right to pry."

"I'm not *that* talkative."

"Beg to differ."

"You knew," she said again. She still couldn't believe it. How she'd braced for the worst, how it hadn't come to pass. How the scars of her childhood seemed to . . . not *fade,* exactly, but soften, their ugliness melting into the background of her being, remaining a part of her but no longer the long shadow over her life. "And you helped me and accompanied me on my travels anyway. It doesn't bother you at *all*? I ended those men's lives, Oskar. Just like—like that—" She made an abrupt motion with one quivering hand. "Nobody should be able to do that. Or, at the very least, they should be able to control it. But I can't, and you're not afraid of me in the slightest?"

He arched a brow. "Do you *want* me to be afraid of you?"

"No." Her bottom lip wobbled. "I want you to—to l-like me."

In an instant he was closing the distance between them and wrapping her up in his strong arms. She made a strangled noise as she hid her face in his shirtfront, allowing herself to tremble, trusting him to hold her together.

"I like you just fine, Gwen." Oskar sounded vaguely amused, but his hand on the back of her head was comforting. "How could I not? One of the things I remember most about that night is that you could have run after you set the fire. Saving yourself could have been your priority. But no—you freed the oxen first. You made sure they could get away. How can I be afraid of someone with a heart that good?" His tone hardened ever so slightly with his next words. "I forbid you to feel any guilt over killing those bandits. They would have hurt you. You did what you had to do to survive. It wasn't your fault."

"I'm starting to understand that some things aren't," Guinevere mumbled. And this, too, felt like defiance. "But there is always this voice in the back of my head. It drowns out even Teinidh. It belongs to Mother and Father. And it blames me for—for most of what goes wrong, because—"

Because you are a monster.

Because those curtains were genuine Marquesian lace and you burned them! What did I ever do to deserve such a child?

Because your freakish nature will be the downfall of this family.

Because it would have been better if she had died!

"Because," said Oskar in the here and now, "you have bad parents."

Guinevere stiffened. She would have struggled free of him, but he held her fast. The simple statement, so bluntly given, sank in. Once she got over her initial burst of indignation, it was almost a relief that someone in this world mirrored her darker thoughts and had no compunctions saying them out loud.

Yet it was also that same relief—the flicker of disloyalty inherent to it—that caused an unexpected flare of temper.

"So what if they're bad parents? They're all I have." Guinevere managed to push Oskar away just then, or maybe it was surprise that caused him to release her. "What good does your judgment do when, of the two of us, I shall be the one left with it? Because you"—*will head for Boroftkrah after dropping me off at Nicodranas, and we will never see each other again*—"are too busy trysting to consider my feelings!"

Oskar blinked. "Trysting?"

"With your women in red dresses!" Guinevere yelled. "Right after you lock me away like a nuisance pet!"

"Let me get this straight." A vein twitched at Oskar's temple. "You tried to sneak out of here and travel to the Menagerie Coast on your own, knowing full well that a bunch of mercenaries hired by a mysterious evil presence are after you and the trunk—*all because you're in a jealous snit?*"

"Did you not read a word of my letter?" she railed. "Jealousy is *not* the reason." In the back of her mind, Teinidh let out such a derisive snort that Guinevere's face flamed. "Or at least it's not the only reason—"

"I think it's a bigger reason than you'll ever admit," Oskar growled. He stepped closer and slipped the straps of the rucksack off her shoulders. "What am I supposed to do with you? Someone who just hares off without even trying to work things out—"

"You lied to me," she said as he tossed her rucksack aside, then moved on to divesting her of her cloak. "You told me you were going to buy sandwiches. But I happened to look out the window, and I saw you walk into an alley with your night dove."

"Night dove?" he echoed, mystified. He threw her cloak on top of the rucksack where it lay on the floor in a sad heap. "Oh, you mean a se—"

Guinevere lurched forward to clap a hand over Oskar's mouth before he could say the much cruder term *sex worker.* He rolled his eyes and gave her fingers a sharp little nip. She gasped and tried to draw back, but his hand was suddenly keeping her wrist in place while he soothed the sting with chaste, butterfly-light kisses to the tips of her fingers.

She refused to be swayed. "How dare you kiss my hand after cavorting with another woman!"

Oskar sighed. He lowered her hand away from his mouth. "That woman was one of the mercenaries, and I was *not* cavorting with her—merely seeking information." He cradled her fingers with his, squeezing reassuringly while he filled her in on what the uniya had told him. "I'm sorry I lied, but I didn't want to alarm you. And, for what it's worth, I *did* find a sandwich shop. It might not necessarily be the best in Wildemount, but it'll do, I think."

"Why are we talking about sandwiches?" In the last few minutes, Guinevere had experienced a staggering range of emotions, from jealousy to sorrow to lingering childhood trauma to anger. Now she had crashed headlong into panic, and she was reeling from the whiplash. "Oskar, whatever's in the trunk, it's valuable, yes, we've gathered that—but what do those mercenaries want with *me*?"

"You mentioned that the trunk is locked and only your father has the key to it. Maybe their plan is to hold you ransom in exchange for that key." Oskar's golden eyes flashed. There was a stubborn set to his jaw that she was coming to know all too well. "But they aren't going to succeed. I won't let them. And I won't let you go anywhere without me, either. For as long as there is breath in my body, you will not face this world alone, Guinevere. Do you understand?"

He burned like fire. Rendered mute by his intensity, she could only nod. Far from relaxing, he glowered at her. "Now, let's discuss this jealousy of yours."

There was something about the look on his handsome face just then that made her slowly back away—not out of fear, exactly, but from some instinct for self-preservation. Without missing a beat, he padded after her all the way across the room, until the door handle settled into the indents of her spine and she could go no farther. He braced a hand over her head, caging her in with his body.

"I was being silly." Her voice was unnaturally high. Breathless. "I do admit to some possessiveness where you are concerned, but I realize that it is entirely misplaced." It hurt to say it, but she owed it to him to be honest about her feelings. Why, then, did he look madder and madder with each word that left her lips? "You are free, of course, to do whatever you wish, with whomever you wish . . ." Her gaze darted to his temple. The vein was back, and twitchier than ever before. "After all, there are no promises between us. I don't know why I do half the things I do, Oskar. You should ignore me."

"I damn well wish I could," he shot back.

And then he kissed her.

CHAPTER TWENTY-FIVE

Guinevere

Kissing Oskar had never been the problem, Guinevere reflected. Her body knew what to do whenever his pressed up against it, their mouths slotting together like jigsaw pieces reunited at long last, falling into a rhythm as old as time.

He was still a little angry with her. She could tell from the roughness of his kisses, the way he formed a fist in her hair and pulled so he could angle her head the way he pleased—not violently, but *firmly*. Firm enough for a shivery coil of excitement to snake low through her belly, its warmth dripping down to the place between her legs. She kissed him back with all of the fervor that she could summon, with all of the fever in her veins. She was tugging at his shirt, and somehow they were separating briefly so he could yank it over his head, and then he was slanting his hot mouth over hers again while she ran her hands all over his bare chest and biceps, relearning him, a lesson she would never tire of.

He deepened the kiss with a muffled curse, one of such gravelly pleasure that her toes curled, and the large fist in her hair dropped down to join its fellow that had snagged at the fabric of her neckline. She was wholly unprepared for what happened next—there was a sharp tug, and the sound of ripping seams burst like a thunderclap through the room as he ripped open her bodice.

"*Oskar!*" Guinevere shrieked. Although she could probably stand to sound a tad more dismayed. "You made me leave six dresses behind in Druvenlode, you can't just go around tearing what I *did* bring—"

"Think of it as a charitable endeavor. Poor Pudding's overloaded enough as it is." Oskar shoved the torn bodice to Guinevere's hips, his topaz eyes glittering as they fixed, hawklike, on her bare breasts. "Gods, princess," he breathed out, all quiet reverence. "How can you think that I'd even *look* at any other woman?"

She preened at that. She couldn't help it. Oh, she was vain. And easily ruined, too—that could never have been more clear than when he bent his head and took her left nipple into his mouth. Suddenly she was the most wanton woman to ever walk the earth, arching into his lips, clawing at his muscular shoulders, chanting his name. Every swirl of his tongue over her taut bud felt like a river of light across her skin. And when he sealed his lips around her and *sucked*—she could die from the sheer pleasure of it. Her world narrowed down to the sweet pulsing of his mouth and the curve of his tusks against her sensitive flesh. She tugged at his soft midnight hair and whimpered and begged, climbing toward her little death but never reaching it. Teinidh was fluttering along with her, spinning and swaying, trailing bright flames through darkest chasms.

By the time both her breasts were slick and flushed from Oskar's attentions, there were overwhelmed tears in Guinevere's eyes. He huffed when he saw them, his finger lightly dashing them away from the corners of her lashes. "You cry too easily."

"It's your fault, this time," she sniffled.

She was so dizzy with want that she could do nothing but rest her head on his shoulder when he swept her into his arms and carried her, as one would a bride, to the sole bed shoved up against the wall. He laid her down over the sheets and took her boots off for her before removing his own, a task greatly hindered by the fact that he couldn't seem to look away from her exposed chest for too long.

She laughed through her tears and held her arms out to him, and his lips quirked in a wry half smile as he crawled on top of her. He plied her with one heated kiss after another, over and over until she was melting into the mattress, drunk off the taste of him. Time spiraled on in wave upon decadent wave, and at some point in that blur of glorious sensation, her torn dress was stripped away and his trousers were rolled down and the wearing of undergarments was consigned to the dustbins of the past, but she was only vaguely aware of any of it. She was floating in her dream of Oskar and all that lovely wilderness brought forth by his kisses, his caresses.

Thus, she was more than a little disgruntled when he propped himself up on his elbows, lifting his mouth from hers with no indication of putting it back where it belonged anytime soon. Before she could voice her annoyance, though, he peered down at her with a solemn tenderness that stole her heart.

"Gwen," Oskar rasped, "are you sure? We don't have to, if you're not sure."

He was hot and hard against the inside of her thigh. It wasn't lost on her that what happened next would be a point of no return.

Guinevere swallowed, searching for the right words. She reached up to trace the line of Oskar's jaw. It clenched into the curve of her palm.

"So much of my life consists of choices made by other people," she whispered. "This is the one thing I get to decide. And even if it wasn't—even if my straits were less dire and I was as free as the leaves blowing across the Amber Road—I would still want it to be you."

He closed his eyes. "I don't deserve you, sweetheart," he mumbled. She turned pink with delight at the endearment, her fingers scaling the ladder of his ribs while his lips trailed an ardent path from her temple to her cheek, then down her neck to the hollow at the base of her throat. His lean hips slotted fully between her spread legs, and the blunt head of his erection nudged at her entrance. A fresh surge of arousal swept through her, mingled with some apprehension. He felt . . . *thick.* Surely all that wasn't expected to go inside her? But she knew Oskar well enough by now—knew that, if she showed even the slightest trace of hesitation, his mulish sense of honor would cause him to put a stop to the whole affair.

So she arched up, hooking one leg over his waist, and the tip of him began to sink in—

Oskar let out an undignified yelp, canting his hips away from hers, one hand pressing into her belly to hold her still. "*Slowly,* Gwen," he said through gritted teeth. "Nice and easy. It's your first time."

Guinevere wasn't so sure that she liked the sound of that. There was so much of the world that she had yet to discover. So much yet to see. And so little time. She began to protest, but Oskar shut her up with another fierce kiss. She returned it, happily looping her arms around his neck, relaxing, giving him free rein to position all the pertinent bits down there if it was *so* important . . .

And then he was wrenching his mouth from hers and gripping her shoulder almost hard enough to bruise, pushing *forward* and *inside,* and it felt odd, it truly did, far bigger than fingers, opening her up. His dark brows knitting together in utmost concentration, he reached down and thumbed at her pearl, his tongue flicking out to lave her nipple at the same time. She keened, her inner walls releasing another wave of wet, admitting more of him inside her. There was a twinge of pain that made her tense, and he went statue-still at once, his topaz eyes searching her face.

"I'm all right," she assured him. "You may, ah, *proceed.*"

He didn't look like he believed her, but he gave a shallow, experimental thrust. It felt sort of nice. Another thrust and her mouth fell open, her eyelids fluttering. He buried his face in the side of her neck as he rocked into her. "Shit," he groaned. "You feel amazing. *Gods.*"

His praise went down like finest ambrosia. Encouraged, she mimicked the rolling motions of his hips with her own, and suddenly he was so deep inside her that she all but arched off the mattress, stretched and filled beyond what she had thought possible. Whatever pain she might have felt, though, was quickly washed away when Oskar gathered her close, raining sloppy kisses all over her face and throat. His next thrust was the most forceful one yet, knocking a sound that was nearly a sob out of her lungs.

"Oskar," she said plaintively, "I'm so full, please, you're so—it's so much—"

He froze again, twitching inside her. "I'll stop," he gritted out, as breathless as she felt. His expression was utterly wrecked, strands of dark hair falling across his flushed, sweat-dampened face. "Let me just—"

He withdrew, so carefully that it almost broke her heart. Wildfire slipped into the fractures, and she dug blunt nails into his shoulders, keeping him halfway in. Keeping him there, with her.

"I didn't say that it was *too* much," Guinevere rasped. "I didn't say to stop."

Oskar's topaz eyes blazed with relief. He pressed his forehead to hers, muttering something that sounded like both a prayer and a curse against her cheek.

Then he slammed back in.

Guinevere saw stars. She truly did. They streaked across her vision and fell into the flames that sang inside her. She gave herself over to the oldest song in the universe, to a rhythm that she'd been made for, to a place where no mercenaries or sinister presences or mysterious trunks existed. A place that was just her and Oskar. The bed creaked and the sheets twisted and their lips caught as they moved together, urging each other higher.

A line was crossed at some point, some boundary hurtled over, and all of his immaculate self-control snapped. He rutted into her mindlessly, until she was crying out from pleasure and raking her nails down his back, both of them lost in delirium. "Good girl," he ground out, slick with sweat, pupils blown wide, a young god above her, his broad shoulders the roof of her world. "Taking me so well in that tight little—"

"Don't say things like that." Some lingering shred of primness made her interrupt in between pants. "It's really not"—he swirled his hips against hers, the tip of him hitting a spot inside her that set off sparks—"*oh,*" she moaned, and then she came, spasming around his thick length. She could swear that his eyes all but rolled into the back of his head when he felt her clamp down. Tendrils of warm, radiant bliss spread through her until she was boneless, until she lay beneath him, sated and pliant, murmuring nonsensical words of encouragement while he drove into her and followed her down into delirium.

CHAPTER TWENTY-SIX

Oskar

Spilling inside Guinevere was a religious experience. Not to say that every moment prior had been anything short of sacred.

He collapsed on top of her, his ears ringing. She prodded him in the ribs. "Oskar, you're heavy."

"Five minutes." He pressed a kiss to the side of her neck. "Just let me catch my breath."

She huffed but reached up to card her fingers through his hair. He closed his eyes, savoring each soothing caress.

"That was rather wonderful, wasn't it?" Her pleased voice drifted in as though from far away, slipping comfortably through the haze of his afterglow. "They say it usually hurts the first time, and there *was* a bit of discomfort, but now I can confidently state that if one's partner is as gentle and respectful as you were—"

"Mmm." Being gentle and respectful had damn near killed him. But he was happy that she was happy.

"You weren't very respectful toward the end, though," Guinevere remarked. "I've no issue with it, I don't think, but it'll take me a while to get used to that kind of love-talk. You may try it again in the future."

He dozed off to the dulcet singsong of her chatter, his face nestled in the valley between her breasts. When he woke up, the fire was burning lower in its hearth and the sky beyond the lone window was pitch-black.

Guinevere regarded him with violet eyes at half-mast, a smile lurking at the corners of her lips. "I *have* heard that men tend to fall asleep right after."

"Sorry." Oskar rolled over but took her with him, so that she was now the one pillowed on *his* chest. "I guess I'm a typical man in this regard."

"Nothing about you is typical," she told him softly, and his heart might have skipped a beat right then and there, but he'd be damned if he would admit it. The room smelled like sex, and her silver hair was delectably rumpled, falling in waves over satiny brown skin that glowed in the firelight. Ah, but he could get used to this.

They ate their sandwiches in bed, not bothering to put clothes back on. She licked a stray drop of mustard off his chin with an impish giggle, and he forgot himself long enough to smile at her. Eventually he poked his head out the door and asked a passing chambermaid to draw a hot bath, and he and Guinevere spent an idyllic—if comical— thirty minutes squeezed into the too-small slipper tub, washing each other.

"Enjoy this," he warned her, ducking so she could lather soap into his hair. "This is your last bath until Trostenwald." He'd decided that they wouldn't stop in Alfield, which was the next settlement after Zadash. Alfield was a small farming town hardly equipped to deal with a rash of mercenary activity.

"I'm sure we can find another waterfall somewhere along the way," she murmured, looking at him through lowered lashes, and he felt his face heat and his cock twitch.

While they were drying off by the fire, his gaze fell on her ripped dress. "I don't know what came over me," he said dourly. It was a waste of a perfectly serviceable garment.

Guinevere chewed on her bottom lip in a way that made him want to do it for her. "I found it rather exciting, to tell you the truth."

"Well, it's not going to happen again. My working-class heart can't take it."

"It shall remain a treasured memory, all the more special for its unique nature," she vowed.

He laughed. He wasn't the sort of man who just . . . *laughed*—but she brought that out in him. And he didn't consider himself the sort of person who cuddled, either, but after they changed into their sleep clothes and went to bed, nothing was more important than curling around Guinevere, tucking her smaller body into his as they lay on their sides like spoons in a drawer, all sparkling and clean and snug.

Now that her magic was out in the open between them, it seemed easier for her to tell him things—things like how Elaras had told her to listen, and what she had heard when she touched the trunk.

"There's something enchanted inside," she said. "But the trunk itself contains an enchantment, too. Where did Mother and Father *get* this? We don't deal in magicked wares; there's a whole other trade license you need to apply for."

If there was one thing Oskar hated more than treehuggers and mercenaries, it was mysteries. But he didn't have any answers for her, so he just held her tighter.

"Oskar?" Guinevere sounded worried, her fingers gliding frenetically along his arm wrapped around her waist. "What if the mercenaries find us in Nicodranas? Mother and Father . . ."

"Where are they staying?"

"At Lord Wensleydale's manor."

His stomach hollowed out at the mention of her betrothed. But she was in distress, and he had to fix that first. "That's your problem solved, then. A fancy lord has more than enough guards. You'll be safer in his manor than you'll ever be on this journey." *Safer than you'll ever be with me.*

It was no competition at all. Oskar had no armies, no piles of gold with which to hire them. It was up to him and him alone to keep Guinevere alive and unharmed until the Menagerie Coast, where he would turn her over to people better equipped to protect her and give her the life she deserved. He would see his duty through until the bitter end.

And then he would let her go.

THEY HAD A SHOCKINGLY LATE start the next morning. Oskar maintained that it was no fault of his.

"How can it not be!" Guinevere's pert nose was the highest point in Zadash as they trooped out of the Song and Supper with all their luggage. "I did my part, didn't I; I nudged you to wake you up and everything—"

"It's not that you nudged me, it's *where* you nudged me," he patiently explained. "I thought it was . . . an overture."

"I was aiming to elbow you in the ribs. I didn't mean for my hand to touch your—your—" She faltered, then bristled. "Am I the sort of woman who would purposefully, without so much as a by-your-leave, grab someone's—someone's staff—"

He let out a bark of laughter. She glared at him as they entered the inn's stables. "You could have inquired as to my intentions. There was no call to ravish me straightaway."

"Would've been unsporting of me to stop once you started begging me not to," Oskar cheerfully pointed out.

"Please, sir," quailed the young stable hand who had been waiting by the doors, "that's six copper pieces for the two horses' keep and hay and water overnight. I—I brushed them down, too."

Guinevere's face could have fried an egg. Enjoying himself immensely, Oskar paid the stable hand, adding a little extra for the latter's trouble.

On their way to Zadash's southern gate, they came across a blacksmith's shop. Guinevere had elected to walk with Oskar and help him guide the horses, but now she let out an excited squeal, grabbed her satchel of wares, and ducked beneath the hammer-and-anvil sign over the entryway before he could even blink.

Bewildered, he waited outside with Pudding and Vindicator. After all, he couldn't just *leave* the trunk there, despite the ever-present Crownsguard patrolling the vicinity. Guinevere skipped back into view a few minutes later, minus the satchel but looking inordinately pleased with herself.

"Go on," she told Oskar. "I'll watch over the horses and our effects."

"What have you done?" he asked, alarmed. It was nothing against her. Not really. She couldn't help the strange ideas that popped into that pretty, whirligig head.

"It's a surprise," she insisted.

Oskar went inside the shop full of misgivings. The dwarf blacksmith was waiting for him with the friendly smile of someone who had been paid very, very well.

"Absolutely not," said Oskar.

"My lady mentioned you might say that," the dwarf replied. "In which case, I am obliged to inform you that we don't offer refunds. The weapons have been paid for, sir. You need only make your selections."

The thing was—it *did* make sense to replace the swords Oskar had lost. He could hardly fend off the mercenaries in close combat with a hunting knife and a plucky horse. He would give the purchased weaponry to Guinevere at journey's end, he decided. Then she could gift them to her betrothed or . . . whatever. It would be no business of Oskar's by then.

After several minutes of browsing, he selected two of the blacksmith's finest swords. They were plain in appearance compared to the ones with engraved hilts or jewels set into their pommels, but the blade was the important thing, and these blades were as sharp as ice, crafted for fighting rather than display.

Gods help him, but he was in a buoyant mood as he left the shop. He had started the morning making love to a beautiful woman, and now she'd bought him a pair of dwarven-made swords. He had to thank Guinevere sincerely.

"You gave away *everything* left in your satchel?" were the first words he barked at her.

"You were the one who believed I should have no qualms exchanging the wares for what I needed," came her lofty response. "And I need you to be adequately armed if you are to protect me from the mercenaries."

But she was clearly fighting to suppress a smile, her frame vibrating as though she wanted to jump up and down, awash in the simple joy of gift-giving. He scowled and took her hand and didn't let go of it until they reached the city gate.

AFTERNOON FOUND THEM ON VINDICATOR'S back, trotting along the Amber Road behind a procession of two covered, ox-driven wagons that bore a ragtag assortment of travelers and all their earthly possessions. One of them was an orange-skinned goblin—a musician who liked to dangle his brightly stockinged feet outside the wagon's canvas bonnet while strumming his lute and singing lusty songs that Oskar fervently hoped went over Guinevere's head. There was an entire army of goblin children, too, occasionally hopping down to run beside their conveyances' spinning wooden wheels, flying kites and blowing soap bubbles out of pipes. As the hours wore on and boredom set in, more than a few of them took to doubling back and pestering Oskar and Guinevere's own party.

"Leave that alone!" Oskar bellowed at the tiny horde of devil spawn who had clambered onto Pudding and were using the pearwood trunk strapped to the mare's back as a drum.

The children ignored him. Where were the parents? He glared at the musician, who was the only adult visible in the wagon a few feet ahead. "Can't you do something?"

The musician plucked a mournful note from his lute. "Those're my sister's kids. They don't listen to me."

"Can't we leave them be, Oskar?" Guinevere pleaded. "They're just having fun, and Pudding appears to like their company."

"I doubt Pudding understands what's going on around her enough to form opinions on people," Oskar muttered.

"She's a very sweet horse," Guinevere said loyally.

"She is," he agreed. "Like treacle. And just as slow."

Offended on their pack mare's behalf, Guinevere turned around with a huff and spent the next several minutes looking straight ahead at the road, shoulders rigid, refusing to talk to him. He poked and prodded at her, stifling his chuckles every time she so very pointedly veered from his touch as far as the saddle would allow. Eventually, he couldn't stand it any longer, and he pressed a fond kiss to the side of her neck, nipping at the sensitive skin. She shrieked with laughter and half-heartedly tried to push him away, but he persisted. Another kiss. Another little nip. She sighed, leaning back against his chest.

"Ah, the bloom of romance!" the goblin musician called out. In a fit of inspiration, he wove a beautiful melody from his lute. The sound of strings was lighter than sunbeams on a forest pond, serenading the autumn leaves and the clear horizon, impossible not to get lost in.

"Oh, my beloved's eyes are violets, her hair spills like a moonlit stream." The fine tenor of his voice rang exquisitely over the open road. "She is a gentle warrior, she handles my sword like a dream—"

"I'm going to kill you!" Oskar roared.

The children cackled. Their uncle hastily vanished into the darkness of the wagon in a flash of bright stockings, the echoes of goblin music still haunting the air.

CHAPTER TWENTY-SEVEN

Guinevere

In hindsight, it had been foolish to believe that the sunny days would hold fast three weeks into Fessuran. Although it wasn't that Guinevere had *believed* it would never rain, exactly—she simply hadn't thought about it.

That was the thing with the weather: one tended to take the good for granted until the bad crept up on them.

Or, in this case, until the skies clouded over, swallowing the sunlight, and a growl of thunder was all the warning that the gods deigned to issue before a blinding deluge fell over the Amber Road.

Vindicator pranced anxiously while Pudding let out a high-pitched neigh of distress. Through sheets of water so thick that they all but plastered to her eyes, blobs of diminutive orange streaked across Guinevere's vision as the goblin children abandoned the mare and raced to the shelter of their wagons.

"Come!" The musician had reemerged and was now beckoning at

Oskar and Guinevere, shouting to be heard over the din of the elements. "Inside, quickly!"

Oskar urged Vindicator forward. The ground had turned to mud, but the stallion prevailed, and soon Oskar was lifting Guinevere into the wagon.

"I have to stay with the horses," he told her.

She gripped his arm. "But—"

He shook her off. "Take care of her for me," he said to the musician, who nodded and ushered Guinevere into the darkness underneath the bonnet.

Guinevere wasn't sure how many children there actually were. They moved around so much that each one seemed to be everywhere at the same time. There were fifteen adults of various races, though, including the musician. They sat comfortably amidst piles of furs, wooden chests, building materials, and a staggering array of clubs and axes.

"She's shivering, the poor dear," tutted the most elderly of the lot, a stooped human woman with white hair and gnarled knuckles. "Rodregg, fetch us some blankets, won't you?"

"Yes, Nan." The musician ambled over to one of the chests and heaved the lid open.

"He's a good lad," the elderly woman confided to Guinevere. "One of my favorites. I wish he'd apply himself to the clan business more— we're fur traders, you see—but unfortunately he wants to focus on his music."

"He couldn't skin a rabbit if it hopped into his lap and held still!" cackled a brunette goblin who bore enough of a resemblance to Rodregg that Guinevere guessed she was his sister.

"If you are quite done assassinating my character, Zugri . . ." Rodregg dumped several heavy wool blankets into Guinevere's lap.

"It's short for Zugrinilka," the brunette goblin explained as she helped Guinevere bundle up. "It means 'the presentiment of doom that overtakes the enemy before battle is joined.' I hope my little hellions weren't bothering you too much earlier."

There were cries of "We weren't!" and "We're *good* kids!" from the innumerable children. One of them asked Guinevere if Pudding would be all right in the rain. She nodded, her teeth chattering too much for her to speak. Her new companions took pity on her and introduced themselves one by one to fill up the silence. Her head spun from all the names, but she forced herself to concentrate, to remember. It was the least she could do.

The old woman everyone called Nan had formed Clan Bonecrusher decades ago. They were nomads who plied their trade all over Wildemount, collecting every lost soul in need of a home along the way. Species didn't matter; they were a *family*. A particularly well-armed one, more than capable of holding their own against the bandits that plagued the wilderness.

When the blankets had finally warmed Guinevere, she hurried to introduce herself and to thank the clan's matriarch, as etiquette dictated, but Nan waved her off.

"Think nothing of it," she said. "We know how it goes. Travelers help one another here on the Amber Road, or we're *all* up the creek without a paddle."

"And where are you off to this time?" Guinevere inquired.

"The Menagerie Coast," said Zugri. Her yellow eyes glinted with mischief. "Where the winters are milder for Nan's old bones."

A chorus of cackling laughter echoed through the wagon. Nan playfully shook a fist at Zugri.

"You're for the Coast as well, yes?" Rodregg peered at Guinevere speculatively. "Forgive my presumption, but a fine lady such as yourself doesn't seem all that destined for Alfield *or* Trostenwald."

Guinevere fidgeted. She hardly felt like a lady in her drenched clothes, half-buried in rustic blankets and her hair a sodden, tangled mess, but her parents would have been delighted to know that her affluent upbringing had shone through. *It's in how you carry yourself,* her father loved to say. *Your mother and I are as common as muck, we come from generations of it, but with you, my girl, we'll finally break that cycle.*

Out loud, Guinevere confirmed that her party was also headed to the Menagerie Coast. Rodregg grinned. "You and your young man are eloping, are you?"

Her first instinct was to protest. But, on second thought, she and Oskar could hardly go around telling everyone who asked that they were transporting a trunk filled with valuable enchanted items. If omitting that fact, though, it was difficult to explain why two people were traveling together all by themselves such a long way, one of them clearly from the upper class, as Rodregg had pointed out. Without knowing it, the musician had handed Guinevere a plausible cover story.

"Yes, we're eloping," she confirmed, and Rodregg clapped a hand over his heart as the other Bonecrushers hooted in delight.

Rain continued to pour well into the late afternoon. While her companions napped or played games with the children or chatted among themselves or threatened to break Rodregg's lute over his head if he didn't stop singing, Guinevere took to checking on Oskar. She stayed at the back of the wagon, fretfully peeking out the bonnet and into the silver-gray blur that the world had become. Oskar was practically a darkened silhouette; he walked between the two horses, their reins in his hands as he scouted the ground ahead, guiding Pudding and Vindicator away from rocks and deep potholes. The hood of his cloak was drawn over his head, but he had to be drenched to the bone . . . yet he continued slogging through the mud and the wet behind the wagon, never faltering. Guinevere's heart ached.

She could have wept in relief when the deluge finally ceased. Nan made the call to set up camp, as the sun didn't look likely to return. The two wagons trundled to a stop at the side of the road, and Guinevere leapt down. Her arms filled with blankets, her boots kicking up sprays of brown slush, she ran to Oskar, who had taken off his cloak and was tethering the horses.

"I'm fine," he insisted in that gruff, tired rumble of his as she attempted to swaddle him in the blankets. "Did they treat you all right?"

"Yes." She arranged a third blanket over his shoulders. He gave up and let her, a faint softness tugging at the corner of his mouth. "They've invited us to camp with them tonight," she added hesitantly. "I think it's a good idea?"

Oskar nodded. "Safety in numbers."

"Let me introduce you to Clan Bonecrusher, then." She wrapped both her arms around one of his, tugging him in the direction of the wagons. "By the way, I told them that you and I are eloping."

He nearly walked into a tree.

TENTS WERE PITCHED ON THE damp ground in a large clearing just off the Amber Road. The Bonecrushers had logs in their wagons, and soon enough, a fire blazed merrily, warding off the post-rainstorm chill. The cozy scent of burning applewood mingled with the cool musk of wet earth.

The clan traveled well stocked. In an enormous iron cauldron blackened from years of use, Zugri mixed up a hearty pottage of cracked wheat, pickled turnips, and mutton that had been cured in salt and honey. Seated by the fire, Oskar and Guinevere threw all shame to the wind and asked for thirds.

"This is the best we've ever eaten while camping," she told him, and he grunted agreeably as he shoveled more pottage into his mouth.

The Bonecrusher beside Guinevere—a half-elf named Iaz— touched her arm. "Big man like that needs his food, and lots of it," she whispered. "Do you know how to cook?"

"No," Guinevere admitted.

"Nothing to it, but you have to learn," said Iaz. "Wherever you two decide to settle down, ask your neighbors for their recipes. There are some basic techniques . . ." And she quickly went through the steps for boiling and frying.

At first, Guinevere listened only to be polite. She and Oskar were certainly not going to be settling down anywhere together; that was merely the fiction that they'd created. The longer she paid attention to Iaz, though, the more an odd little daydream began to form in her head. A daydream of Oskar coming home to a hot meal on the table, prepared by her. Perhaps she'd still be wearing an apron when he came in. Perhaps the house could be by the shore of a shimmering mountain lake, surrounded by trees. And he would be the first thing she saw every morning, and every night she would fall asleep in his arms.

There would be no jewels or silks in that life. No balls or high teas or pianofortes—none of the things that she was used to. Could she be happy?

But there was no point to this mental exercise. She could never abandon her duty, and Oskar would never want to be saddled with her for the rest of his life. Stricken, she banished that impossible future to nothingness.

After supper, the children were sent to bed, and the adults passed around their homemade grog—a potent spiced drink that, in contrast to Zugri's pottage, Guinevere found utterly vile. She imbibed enough to be courteous; Oskar, on the other hand, seemed to enjoy it. Rodregg broke out his lute, and, with some good-natured moaning and groaning, his kinsmen let him perform. Drinks flowed and music lilted and firelight flickered, and it was such a beautiful night, there beneath wisp-clouded velvet skies, there in the heart of autumn. Guinevere soaked up every moment the way a plant soaked up the sunshine. She was at peace, and all was right in the world . . .

"What're you so aloof for, boy?" Nan yelled across the campfire at Oskar, waving her bottle of grog at the space between him and Guinevere as though it were a personal affront. "You stole her away from her lord father, the least you could do is cuddle!"

"Hear, hear!" the Bonecrushers shouted raucously.

Guinevere considered it a small miracle that she didn't panic enough to manifest Teinidh and burn the whole forest down. As it was, she could only blush furiously and avoid Oskar's gaze.

"There's really no need—" she started to tell the Bonecrushers, only for the rest of the sentence to wither in her mouth, suddenly dry as Oskar draped a heavy arm over her shoulders, hauling her close to his brawny frame that she had already memorized with her hands.

"Regretting your lie already, princess?" he murmured in her ear.

She couldn't respond. There was just . . . *something*—about being claimed so openly, even if it was a charade. Their audience cheered, and Rodregg switched from a lively dancing tune to a familiar soft ballad. He was continuing his song from earlier.

"Oh, my beloved is the bronze of the linden trees, she sets fire to my soul," the musician crooned. "She smiled at me as she went down on her pretty knees, she swallowed me whole—"

Oskar threw a turnip peel at him. The rest of the clan thought this was great fun, and they joined in. Poor Rodregg was pelted with more turnip peels, leaves, and the occasional pebble, but he valiantly kept strumming his lute.

"Oh, everyone's a critic, it's brutal out here," he sang in the same tune but in a much louder voice, caught in the agony of creation. "You're all bastards, that much is exceedingly clear . . ."

CHAPTER TWENTY-EIGHT

Guinevere

"One day I'll be famous and you'll all be sorry," Guinevere sang as she and Oskar walked to a nearby stream the next morning. "So put that turnip down, my horrid sister, Zugri."

"Sing something else," Oskar begged her. "Anything. I couldn't sleep last night because that accursed jingle kept running through my head."

"It's stuck in mine, too." Guinevere offered him an apologetic smile. "Rodregg has an ear for melody, you have to admit."

"But his lyricism leaves much to be desired."

Oskar was carrying a chest full of the used bowls and spoons from last night's supper. He had volunteered to do the washing, and Guinevere was accompanying him because she wanted to be useful, for once. Not that she knew how to wash dishes, but how hard could it be?

"Where is the soap?" she asked brightly, sorting the utensils as she and Oskar crouched by the stream.

"And so her diabolical plan is revealed," Oskar muttered, opening a round wooden container filled with . . . something. "She wishes to bathe while I toil away."

Guinevere chuckled. "The soap for the *dishes,* Oskar."

He blinked. "Why would you waste soap on cleaning the dishes?"

"What are we supposed to use, then?"

He showed her what was inside the container. The ashes from the campfire.

A few minutes later, Guinevere was trying very hard not to cry as she dragged her bare fingers through the black muck, sprinkling it into the bowls and scrubbing, scrubbing. She could feel the grit seeping into the crevices under her nails, along with bits of grain and mutton. This was the worst thing that had ever happened to her. She put on a brave face and muddled through, all the while praying that Oskar wouldn't notice her distress.

When he hadn't made any remarks by the time the last bowl was rinsed off in the stream and placed back in the chest, Guinevere started to hope that she'd gotten away with it. They stood up, and she turned to head back to the campsite, but he stopped her with a hand around her waist.

"If it makes you feel any better . . ." His grin was gentle in the early morning light, but there was a trace of ruefulness to it. "That's probably the last time you'll have to do it."

She turned her nose up at him. He kissed it, then darted another quick peck to her lips. Which was a pity, as she would have quite liked for it to last longer.

"You know, Oskar," Guinevere mused as they retraced their steps to the clearing, "you haven't been as grumpy lately."

"I threw a turnip peel at someone last night," he reminded her.

"The old you would have thrown a rock," she countered. "You have also been smiling more. And sometimes you *laugh.*"

This time, the bend in his grin was devilish. His golden eyes swept her from head to toe, poured over her like honey. "Maybe it's because you're just so good at—*it.*"

She almost walked into a low-hanging branch, so flustered was she. But she was pleased, too. "Thank you," she said primly. "I—"

"At washing the dishes, I mean."

Guinevere half burst into giggles, half choked on outrage. She took a threatening step toward Oskar, and he held the chest of bowls and spoons higher in front of him, like a shield.

"If any of these fall, *you're* doing the rewashing," he warned.

"Just you wait until we get back to camp and you can't hide behind them anymore." A thought struck her, and she looked around. "Speaking of, we should have been back by now, don't you think? Did we take a wrong turn?"

A wrong turn wasn't possible, though. Not when the stream was only a stone's throw away from the campsite, not with a veteran woodsman like Oskar. They both went still as they attempted to get their bearings.

With its moss-covered rocks and floor of bracken and canopy of red and gold, this part of the forest looked like any other. But something was slightly . . . *off,* like what should have been a closed door only three-quarters settled into the wall.

Oskar slowly placed the chest on the ground. When he straightened up, his right hand dropped to the hilt of one sword.

"Stay alert," he told Guinevere in a soft voice that somehow rang unnaturally loud in her ears, and at last she realized what was bothering her about their surroundings.

In the course of her travels, she had come to realize that the forests were never truly silent. There were always birds singing and insects whirring away, always the snap of twigs and the rustling in the undergrowth.

None of those ambient noises was present now. The world was as still as glass.

Guinevere listened the way Elaras had taught her. And the eerie quiet was replaced by the roar of magic everywhere, woven into each blade of burnished grass. Teinidh stirred uneasily within the caverns of her soul.

"It's an illusion," said Guinevere. "This whole area." She remembered sparks flaring from purple fingers beneath the onslaught of a stallion's hooves. "The mercenaries had a magic user with them, didn't they? That gnome."

Oskar drew his sword. "Get behind me. No matter where I turn, you have to make sure you're *always* behind me. Understand?"

She nodded, stepping into place as he'd instructed. She tried to peek over his shoulder, but his next command quickly put a stop to that.

"Face the other way. If you spot even the tiniest movement, anything at all—scream."

Guinevere nodded again, then realized Oskar couldn't see her. "Yes."

When she faced away from him, her view consisted mostly of bushes and tree trunks. She was more or less calm, thanks to Oskar's own steady, no-nonsense attitude, but it was a fluttery sort of calm, like a veil had been thrown over the apprehension that was struggling to break free.

Suddenly there was a glint of silver leaping out of the autumn foliage, and Guinevere was too startled and afraid to scream. She gasped instead, but it was all the warning that Oskar needed. Swiftly, he spun on his heel and one arm shoved her behind him while the other raised his sword at a slant. A dagger bounced off the curved blade.

And a second one flew into Oskar's shoulder.

Guinevere screamed then.

There was a subtle twist in the air as the net of illusion magic shifted, and three figures came charging out from bushes that had not visibly contained a single living soul scant seconds prior. There was the leonine katari, the reptilian dragonblood whom the purple gnome had called Bharash, and the uniya, whose name, Oskar had said, was Selene.

"You should have taken the deal," Selene called out to Oskar, right before she and her cohorts descended on him and Guinevere.

Guinevere couldn't pinpoint the exact moment Oskar wrenched the dagger from his shoulder, or when his sword blocked the enemy's first strike. Everything was a blur. He had switched his weapon to his left hand while the injured right arm reached back, guiding her with every movement he made so that she was always shielded by his body even as he slipped them through every break in the mercenary ranks.

But Guinevere was surprised to find that she didn't *need* to be guided. Years of dance lessons came rushing to the forefront. No one could escape more than a decade of waltzes and tangos and quadrilles without developing impeccable timing and a sense of rhythm. What had been the blur of battle soon began to take on a certain logic, and her footwork synchronized perfectly with his, stepping parallel to where he stepped, turning when he turned. He'd told her to ensure that she stayed behind him, and so she did. The back-and-forth of attacks and countermeasures was her rhythm. The slam of steel against steel was her beat. Whirling around her were the katari's claws and the dragonblood's morning-star flail and the uniya's multitude of daggers, but as long as she kept time with Oskar, she would be all right. He was her dance partner, and he would keep her safe. She would follow his lead until the ends of the earth.

They couldn't keep it up forever, though. It was still three against one. Oskar began to falter in the face of the relentless assaults from all sides, his blocks clumsier, his swings far too wide.

Where was Teinidh?

For the first time in her life, Guinevere wished that the wildfire spirit would manifest. She wished it with every inch of her body. She could *feel* it, the flames within her, fanned by terror. But they could never seem to hit critical mass, the point of breaking free. There was something holding her back, and she couldn't, for the life of her, figure out what it was. Teinidh wailed and gnashed against the walls of her prison, and the seconds hurtled agonizingly by . . .

And the katari's great paw swiped across Oskar's ribs, sharp claws cutting through fabric and through skin. In doing so, however, the feline humanoid had left a flank wide open, and Oskar wasted no time in lunging forward, driving the dwarven-made sword into his opponent's furred stomach.

Blood went *everywhere.* Some of it spattered on Guinevere's face. It was worse than the ashes. The katari staggered back and fell and then moved no more, his sightless eyes clouding over. Enraged, the two surviving mercenaries fell upon Oskar with a vengeance. He resorted to dodging and darting out of reach rather than fighting back. Guinevere kept pace with him, and they led the enemy in a frantic circle through the woods. She wondered why Selene was no longer throwing her daggers and why Bharash had yet to use his breath attack, then realization hit her like a flare of lightning—the mercenaries wanted her in addition to the trunk. That first dagger had been flung at Guinevere because the uniya knew that Oskar would block it and fail to guard against the second.

But, when it came right down to it, the mercenaries needed her *alive*.

Bharash and Selene cornered Oskar and Guinevere up against a tree trunk. Their weapons went slicing through the air toward Oskar at the same time. There was no opportunity to second-guess, to hesitate. Guinevere ran out from behind Oskar and placed herself in front of him, shaking, tears of fright welling up in her eyes.

I'm going to die, I'm going to die—

The mercenaries snatched their arms back suddenly. Both the dagger and the morning star veered away mere *centimeters* before they would have collided with Guinevere.

Everyone froze.

"Why are you *crying?*" Bharash asked Guinevere. In spite of the confusion evident in his tone, his deep voice still boomed like thunder.

Guinevere wasn't just crying; she was *bawling*. Fat tears rolled down her cheeks, and sobs wracked her frame. She was so, *so* scared, and the weapons had nearly *hit* her, but she had to save Oskar.

"She does that a lot," Oskar told the dragonblood. Right before he pulled her close and whispered "run" in her ear, and shoved her with all his might.

Into the bushes. Away from the field of combat.

Steel rang against steel once more, but Guinevere only heard it. She'd started running, and there was no time to look back. She thought about Clan Bonecrusher and their vast array of clubs and axes. She had to find the campsite, she had to get help—

She'd barely gone a couple of feet before she tripped over a figure lurking in the undergrowth. Namely, the purple gnome who was in league with the mercenaries.

He was covered in bandages from when Vindicator had trampled him several days ago. He'd been blending in with the bushes, casting his magic with stiffly held arms and broken fingers. Guinevere crashed into him and the spell broke, air warping, colors flashing, rocks and trees rearranging themselves until the path between the campsite and the stream became recognizable and the normal sounds of the forest rushed back in.

"There they are!" someone yelled. It sounded like Rodregg.

And the ground was shaking, and a collective, guttural battle cry was rending the heavens, and the woods were bristling with clubs and axes as the Bonecrushers charged. They raced past Guinevere and swarmed Bharash and Selene from all sides.

The purple gnome shot Guinevere a look of pure venom. He creakily waved his bandaged arms, preparing to cast a spell. She could only stare at him, reeling, not knowing what to do.

Teinidh, she begged.

In the darkness of her heart, embers glowed. A crown of fire rippled and turned, and eyes like craters looked at her, hollow and resigned.

Thin, ghostly shackles were wrapped around Teinidh's molten form, chaining her to this place that was not a place.

When we were younger, I could go off at the slightest provocation. Teinidh sounded shivery and far-off, like a dying candle. *But spending time in this world means growing attached to things. A nice house. A parent's love. The open road. The shape of someone's smile.*

I don't have time for this! Guinevere snapped. *We have to help Oskar!*

How, when you're afraid that we'll hurt him? Shackles spun around flame. Guinevere could only watch, because here it was, at last, laid bare. Finally, she knew. Finally, she understood why. *You're afraid that he'll burn along with the rest. You're afraid of losing him. That fear eclipses everything else.*

In the material realm, the realm of clashing blades and blood-soaked grass, the purple gnome held up a palm, his eyes locked on to Guinevere. Magic crackled at his fingertips, and—

—and he was consumed by a ball of fire.

At first, Guinevere thought that she'd surmounted Teinidh's shackles. Then she thought that perhaps *his* spell had gone awry. Then she turned and saw Zugri, advancing through the undergrowth.

A strange triangular mark had appeared on the goblin's forehead. It glowed in the same crimson light that now filled her eyes.

Zugri was a runechild. Beneath that domestic, motherly exterior lurked a natural font of arcane energy. Her eyes narrowed, and the fire intensified until there was nothing left of the purple gnome, only a pile of soot and the odor of charred flesh. The bright flames licked through the bushes, spreading fast, and Guinevere was no stranger to *this*. She braced herself for inferno. For the fire to sweep out of control and obliterate everything in its path. But it didn't. Zugri banished every single smoke-laden tendril with one wave of her hand.

All her life, Guinevere had known fire magic only as the great destroyer. She hadn't realized that it could be manipulated so artfully, that one could choose what to burn and what to save.

I wish I could learn.

The desire gripped Guinevere as she watched the rune melt back into Zugri's skin. As she listened to a cry of victory rising up from the Bonecrushers, and Oskar shouting for her amidst the clamor. As she smelled the lingering remnants of smoke and felt only the coolness of autumn.

I want to learn.

CHAPTER TWENTY-NINE

Oskar

Bharash and Selene had managed to escape, but not before injuring several of the Bonecrushers. This particular area of the woods had turned into an infirmary, with Iaz, the clan's lone healer, rushing to and fro among the wounded—the stabbed, the spiked, and, in the case of those who were unfortunate enough to have been in the way of the dragonblood's breath attack, the frostbitten.

Oskar felt absolutely terrible, in a way that had nothing to do with his own ailments. Iaz had cleaned and bandaged the dagger wound in his shoulder before leaving Guinevere to take care of the claw marks across his ribs, and he spoke gravely to her as he sat shirtless on the forest floor, the upper half of his body slightly reclined against a large slab of rock.

"We can't stay with them, Guinevere."

"I know," she replied in a soft voice.

The day before, the Bonecrushers had insisted that Oskar and

Guinevere join their caravan, as they were all headed in the same direction anyway. But that was no longer feasible. With two of the mercenaries dead, there was every possibility that the surviving ones would call for reinforcements and grow increasingly more desperate and ruthless as the Menagerie Coast drew nearer. All the members of Clan Bonecrusher were packed into the two wagons, their children included. The worst-case scenario was untenable, its cost too dear. This wasn't their fight.

Guinevere uncorked the fresh bottle of the homemade grog that Iaz had pressed into her hand earlier. She glanced at it and then at Oskar's exposed torso, gnawing on her bottom lip with trepidation. "Are . . . are you ready?"

Oskar nodded, fighting back a tender grin. His poor darling. There was no reason for her to be so nervous. It was only going to be a temporary sting, and he'd experienced much worse.

She splashed the brew over the gouges along his ribs. "Fuck!" he yelped, the burning pain making him see double. "Just kill me!"

"Well, no one wants that," she chided as she set the bottle down and prepared the bandages.

"This is only a wild guess, you understand, but Bharash and Selene might beg to differ."

"I couldn't give a fig about their opinions."

"That might be the meanest thing I've ever heard you say."

Guinevere seemed oddly pleased by his remark. She was still a little flushed from adrenaline, her eyes the color of dusk. There were grass stains on her skirt and twigs in her silver hair, and the katari's blood had dried in specks on her face. Her beauty had taken on a wilder aspect. It was as though she were in bloom, out here in the autumn woodlands.

It took a couple of tries for her to successfully wind the bandages around his rib cage, after which they headed back to the campsite, where a few Bonecrushers had stayed behind to watch over the clan's belongings and had already been informed by a runner of what had transpired.

"You'd been gone quite a while," Nan told Oskar and Guinevere, "so I sent a search party out. We thought you'd run afoul of a bear, maybe. We certainly weren't expecting to tangle with the Spider's Web this morn."

"That's their name?" Oskar struggled not to roll his eyes. "A little too on the nose for my tastes."

"They're a mid-level group," said Nan. "The kind you hire if you can't afford the Ceaseless Reach or the Order of Darkness."

"Now *those,*" said Oskar, "are proper mercenary names."

"We're getting off topic," Nan said firmly. "What I want to know is *why* my kinsmen ended up fighting them today."

After silently listening to Oskar and Guinevere's faltering confession, the Bonecrusher matriarch waved off their apologies for lying in the same manner she'd waved off their gratitude for the clan's assistance the previous afternoon. "Travelers help one another," she intoned. "Of course, if one of us dies, we will come after you and the Spider's Web with the vengeance of a thousand axes, but I don't think we need to worry about that. Us Bonecrushers are as tough as nails."

"Still," said Guinevere, a slight tremble to her bottom lip, "we shall take our leave of you at once. It's not safe to continue on together."

The elderly woman gave a reluctant nod. Oskar thought about what it took to transport an entire clan from one end of Wildemount to the other, keeping everyone alive as they followed you and the seasons and the trade winds. There had to be limits to compassion. He couldn't fault the matriarch in the least.

By the time Oskar had pulled on a fresh tunic and finished strapping all the luggage to Pudding, the rest of the clan had drifted back to camp, some with noticeable limps. They cheerfully thanked Oskar and Guinevere for the "cracking good battle," and farewells were warmly exchanged. Oskar had just helped Guinevere onto Vindicator's saddle when Nan shuffled over and pressed something into his palm.

It was a pendant. A translucent milky-white moonstone that was marbled with swirls of blue and pink, attached to a length of thin black leather.

"That is a Vigilance Stone," said Nan. "The clans in the Cyrios

Mountains trade us moonstones, and Zugri infuses them with detection spells in her spare time. We do not sell these; they are for use within the clan, or gifted to those we consider friends. The moonstones glow when they are within thirty feet of those carrying evil in their hearts. Rodregg wears one of these pendants, and that's how the search party knew where to amass even though the illusion spell hid you from sight."

Oskar went through the motions of putting the pendant on. Once it hung from his neck, the barest downward tug the only indication of an added weight, that was when the significance of the gift truly sank in, along with the realization that perhaps compassion could be endless, after all. He peered down at Nan and said, sincerely, "Thank you."

This time, the Bonecrusher matriarch didn't wave off his thanks. Instead, she reached out to pat his wrist. "It's not too late to *actually* elope with her, you know."

"Goodbye," Oskar said flatly, turning away.

Nan's creaky, wheezing laughter rang out behind him. "May we meet again."

ONCE HE AND GUINEVERE HAD left the Bonecrusher encampment far behind them, Oskar began to consider the Amber Road.

Apart from their party, the wide strip of well-trodden, yellowish dirt was completely deserted today. The steady *clip-clop* of the two horses' hooves echoed in the still air. Gray clouds lurked on the horizon, hiding the next bastion of civilization—Alfield—from view.

All the empty space fed into Oskar's lingering wariness from that morning's ambush. He had the Vigilance Stone to serve as warning, but what good was a detection spell at a range of thirty feet out here in the open?

He made a decision. He steered Vindicator left. Out of the road and into the forest.

"You are absolutely certain that it's safer this way?" Guinevere asked anxiously a few minutes later. They'd dismounted, as the trees grew too close together and the ground was too steep and entangled for riding. Oskar was holding on to Vindicator's reins while Guinevere managed Pudding.

"The Web's magician is dead," said Oskar, "so they can't lead us astray with illusions anymore. On their end, it would be easier to keep watch for us on the Amber Road than to track us here in the thick of the woods."

She nodded at once. He wanted to tell her once again to quit trusting people so quickly, but not as much as he wanted to fold her trust into a pocket in his heart and spend the rest of his life proving himself worthy of it.

They traveled on foot for miles and miles, passing dense palaces of bramble and abandoned shacks that they raided for additional supplies, splashing through streams and crossing crude wooden bridges stretched atop rushing rivers, guiding the horses around towers of deadfall.

When night fell, so, too, did another fierce rain, and they sought shelter in a cave large enough to accommodate the horses after Oskar had checked it thoroughly for bears or big cats. He doubted that the Vigilance Stone could detect predatory animals that were, after all, only following their natural instincts and knew nothing of good and evil. Elaras the treehugger would have been proud of him.

Oskar built a fire using wood chunks obtained from the last abandoned shack they'd passed. While Guinevere warmed up in its feeble glow, he fed the horses and then plucked and skinned the partridge that he'd caught earlier. He cooked it on a spit over the fire, and he and Guinevere ate it with their hands, washing it down with rainwater collected in flasks that they'd set outside.

Afterward, they curled up together by the cave wall, keeping each other warm under one of the Bonecrushers' fabulously cozy blankets. Guinevere had gotten progressively quieter over the last several hours, and it wasn't due to exhaustion—an exhausted Guinevere was even *more* talkative, as Oskar had learned. No, something had begun weighing on her mind as the day drew to a close, and he waited patiently to find out what it was.

"Oskar." She wouldn't look at him, her cheek pillowed against his shirtfront. Her voice was a softly wounded thing amidst the melody of the pouring rain that wove all around them like a second blanket. "I . . . I really want to learn how to control my magic. It frustrates me so much, that I could have saved you earlier—"

"You *did* save me," he cut in, holding her tighter. "You broke the illusion spell by tripping over that magician—"

"Not on purpose—"

"Saved me all the same," he insisted. "And, before that, you stepped in front of me before I got skewered and my head bashed in. Which, by the way," he added, his own words unearthing a skein of anger along with the chilling memory, "you are not allowed to do that ever again."

"You just said you would have gotten skewered and your head bashed in otherwise."

"That doesn't matter. Always help yourself first, Guinevere."

"No," she mumbled even as she burrowed deeper into him. "Travelers help one another. That's what Nan told us. We are travelers together, Oskar, and I will help you in any way that I can. So I—I will practice more. I will use what Elaras taught me back in Labenda. And perhaps one day I can be of as much aid to you as you have been to me."

Oskar was torn. On one hand, a vengeful wildfire spirit would certainly come in handy during battle. But the convenience of Teinidh would never justify the cost to Guinevere. She was a gentle, genuinely kindhearted girl. He had no wish for her to end up like him, hardened and embittered by what it took to survive in this world.

"For what it's worth . . ." Oskar lifted Guinevere's dainty wrist to his lips and kissed the back of her hand. "Your magic is not an abomination, despite what your folks say. I would love for you to wield it without shame. But it has to be on *your* terms. If you don't feel ready, then don't force yourself. Just believe in my ability to keep you safe, because I won't ever let you down in that regard."

She was silent for a while, considering his words. Then she wrapped her arms around his waist until they were as close as two people could be in their clothes. He rubbed her back soothingly, and he truly meant it when he said, "Whatever you decide, everything's going to be fine, and you're going to be brilliant, Gwen. You always are."

CHAPTER THIRTY

Guinevere

"How do you learn to stop being afraid of something?" Guinevere asked Oskar the next morning.

Yesterday's mid-battle revelation weighed heavily on her heart. But she didn't want to tell Oskar exactly *what* she was afraid of, the reason that she couldn't summon Teinidh when he was around; her feelings for him, all-consuming though they might be, were still too new and fragile for her to even hint at them out loud. So she settled on that nebulous, nameless *something,* and she prayed that he wouldn't press her any further.

Oskar mulled her question over as they walked side by side through the forest, between Pudding and Vindicator. Finally, he shrugged. "Maybe 'stop being afraid' is the wrong term. Maybe it's about being afraid of something and yet confronting it anyway. I've done it before. It's not pleasant, but it's always worse in your head than it turns out to be in reality."

She cocked her head at him. "I can't imagine that *you* would ever be afraid of anything."

His high cheekbones flushed a darker shade of oakmoss. "Being underground," he muttered, in such a low and vaguely embarrassed tone that she almost thought she'd imagined it. "I can't stand it. The endless dark, and all that earth over my head—but sometimes my mother forgot to bring her lunch with her to work. I'd wake up and I'd see it on the table, and I'd go down into the mines to give it to her."

Guinevere's heart gave a bittersweet wrench. Oskar had been selfless even as a boy. She wished that she could have known him then. Her hand found his beneath the autumn leaves, and their fingers laced together and didn't let go.

"Oskar," she ventured after a few minutes of companionable silence had passed, "where was your father in all this?"

"I never knew him. He was a military man—a captain of the Righteous Brand. Once Ma told him she was expecting, he got himself assigned somewhere else."

I'm sorry, Guinevere nearly said, before remembering at the last second that she was supposed to stop apologizing for things that weren't her fault. She swallowed the words, biting her lip.

"You were about to say 'I'm sorry,' weren't you?" Oskar drawled.

"Well, *someone* has to be!" she burst out, aggrieved on his behalf. "How dare that man abandon you and your mother!"

"It was probably for the best," Oskar said. "He was, by all accounts, a wastrel. He would have made us miserable."

"I suppose that I'm sorry *for* him," Guinevere sniffed. "He missed out on raising someone like you."

The flush returned in full force to Oskar's handsome face. "Ah, Gwen." He squeezed her hand. "Don't say things like that."

And something about his tone and the look in his eyes reminded her too much of that odd little daydream she'd had by the Bonecrusher campfire, and so she didn't ask him why.

FOUR DAYS INTO THE HIKE through the forest, Guinevere's good cheer began to erode, along with the brisk can-do attitude that she'd determinedly adopted after her outburst in the Labenda Swamp.

Because, yes, she *could* do this, but surely no one should *have to*. The walking was endless, the rain constant. She couldn't even *remember* what her formerly lovely boots had looked like prior to these interminable miles; they were rock-scuffed and mud-caked, the laces limp from the perpetual damp. Her hair had long passed tangled and was well on its way to matted, and every bone in her body ached.

And yet, she felt that she could still have held up admirably despite all these things, were it not for the fact that Oskar had somehow become . . . *annoying*.

It had started two days before. She'd woken up half out of her bedroll and half in his, his—*protrusion*—also very much awake, poking into her backside. Startled and intrigued, Guinevere had squirmed against it . . . and Oskar had stirred, stopping her motions with a firm hand on her hip before leaning in to give her a sleepy kiss. Then, just as the first faint embers of a familiar heat spiraled from her center, he'd rolled away and gotten up to prepare their breakfast as though nothing had happened.

Ever since then, she'd been far too aware of him. Of the way his muscles rolled beneath the clinging fabric of rain-slicked clothes. Of the veins on the backs of his large hands and his long, thick fingers stroking Vindicator's glossy flanks. Of his lips—and the smiles that had been coming easier to them lately—a soft valley between two sharp tusks that was the perfect place for her own mouth to land.

It seemed to Guinevere that she was wet between her legs all the time now, her mind a fever of memories and fantasies. But Oskar remained blissfully unaware of all the torture that he was putting her through. They were making good time, and he was loath to let that go, he said, and so he insisted that they walk as much as they could each day, sleeping early and rising at the crack of dawn, stopping only for quick meals. She'd once tried to cajole him into an afternoon nap, as was customary in Rexxentrum, and he'd made a show of looking around for a feather bed. He'd only been teasing, and she should have loved that he was now comfortable enough with her to tease, but her imagination ran wild with visions of her and Oskar tumbling into all manner of beds—or *right there,* on the forest floor—and at that moment she'd wanted nothing more than to shove him into the nearest river.

Infuriating man.

The last straw broke in the early afternoon. Guinevere and Pudding were lagging behind Oskar and Vindicator. There was a pebble in Guinevere's right boot; she could feel it rolling around in there, and it was *almost* as annoying as Oskar was, with his broad shoulders and his powerful thighs and the firm way he was holding the stallion's reins as they walked.

"Oskar," Guinevere called out, "could we possibly stop for a—"

"I see a stream a ways up ahead, Gwen," he replied without so much as glancing back at her. "Let's eat our lunch there."

She started to explain that she didn't want to stop because she was hungry, she wanted to stop because there was a pebble in her boot, but he had the audacity to continue, "Come along, princess. It's only another few minutes' walk."

Yes, she thought sourly, and then after that few minutes' walk they would stop for also a few minutes to eat their bland rations and then there would be *thousands upon thousands of minutes* of more walking, and it would never end, all the way to the Menagerie Coast, and she would be a saint if she hadn't killed Oskar by then, but he saw nothing wrong with *interrupting her while she was still talking*—

With stern finality, Guinevere dropped Pudding's reins and sat down on a fallen, mushroom-speckled log. The dappled mare looked from her to the rest of their party and let out a mournful neigh. Only then did Oskar turn around.

He arched a brow at Guinevere. She pointedly removed her right boot and shook the pebble out of it before just as pointedly slipping the boot back on. Then she simply sat there, refusing to budge.

Oskar took his sweet time tethering the horses. When he finally went over to the log, he crossed his arms and studied Guinevere with an impassive expression. She scowled, staring up the length of him—at the sinewy forearms and the wide chest, the stubble-dusted jaw that she longed to press her lips to, the white tusks gleaming in the muted autumn light.

"I'm usually the one who's in a mood, not you," he remarked. "What's wrong?"

"I'm sick of this forest," she grumped.

"Well, sitting here isn't going to get us out of it any faster."

"I'm tired."

"I know," he said, not without a trace of sympathy. "We'll nip back onto the Amber Road once we're close to the Wuyun Gates. Then we'll be able to ride again."

"And when is *that* ever going to happen, pray?" She knew that she was being unreasonable and churlish, but for some reason she couldn't stop. "For all I know, you are leading us in circles—this is not a smirking matter!"

"Sorry," Oskar said, still smirking, not sounding sorry at all. "It's just . . . You'd been doing so well all this time that I almost forgot you're a spoiled city princess. But I definitely remember now."

Guinevere shot to her feet and launched into a rant that had been days in the making, wagging an admonishing finger under his nose. "First of all, Oskar, when a lady is in a temper, she must be soothed with sweet words, *not* insulted beyond belief! And where do you get off, insulting me when this is all *your* fault in the first place, for being so—"

He stepped into her space and pressed one hand into the small of her back, gathering her close as he ducked his head. The rest of her litany faded into oblivion when his lips found her neck and sucked a bruise into the delicate skin, so quickly and fiercely that her knees almost gave out.

"This, ah, isn't a kissing matter, either," she managed to rasp, sinking her fingers into the slopes of his shoulders for balance.

"It isn't." His horrid, clever mouth worked on another bruise higher up. "But kissing is a much better use of our time."

"We aren't even *actually* kissing," she complained.

His sudden laughter was as deep and golden as his eyes. He gave her chin a brief peck before nudging it into position with his thumb and index finger. "You," he breathed out against her lips, "are so much work, sweetheart. So why is it that I'm having the time of my life?"

And he kissed her, sweet and slow, and she heard herself sigh as she kissed him back. He stroked her hopelessly tangled hair, and she cradled his face in her palms, her thumbs tracing its dear contours, running along tapered ears and curves of ivory. He hummed in pleasure and, emboldened, she nipped playfully at his plush bottom lip. The kiss turned heated, all tongues and urgency, and then he was walking forward and she was walking back, their mouths still connected, and soon his body had caged her in against a tree the same way he'd once pinned her to the door in that little room in Zadash.

More greedy kisses, more hungry touches, the hardness of him unmistakable on her stomach. His large fingers tugged at her bodice, baring her breasts to the cool woodland air. A fresh surge of desire spiked through her as he covered each one with his palms, squeezing, his hips rocking insistently.

"We can stop," he panted. "We don't have to do this here."

"Don't you *dare* stop," she said as imperiously as she could manage. As imperiously as anyone could sound with their breasts hanging out of their dress. It worked, because he didn't argue with her any further.

After a long and lovely, delightful while, she let out a whine of protest when his lips drew back and his hands fell away, but those lips darted a quick kiss to her forehead, and those hands spun her around, coaxing her into a position wherein she was bracing her arms against the tree trunk.

"What—?" Leaves crunched behind her. She peeked over her shoulder to see him on his knees amidst the grass and the roots. His black hair fell in disheveled waves, his pupils blown wide with lust. How thrilling it was to be able to reduce a man to this. To make his hands tremble against her legs as he lifted up her skirt and pulled her underwear down.

And then he was spreading her thighs and looking at—at *her.*

"Oh," Guinevere groaned softly, hiding her face in the fold of her arm, feeling ever so shy. But apparently not shy *enough*, because she was sort of—*wiggling*—toward him, rather than denying him access. Aside from putting her life on the line several times, the journey south had also unearthed hidden depths of trollopery within her. She probably should have minded a bit more.

"You're just as pretty between your legs as you are everywhere else." Oskar's voice was gravelly with wonder. His hot breath fanned against her intimate place, and she squirmed, a bead of moisture dripping out of her and down the inside of one thigh. "So pink and glistening," he continued in that deep rumble that was sending goosebumps along her spine. "Like . . . like rose petals. Covered in morning dew."

He abruptly fell silent. She could *feel* his embarrassment, suffusing the air. Despite herself, she giggled. "Did you take poetry lessons from Rodregg, by any chance?"

Oskar pinched her bottom in retribution. Guinevere gasped, and then his tongue was licking a long stripe over her entrance, and she *moaned*.

It felt like nothing she had ever experienced before. Like her entire being was afloat in the tide of some dark heaven. Oskar lapped at her long and deep, his wicked tongue drowning her in waves of pleasure with each velvety caress. Guinevere threw back her head with a strangled cry, her fingers clawing at the rough bark of the tree trunk, which was the only thing anchoring her to the ground. She writhed into his mouth, her buttocks resting against the crescents of his tusks as his lips pulsed and his tongue stroked and finally, *finally* touched the secret pearl and swirled over it, again and again until her toes were curling and she was screaming, her mind a whirlwind of autumn leaves.

It was the kind of orgasm that could make a girl go blind. Guinevere had yet to recover from it when Oskar wrapped her hair around one hand and gave a gentle tug, urging her head back toward him until their lips met in a sweeping, utterly filthy kiss. She tasted herself on his tongue. She heard her own muffled whimper as the knuckles of his free hand brushed against her left nipple, teasing and compulsive all at once.

When he released her, she sagged against the tree trunk, caught in a strange halfway state between relaxed and excited for what would come next. She listened to his ragged breaths, to the sound of him fumbling with his trousers, to the cries of distant birds. At the corner of her eye, Pudding and Vindicator were grazing, oblivious to the debauchery only a few feet away.

At least, Guinevere *hoped* that they were oblivious.

She didn't believe she had it in her to come again, but when Oskar's thick length slipped between her legs, rubbing against her wetness, sparks flew within her and she began to ascend once more. He took her by the hips, adjusting her to his liking, and the blunt tip of him notched inside, stretching her inch by inch, so slowly that it was almost agonizing. She wheezed and he cursed, she squirmed and he sank in deeper, until at last he had sheathed himself completely and she was so deliciously full, and it was too much and not enough. Another halfway state, another prelude to ecstasy.

"Oskar." Her lips grazed tree bark as she said his name. "Please, I need . . ."

"I know what you need," he growled. "You're a bit of a brat, aren't you, Gwen?" She gave a limp, half-hearted shake of her head, but he persisted, sounding so very *mean,* and, gods help her, but she clenched tighter around him. "You were in such a bad mood all day. Picking fights with me when, in fact, all you wanted was my cock inside you."

He didn't even give her the opportunity to admonish him for such crude language. His hips snapped against her buttocks in a forceful thrust, and she ceased to think at all, forgetting all about propriety, knowing only wildfire.

CHAPTER THIRTY-ONE

Oskar

To say that Oskar had never thought about making love to Guinevere again would have been a lie.

After Zadash, there'd been entire stretches of the Amber Road and this forest when it was *all* he could think about.

He just hadn't wanted to pressure her, even if he hadn't been able to resist stealing the odd kiss here and there. She was technically betrothed, and what had happened at the Song and Supper might have been a fluke. He had been content to wait for her overture . . . until he realized that she was just like him, cranky when she wanted *it* but wasn't getting any.

Ah, his sweet Guinevere. So shyly mischievous and tasting of snapdragon nectar, spreading her legs for him and making all those lovely little cries while he plowed into her. Despite having already climaxed, she was still so tight, and he knew that he wasn't going to last much longer. Desperate to make it as good for her as it was for him, he hunched over her, one hand sliding to her chest, the other to the place where they were joined.

"Oh, oh, Oskar," she sobbed, even as she undulated into his ministrations, "I'm not sure I can bear it."

"You can." He bit into the graceful round of her shoulder as he played with her breasts and her bundle of nerves, as his hips stuttered against the burnished cheeks of that perfect derriere. Her inner walls rippled around his shaft, and he nearly passed out from how incredible it felt, but he had a job to do, damn it to the hells. "That's it, sweet girl," he ground out. "Come again, because you deserve it, taking on the road even though you were afraid, taking me on like you were made for this. With your pretty mouth, with all those stars in your eyes—with the way you fit me like a glove—" The voice was too broken to be his, surely, each word laced with sheer yearning. Her thighs shook as she rocked back against him, whispering a stream of nonsensical encouragement. "Come all over me, princess." He sounded like he was begging. He didn't care. "Let me feel it."

And she went off, and she clamped down, and she screamed out, almost hauling him to the peak with her. The thin thread of self-control that was holding back his baser instincts *snapped*, and he straightened up, his hands on her slender waist, setting a punishing pace.

Guinevere clung to the tree as though for dear life as Oskar knocked the breath out of her lungs with each thrust. Her snug, wet heat; the sight of her with her skirt tossed up; the lingering taste of her on his tongue; the way he was nearly lifting her much smaller body off the ground—it was all too much for him. His hand slammed into the trunk above hers and everything went tight and the world went blank, and he came with a roar, startling the horses.

It wasn't until Oskar had slumped over Guinevere, wringing out the last drops of his spend into her, that he became aware of the fluttering of feathers overhead, which indicated that he'd startled a flock of birds out of the trees, too. He and Guinevere looked around blearily and froze as they made eye contact with Pudding and Vindicator, who had stopped grazing and were giving them baleful stares.

Oskar would never be certain whether it was himself or Guinevere who started laughing first. He thought that it might have been him.

THAT NIGHT, AFTER SETTING UP camp, Oskar reached behind him to scratch an itch in his lower back—and the battered seams of his well-worn tunic's right sleeve promptly gave way.

Guinevere clapped a hand over her mouth, muffling a giggle into her palm. It was so charming that Oskar forgot to be embarrassed. Then she was a whirlwind of activity, rifling through her pack until she pulled out a brown leather case, perching on a mossy stump by the fire, unrolling the case over her lap to reveal a small collection of sewing implements. He watched her do all of this far too idly for a man whose sleeve was hanging on to his shoulder by a literal thread.

"Take off your shirt," she chirped.

He raised an eyebrow at her. She blushed but didn't back down. "So I can mend it. *Honestly,* Oskar."

He schooled his features into an exaggerated look of disappointment. What was going on with him? He didn't *tease*. Yet here he was, damn near pouting at her.

Her lush lips quirked against another giggle, and she crooked a finger, beckoning him near. He went to her, as he always would, dropping to his knees in front of the stump, helping her peel off his ruined tunic, excitement singing through his veins as he leaned in . . .

But Guinevere was a woman on a mission. She didn't even realize that he was angling for a kiss—she was too busy draping the tunic over her lap. "All right, Oskar, you asked me a while ago to teach you how to sew, so this is how." She unraveled a length of thread and snipped it loose from its spool. The scissors in her hand were quickly replaced by a needle. "First, you push the thread through the eye . . . Could you budge up, please? You're blocking my light."

Oskar unpuckered his lips and grouchily scooted to the side.

It wasn't long, though, before he started taking a genuine interest. Guinevere was completely in her element. Her slim brown fingers were impossibly nimble in the firelight, the needle flashing silver like a comet through a sky of old linen, each stitch smooth and neat. As she worked, she explained what she was doing in that soft, cultured voice of hers, and everything about this moment wove a spell through Oskar's heart.

He could have observed and listened to her forever, but the last stitch eventually fell into place, and she packed her sewing kit away. Beaming, she held up the tunic. The sleeve looked as though it had never ripped in the first place. He couldn't even see the stitches unless he squinted.

"You're amazing," he blurted out.

She lowered her lashes bashfully. "It's the only thing I do well."

"I wouldn't bet on that." He cradled her face in his hands, urging her to meet his gaze. "You light up every room you walk into. With you, hiking through interminable wilderness is actually bearable. You're very good at making people happy."

You're very good at making me *happy.*

He couldn't bring himself to say it. There was a permanent goodbye at the end of the road, and there were some things that could never be taken back. So he pressed his lips to hers instead, closing his eyes as she responded in that sweet, warm way that he couldn't get enough of. The newly mended tunic slipped from her grasp, falling to the forest floor in a heap, but neither of them cared overly much. Maybe *he* could teach *her* how to do laundry.

CHAPTER THIRTY-TWO

Oskar

The rest of the week passed in a tranquil haze. There was the monotony of slogging through rain and mud—or, when the weather was not being quite *so* rotten, somewhat drier mud. There were consecutive meals of hardtack and barely ripe berries, and freezing nights in damp bedrolls, and tough scrambles over steep slopes.

And yet, through it all, there was also Guinevere. Chattering away about anything and everything. Singing Rodregg's song whenever the melody entrenched itself back in her head. Complaining about all the walking they had to do. Keeping Oskar warm in the evenings with that delectable, terrifyingly addictive body. Skipping ahead of him, the curtain of her hair swaying silver amidst the scarlet fumes of autumn.

She entertained him like no other and brought out an affectionate side that he hadn't even realized he was capable of. The Vigilance Stone never glowed, not even once. When Oskar allowed his guard to relax, he had to admit—much to his chagrin—that he was having fun.

The undergrowth eventually thinned out and the trees grew more scattered. Through the gaps between the trunks, he could see the rolling grasslands of the Marrow Valley. They were almost to the Wuyun Gorge; at the tip of that would be the gates, followed by the Coast, which in turn would be followed by . . .

Journey's end.

Her journey, anyway. As for Oskar, he would have to turn around and go back the way they'd come, which was—*fine*. It was what it was. He'd made that choice when he strong-armed her into accepting his escort.

For some reason, though, the prospect of traveling the Amber Road without Guinevere by his side seemed unbearable.

He was getting far too used to her.

They left the forest's dense embrace under a sky that, while overcast, had yet to spit out rain. The entrance to the Wuyun Gorge was only a short gallop away through tall stalks of golden grass. Leading into it was the Amber Road, dotted with wagons and carriages and figures on horseback as far as the eye could see.

Oskar turned to lift Guinevere into Vindicator's saddle. But, for someone who'd haughtily declared a few hours ago that walking was a fool's game, she was strangely hesitant now.

"I actually might prefer to just sit here for a little while," she told him painstakingly. "Why don't we have an early lunch?"

They'd eaten an uncommonly hearty breakfast of roasted mushrooms and quail eggs not too long ago, the six approved gods having smiled down on that morning's foraging attempts. Oskar wasn't hungry yet. But he heard himself say, "All right."

Because, once they entered the ravine, it would be less than a day's ride until the Amber Road came to an end at the Wuyun Gates. Their time together was fast running out, and it was with a pang that Oskar realized he would do whatever it took to make the remaining hours last longer. To grab hold of them and never let go, to spin them into years and years until they became a tapestry that encompassed all of forever—

No. That line of thinking led to madness. And *her* thoughts were probably along the lines of how damn tired she was, and how she wasn't eager to be back on that dusty, crowded road anytime soon.

They sat down in the long grass and broke out the last of the hardtack and some forest fruits that they'd picked yesterday. They didn't bother securing the horses, as they'd learned that Pudding and Vindicator weren't prone to wandering off as long as there was the promise of food—and, indeed, the black stallion leaned in over Oskar's shoulder and shamelessly nosed for crab apples while the gray-and-white pack mare did the same with Guinevere.

Guinevere was happy to share her fruit, Oskar a little less so. She shot him a sympathetic grin as she patted the bridge of Pudding's nose. "I'm going to miss the horses," she said wistfully.

What about me? "You don't have to miss them," Oskar grunted. "We bartered for them with your parents' merchandise, so they technically belong to your family. You should keep them."

"I couldn't possibly," she protested, her violet eyes wide. "You're so much better with them than I am. And . . ." She hesitated, swallowing. "And you're going to need them more."

Yes, because once she arrived in Nicodranas and Lord Wensleydale started wooing his would-be bride, she would have her pick from stables full of the finest destriers and most impeccably pedigreed mares that gold could buy. Amidst the affluence of that new life of hers, Pudding and Vindicator would soon be nothing more than distant, bargain-bin memories. As would Oskar.

He gave what he hoped was a flippant shrug. "If you don't want them, I'll be happy to take them off your hands."

"I never said I *didn't* want them, only that—"

"There won't be a place for them," he finished for her. He had an uneasy feeling that they weren't talking about the horses anymore. Or, at least, not *just* the horses.

They finished eating in desultory silence. Once she'd choked down the last of the hardtack and wiped the crumbs off her skirt, Guinevere busied herself with picking wildflowers from a vibrant cluster an arm's length away. It was high time to get going, but Oskar's body refused to obey his common sense. Instead, he watched as she skillfully braided the stems together into a circle, taking care not to damage the delicate blooms. She'd always been good with her hands. Aside from the night she taught him how to stitch, there'd been nights when she sat by the campfire with needle and thread, embroidering a patch of roses on the collar of his one good jacket, her tiny nose scrunched up in utmost concentration. He was going to miss the sight of that. The sight of *her*.

But the memory of firelight gave him an idea for a relatively safe topic. "Any luck practicing with your wildfire spirit?"

Guinevere frowned down at her task. "I wouldn't be so eager to wish for that, if I were you. Teinidh's hard to put out once she gets started."

She'd told him of a few incidents from her childhood while they were traipsing through that forest. Her mother's singed eyebrows, the scorch marks that devalued formerly priceless furniture and art, the burns on tutors with loud voices and heavy hands. For each tale, Oskar had assured her that it hadn't been her fault. He never grew tired of saying it, because it was what she needed to hear—and maybe if he said it often enough, she would believe it. She wasn't automatically apologizing for every single thing anymore, and that was a start.

"All done!" Guinevere held up her handiwork for Oskar's perusal. It was a profusion of crimson flowers set like rubies into a band of leaves and stems.

"Very nice wreath," he said.

"It's a flower crown." That was the only warning she gave before plunking it over his head.

"Guinevere." Oskar levied his most fearsome scowl upon her. "Kindly take this thing off me."

"Whatever for?" she protested. "You look rather dashing!"

"I don't *want* to look dashing," he snapped, "and I don't want to wear a damn flower crown, either."

"But—but I made it for you."

Her beautiful face took on a plaintive expression. Hah. That wasn't going to work on him this time. He would harden his heart, by the gods.

Her bottom lip wobbled.

Fuck.

Minutes later, Oskar was holding Vindicator still while Guinevere slipped another flower crown around the latter's head. The stallion eyed Oskar with something like distress, but no one could help either of them now.

"We'll get through this together, old friend," Oskar muttered to him.

Pudding merely shot him an amiable grin, her eyes half-closed beneath her own flower crown, while Guinevere surveyed the three of them with her hands on her hips, her satisfied smile as radiant as the sun.

"Why aren't *you* wearing one?" Oskar demanded.

He sounded like a rude son of a bitch, but Guinevere was unfazed. She pointed to the once colorful patch on the ground. "There aren't any flowers left."

"Not very environmentally friendly, now, is it?" he said under his breath as he tucked their waterskins back into the rucksack dangling down Pudding's side.

"Sorry?" Guinevere looked over at him, all sweet, blissful innocence. "I didn't quite catch that."

"Nothing, dear."

It came so easily to him, that endearment. It rolled off his tongue the way a breath was exhaled by the lungs, an action that required no mulling over. It simply . . . *was.*

"Oh, Oskar," Guinevere scoffed, and she turned away from him, but not before he saw her smile brighten even more.

❧

VINDICATOR'S NEW ACCOUTREMENTS APPEARED TO have thoroughly sapped him of his pride. There was a distinct lack of vigor in the stallion's steps as he bore Oskar and Guinevere across the golden grasslands and into the procession of travelers entering the Wuyun Gorge.

As their party eased into an open space between two other groups, the five human riders behind them didn't bother hiding their stares— first at the flower crowns on Oskar and the horses, and then at Guinevere, at which point the staring turned to outright gawking. Some of their jaws actually dropped.

Oskar shot them a nasty glare over his shoulder, his arm tightening around Guinevere's waist. Then it was *her* turn to look around, wondering what bee he had in his bonnet. Or, to be more accurate, in his flower crown.

But soon her attention swiveled back to what lay in front of them. It truly was an incredible sight. Oskar had passed this way before, but he was far from immune to the awe it inspired. The Wuyun Gorge was a large ravine that snaked down in a stony gash through the center of two mountain ranges—the rugged Cyrios, which cordoned off the Menagerie Coast from the rest of Wildemount, and the Ashkeeper Peaks, the forested and treacherous spine of the continent that separated the Dwendalian Empire and the Wastes of Xhorhas. From left to right, there was only ridge as far as the eye could see, holding up the gray sky like the shoulders of giants.

The heart of autumn had burst upon the world. The mountains looked as though they'd been dipped in fire, their vast slopes boasting endless waves of scarlet and ocher and magenta, the highest peaks wreathed in silver mist. And slicing into the middle of it all, the burnished carpets of foliage abruptly giving way to platforms of barren red rock, was the enormous gorge, which lay as though in wait.

"I feel . . . small." Guinevere's soft voice threaded through the chime of hoofbeats and wooden wheels echoing all over the road. "But not insignificant. Like I'm a part of something greater. Like maybe I'm meant for better." She turned back to Oskar then, sharing this moment with him, her violet eyes alight, her pale hair streaming in the wind. "Like—I don't know, Oskar. Who could ever describe this feeling? I don't have the words."

"I do," he said, staring at her, framed as she was against a backdrop of open road and high mountains. "I feel like the look on your face."

CHAPTER THIRTY-THREE

Guinevere

All things considered, it was a miracle that she didn't fall off Vindicator's back once they entered the Wuyun Gorge. She was half out of the saddle, so busy twisting from side to side, taking in every inch of the walls of sheer rock that surrounded this final stretch of the Amber Road.

It wasn't proper, of course. Ladies were supposed to sit quietly on their horses, backs straight and eyes gazing straight ahead. But ladies weren't supposed to disrobe in the woods and let a man kiss them between their legs, either, so Guinevere felt that this was a moot point.

Once she arrived in Nicodranas, she would have to be a lady again, but for now she could have her edifices of stone and her deep ravine. She could have Oskar behind her, a steady presence, letting her take it all in with an easy alertness that made clear he was prepared to catch her if she *did* begin to fall.

Despite the gorge's harsh, arresting beauty, the journey through it was a slow and plodding affair. Not only was the path extremely steep in several places, but it was also varying levels of narrow; there were certain intervals wherein the many travelers had to proceed in single file. Everyone spoke quietly and pitched in to help the larger conveyances rattle up and down the inclines without making too much noise.

When Guinevere inquired as to why this was, once Oskar returned to her after lending his assistance to the wagon in front of them, he explained that the whole valley was a landslide risk, and she found herself wishing that she hadn't asked. She still gazed up at the cliffs with awe, but there was now a healthy dose of wariness as well.

They were trekking at a slower pace than Oskar had accounted for. When the sun began to set, the Wuyun Gates were still a two-hour ride away. But there was no question of stopping for the night; the darkness came down fast, spilling into the ravine like a wash of ink. As their fellow travelers set up camp, Oskar and Guinevere staked out a spot under an overhang, making sure that the pearwood trunk was tucked safely between their bedrolls and the rock face.

Supper was salty strips of Clan Bonecrusher's preserved mutton and more forest fruit, eaten in the dim glow of other people's fires. It was the coldest night yet, perhaps because of the altitude, and Guinevere's teeth chattered so hard that she almost couldn't partake of her meal, despite being famished. Oskar did his best when they went to bed, wrapping her up in blankets, but it still wasn't enough. The chill was a knife in her middle, spreading outward, all the way to the tips of her fingers and her toes.

Finally, she couldn't take it anymore. As campfires were snuffed out one by one all along the ravine, a shivering Guinevere crawled into Oskar's bedroll.

He folded her into his arms at once, climbing on top of her so that there would be space for them both. Pinned down by his solid weight, she happily soaked up the heat emanating from his broad frame. How nice it was to be held without hesitation. She wondered if Lord Wensleydale would be this affectionate, this warm—

Just like that, the chill tore through her again. She couldn't even imagine doing this and more with any man other than Oskar. It felt horribly wrong. But she would have to, wouldn't she? A lord needed heirs, and it was her duty as his wife to provide them.

"Am I too heavy?" Oskar asked. "You've gone tense."

Guinevere was slow to respond, and he started to move off her. But she grabbed at his tunic with desperate fists, keeping him in place. "It's fine," she croaked. *Heavier, heavier,* she thought wildly. *More real. I need this to last, even if the Amber Road won't.* "Kiss me."

And when he did, she parted her lips for him at once. His tongue tangled with hers and swept and rolled, leaving no inch of her mouth untasted. The flower crown was a thing of the past, having been snatched up and gobbled down by another traveler's mule earlier; already she missed the way he looked with the leaves threaded through his dark hair, the petals trailing down to his pointed ears, but it was a small price to pay for being able to card her fingers through his thick mane unimpeded.

When those fingers had stroked and tugged their fill, they drifted lower. Her shyness, too, was a thing of the past. There was no time for it anymore. They were running out of road. He muttered oaths against her lips as her hand disappeared into his trousers, down to where he was already hard, as though he'd been waiting for her all his life. She wrapped her fist around him, marveling at the heat of it, the girth, the texture like silk stretched over bulging steel.

Oskar's kisses turned sloppy as he thrust into the circle of her fingers. He finally gave up on kissing her mouth altogether, yanking his tunic over his head before settling into the easier angle of her neck as he cupped and squeezed her breasts through the fabric of her bodice. Guinevere squirmed beneath him, the flame of want soaring higher, warding off autumn's icy sting. Soon he'd lifted up her skirt and positioned his lean hips between her spread thighs, lying almost flat atop her as the blanket fell all around them like a second veil of night. There were no more campfires left in their little slice of the Wuyun Gorge, but the clouds had decided to thin at some point, one of the two moons and a few faint stars shining in the misty velvet black over Oskar's head. The ravine was narrow, and everyone wandering through it had more or less kept pace with one another all day. There was an encampment of sleeping travelers about twenty feet to Guinevere's left, and another group was half that distance directly across from her and Oskar. It was the height of folly to do this here and now. The last holdout of common sense in a lonesome corner at the back of her mind—that one tiny part of her that wasn't drowning in lust—understood that all too well. But . . .

But by tomorrow afternoon, they would be in Nicodranas. There was no more time. There was no more road.

"You have to be quiet, sweetheart." Oskar's voice was a hoarse whisper in the dark, fanning against her temple. "Do you think you can be quiet?"

"Yes," she mumbled into his neck, inhaling the scent of forest and leather, of sweat and salvation and Fessuran. She would be quiet. She would do anything for him.

He tugged the gusset of her underwear to the side and pushed in. It was always such a lovely shock, those first few inches. She arched silently, her breasts pressing against his wide chest as she savored the feeling. Had they been in the woods, she'd be howling at the moon by now. But they were in the gorge, surrounded by people who had to be kept none the wiser, and so she swallowed it all down even as the space beneath her heart exploded into a million butterflies.

Oskar's mouth dropped to her throat. He nibbled at the skin there, but not hard enough to bruise it again. There could be no evidence when he handed her off to her parents and another man. Yet the sharp tip of his left tusk caressed her jawline, raking up trails of shivery sensation, and that would have to be enough. She'd take it. She would take what she could get. He worked his whole length into her with painstaking slowness, his muscular frame trembling from the strain of holding back, and she looped her fingers into the cord of the pendant that dangled from his neck, tugging at the Vigilance Stone until their lips met once more. She kissed him, she took him, and with one last careful nudge he was all the way in, and, gods, it was a good thing that his tongue was currently keeping hers occupied, lest their hapless fellow travelers be in for a rude awakening.

It was only then that Guinevere began to question how they were to do this. Sex, as she had learned, came with all manner of distinct sounds, especially the way she and Oskar both liked it, hard and fast, slap of skin on skin. She couldn't fathom how they'd be able to get away with this.

It wasn't long before he *showed* her, though.

He wedged one large hand under her buttocks, lifting her lower half up slightly. He rolled his hips against hers, never fully withdrawing even as he created a delicious friction. It wasn't a thrusting, but a rocking, a slow drag alongside her inner walls. It was the gentle kind of intense that made her feel like she'd go up in smoke. Her legs locked around his waist, her toes curling. Her mind melting. The pleasure that spiraled through her long and undulating. Taking its sweet time.

The tip of him hit that perfect spot inside her, the one that made her breath hitch, that made her body go into a full spasm. She felt rather than saw his lips curve against her neck in a wicked grin. He came back to it, again and again, and she was going to scream, she truly was—

Frantic, Guinevere sank her teeth into Oskar's bare shoulder. He let out a hiss, twitching inside her before he picked up the pace, just a little bit. If anyone happened to wake up and glance over now, they would see two forms writhing under a blanket. They would know.

And was it the danger, Guinevere thought, that was making her burn up? The illicit thrill of it? She was almost *there*. She just needed one last push . . .

Oskar apparently did, too. Without warning, he reared up, practically folding her in half, clapping one hand over her mouth. He drove into her with rapid, shallow thrusts. They were hardly being subtle, but at this point Guinevere was too far gone to care. She muffled her screams into his palm, and she watched the stars over his shoulder as he slammed into her, folds of blanket tangling between their bodies. And soon those stars were blurring before her eyes and she was coming, dragging him along with her, desire and desperation unfolding all throughout this vast ravine.

Was she truly to never feel this way again, after tomorrow? Oskar collapsed on top of her, and Guinevere gathered him into her arms, kissing his temple as he nuzzled at her clothed breasts, wringing out the last drops of his spend inside her with a few more limp thrusts. She was sated, yet hollow. *End of this* was all she could think, there in that place of rock and starlight. *End of road.*

CHAPTER THIRTY-FOUR

Oskar

Nicodranas.

It was as colorful as Oskar remembered, its eclectic jumble of architectural styles speaking to the diverse array of cultures that had made this port city their home. The cobblestone streets sloped and curved, affording panoramic views of the sun-dappled Lucidian Ocean, stirred by balmy breezes that delivered the shoreline's tang of salt and dried fish to the innermost sprawls.

Guinevere hardly spared a glance for anything as they led the horses through districts that were a riot of color and noise. That was strange. She had burst into every settlement they'd passed through along the Amber Road with innocent eagerness, soaking up all the sights that were new to her. Oskar had assumed that Nicodranas wouldn't prove any different in this regard, particularly because it was her first time on the Menagerie Coast.

But she didn't marvel over display windows of curios and jewels and silks, or outdoor stalls where vendors and customers haggled over piles of spices and dates. She showed no interest in the palm trees that waved in the wind or the cawing seagulls that streaked overhead. She didn't look at the street performers juggling and playing music and casting little spells, or at the Clovis Concord's Zhelezo that patrolled the city in mismatched armor that was so different from the deep uniform red of the Dwendalian Empire's Crownsguard. Instead, her violet eyes were practically glued to her feet, the letter her father had written to tell her of her betrothal crumpled in one small fist.

She had shown the address on the letter to a tanner near the city gates, and after about half an hour of walking, they were drawing near the fifteen-foot-tall stone archway crowned with a large opal that the man had described—one of eleven that marked the entrances to the imaginatively named Opal Archways district, where Lord Wensleydale's estate was located.

Guinevere walked through it as though she were walking to her execution.

Oskar concluded that she was nervous about reuniting with her parents and meeting the stranger whom she was to marry. He ached to pick her up, deposit her onto Vindicator's saddle, and ride off with her in the opposite direction. Back toward the Wuyun Gates, back toward the Amber Road. The urge gripped him like a fever.

But that was kidnapping, and it was frowned upon in civilized society. There was also the fact that the neighborhood they were currently in was a study in gilded elegance, each house grander than the one before, with manicured lawns and windows bedecked in curtains of finest snow-white lace. The streets were less crowded compared to other areas of the city, and the silk-clad, bejeweled folks who *were* out and about all sported the pinched features and perennially turned-up noses characteristic of nobility. Even the oil lanterns mounted to the poles boasted all sorts of fancy embellishments, which struck Oskar as ridiculous, because why would a lantern need to be carried on the backs of golden dolphins leaping up from golden waves? Who even *cared,* as long as it did the job of providing light at night?

It couldn't be denied, however, that this was the world to which

Guinevere belonged. Here in the Opal Archways, there was neither hunger nor hardship. Judging from the residents' expressions of alarm that would have been more appropriate for a dragon attack, the most distressing thing that could happen here was the arrival of a pair of grimy, shabbily dressed travelers.

Not even Guinevere's considerable beauty could save her from censure. People were actually *crossing the street* so as to avoid walking right by them.

"Oskar," she whispered, and her next words filled his heart with ice, "could we possibly change before we call at Lord Wensleydale's estate?"

Could we *possibly change . . . ?* She was ashamed not just of herself, but of him. He was thinking about the meeting with Lady Foxhall again. The way Guinevere had tried to hide her humble attire with her cloak, the way she had hesitated to introduce him.

He was too tired to be angry. The journey was drawing to a close, and all the lies he'd told himself about what mattered and what didn't were shattering left and right.

Princesses didn't marry blacksmith's apprentices.

He wasn't even a blacksmith's apprentice anymore. He was literally an unemployed bum wandering around Wildemount. What kind of life could he give someone who'd once had everything?

They ducked into an alleyway between two houses. Oskar blocked it off with Pudding and Vindicator but also kept watch while Guinevere changed. The furtiveness required of being in a city was a far cry from swimming naked in a lake or making love in the forest with the eyes of creation upon them. They were back in reality now. Back to hiding bits and pieces of themselves.

Feeling a light tap on his shoulder, Oskar turned around to find Guinevere in a clean if wrinkled blue dress, one that she hadn't worn before. He realized now that she'd been saving it for today. But even a fresh garment couldn't disguise the tangles in her silver hair or the dust all over her skin or the fact that she was thinner than she'd been when they first set out on the Amber Road.

Gods, what had he done to her?

"Your turn," she said, not quite meeting his eyes.

She took watch while he changed, resentment simmering through him. He selected his least beat-up linen shirt and the black jacket that Guinevere had embroidered with roses in happier times. When he was done, he yanked off the Vigilance Stone and shoved it into his rucksack before she could give any indication of what he already knew—that the leather strap and its lone cheap gem were out of place amidst all the gold-chained, diamond-encrusted pendants dangling from aristocratic necks that they'd seen thus far.

"Do I pass milady's muster now?" Oskar hated the bitterness in his voice, yet he was powerless to do anything except feel it.

Guinevere appeared startled by such a question, but she eventually nodded, biting her lip. Her gaze lingered on the adorned collar of his jacket, and he silently willed her to say something, *anything.* Just the slightest acknowledgment that all that had happened had happened. Because that was what she had reduced him to.

But she didn't breathe a word, and they left the alleyway and continued on, until at last they came to a house that fit the tanner's description and was in the location that he'd stated.

It was a house in that it was a place where people slept and ate and passed their days. However, Oskar had seen smaller villages. *Mansion* was the more appropriate term, perhaps even *palace.* It loomed on an incline over a seashell-flecked granite driveway shaded by palm trees. Its façade was all graceful lines and snow-white alabaster gleaming in the bright coastal sunlight, capped by a painted roof that rested on bas-relief carvings of Minotaurs, which were the symbol of House Wensleydale.

There were guards everywhere. Not the Zhelezo, but a private security force. Oskar derived some comfort from that; laying siege to this estate was probably above the Web's pay grade. As he and Guinevere started up the driveway with the horses, the guards crossed their spears together, blocking the path.

A captain-of-the-guard-looking fellow stepped forward, assessing Oskar's and Guinevere's appearances and their luggage. "Deliveries are through the servants' entrance out back," he told them with a sniff.

Oskar jabbed his thumb in Guinevere's direction. "Even when I'm delivering *her*?"

The probable captain's eyebrows nearly disappeared into his helmet. Guinevere showed him her father's letter and explained the circumstances that had led to her showing up on Lord Wensleydale's doorstep several days behind schedule and with only one escort.

Servants were summoned—grooms to take care of the horses, and a butler to ferry Oskar and Guinevere to the gardens, where "Master Illiard" and "Mistress Betha" apparently were. Even as Oskar followed Guinevere and the butler, the pearwood trunk tucked under his arm, he wondered why he was doing so. He had fulfilled his duty. He was supposed to be heading back north by now. Why wasn't he? Why hadn't Guinevere sent him away yet?

The stately gardens were to the left of the mansion. No wildflowers here, no overgrown grass. Everything was perfectly calculated, from the neat beds of red chrysanthemum and purple phlox and white verbena to the glimmering marble fountains to the trellises of morning glory and firecracker vine. Wensleydale must be retaining an army of gardeners in addition to his army of private guards. Two figures were standing beneath an arbor, looking out over the sweeping grounds beyond. They turned at the sound of footsteps and were rushing over even before the butler had finished announcing Oskar and Guinevere's arrival.

But they stopped within arm's length of their daughter, their postures making it clear that they were prepared to turn right back around and run in the opposite direction at any moment. That was the moment it truly sank in for Oskar that Guinevere's parents were afraid of her, and rage made his vision go dim and his fists clench.

Guinevere had inherited her pale hair and violet eyes from her father, Illiard. She'd gotten her copper complexion, slim build, and delicate features from her mother, Betha. Both parents were as well attired as any noble in the Opal Archways, but there was a conspicuous absence of jewelry.

Of course. The jewelry would have been the first to go when the coffers started running out.

"Heavens, Guinevere, you look a fright!" Betha declared in a strident tone that contained no trace of her daughter's sweet lilt. "What has happened to you?"

"And where in blazes is the—" Illiard caught himself, finally registering Oskar's presence as the butler discreetly took his leave. "You're not one of the guards I hired."

As Illiard's and Betha's gazes fell on him and hardened with suspicion, Oskar set the trunk down on the ground and opened his mouth to explain, but Guinevere spoke first. Her voice quavered at certain points, and she had difficulty maintaining eye contact, but she told them everything—everything within reason, anyway. Oskar felt that she was rather embellishing the role he'd had in their continued existence in the material realm, while downplaying hers. Or, to be more accurate, that of her wildfire spirit. She divulged nothing about the presence that Elaras had sensed, and Oskar was quick to realize that she didn't want her folks to know that she'd studied magic, however briefly. He was of the opinion that they *should* tell Illiard and Betha and pressure them to provide answers to the mystery that had been hounding their steps across Wildemount. But Guinevere wasn't ready, and of course Oskar would follow her lead, even if he had his misgivings.

He watched her parents like a hawk as they listened to their daughter's harrowing tale of survival. They were visibly alarmed when she got to the part about the mercenaries—Illiard, in particular, looked around wildly until the sight of Lord Wensleydale's guards hanging around the periphery of the sprawling gardens soothed him—but that was the height of the emotions that they showed. It was an alarm that eclipsed even the concern they expressed for their only child's well-being. Then again, Oskar thought sardonically, she'd made it to them, her dowry safe and sound, and that was the important thing.

"I cannot believe you lost Bart and Wart, Guinevere!" Illiard groaned. "Those two beasts were as children to me."

"I know," Guinevere whispered, her shoulders hunching like she was trying to make herself smaller.

"She didn't *lose* them," Oskar snapped. "The bandits are solely to blame."

"Yes, the bandits, who nearly took my most prized possession because you—" Illiard rounded on Guinevere, but at that moment she tugged imploringly at his sleeve. A mute, desperate gesture, the kind given by a child who had rarely known love but was still reaching for it. He flinched at her touch, and Oskar wanted to punch something. Preferably the other man. Right in the face.

"Father, please," Guinevere said, "what's in the trunk? Why does the Spider's Web want it? Oskar and I have carried it all the way from Druvenlode to Nicodranas. We have risked our lives for it. And, before that, it sat in the corner of my room all those years. I think—I think I deserve to know."

The way her parents gawked at her, Oskar could tell that this was the first time Guinevere had asserted herself in a long, long while.

Betha was the first to recover. "I never!" she huffed. "Such impudence. You've picked up some rather deplorable habits on your little adventure, I see." She glared at Oskar like it was all his fault.

But Guinevere held fast, ignoring her mother, looking her father in the eye. Eventually, a flush rose to Illiard's pale cheeks. "It's jewelry," he said, sullen and defensive. "A whole bunch of them—a matched set. Very valuable. I won them in a round of cards shortly before you were born. The chap who bet them was a sore loser and he tried to call me out, but I won fair and square, and the whole den can vouch for that. Maybe he nursed that grudge these last two decades and hired the mercenaries to track me down and get it all back." His flush deepened at the skeptical expression on Oskar's face. "I may have boasted about your dowry, girl," he admitted to Guinevere, scratching his head. "Once Wensleydale signed the papers, I took myself down to the Withered Bird and had a pint too many. Bought several rounds for some sailors, too, and I maybe told them things I shouldn't've."

Betha was apoplectic. "*This!*" she screeched at her husband. "This is why we hardly have any money left! Why you couldn't afford to hire more guards for the trunk! You mismanager, you utter *fool,* letting total strangers leech off you—and not only that, but also running your mouth off about the Parure—"

"I was in high spirits, wasn't I?" Illiard roared. He jerked his head at Guinevere, who shrank back. "Never thought we'd be able to marry *her* off, what with—"

"What's the Parure?" Oskar interrupted, because he had the unsettling premonition that, were Illiard to finish his train of thought, once again denigrating Guinevere with the effortlessness of habit, Oskar would beat him to within an inch of his life.

Betha blinked at Oskar several times, her fury momentarily thrown off-kilter by his question. "The—a parure is the term for a matching set of jewelry."

"That's *a* parure," said Oskar, his eyes narrowing. "What's *the* Parure?"

"It's—it's just what the original owner called it," Illiard scrambled to reply.

Oskar didn't like this one bit. He knew guilt when he saw it. He knew the hunt, too. Guinevere's parents had the tense look of prey run to ground.

Before he could call them out on it, however, a new voice echoed through the gardens. A deep, cultured voice, the kind that could only have been a product of generations of voices that expected the orders they gave to be followed.

And that voice said, "I *do* beg everyone's pardon! I was out riding."

Fitzalbert, Lord Wensleydale, strode toward them with an air of quiet, unshakable confidence. He was a tall, trim man in his late thirties, with piercing blue eyes and thick blond hair streaked with hints of silver. He wore a frock coat of emerald-green wool over a cashmere waistcoat and a crisp white shirt, as well as buckskin breeches and spurred boots of such handsome leather that, were they ever to gain sentience, they would surely kick Oskar for daring to be in their presence.

Guinevere's parents instantly changed their attitudes.

"Oh, it's quite all right, Lord Wensleydale!" Betha trilled. She gingerly nudged Guinevere forward. "Permit me to make known to you my daughter, Guinevere, here at long last!"

Guinevere dipped into a graceful curtsy. When she came back up, Wensleydale's blue eyes widened as he beheld her face, and he broke into a dazzling smile.

Wouldn't you know it, Oskar thought sourly, he *did* have all his teeth. And he *wasn't* too old.

In fact, he looked like a fucking prince from a fucking fairy tale, and Guinevere was smiling back at him, and, *fuck,* Oskar had to get out of here at once. He should have left as soon as they got to the estate. It wasn't as though she needed him anymore.

But . . . no. He couldn't leave her yet. Not when her parents were acting suspicious about the trunk's contents. Of course, it was highly likely that his low opinion of them—one that had been formed before they even met—was coloring his view of the situation, but he had to confirm that first.

He would make sure that Guinevere was safe here, and then he would go.

"Apologies for the state of her, m'lord," Illiard said nervously. Guinevere's smile faded, and Oskar decided that he wouldn't leave until he'd thrown her father into a ditch.

"You cannot be implying, Master Illiard, that my betrothed could look anything less than a vision." Wensleydale took Guinevere's travel-roughened hand and pressed a gallant kiss to her knuckles. Oskar added throwing Wensleydale into a ditch to his list of things to do before leaving. "Such slander shan't be countenanced."

"You are too kind, Lord Wensleydale," Guinevere murmured, relaxing, glowing for him like he'd lain the world at her feet.

Oskar couldn't even be mad—because, if Guinevere had to marry someone, it might as well be a wealthy and powerful man who could defend her not only from mid-level mercenaries but also from her stupid parents. He might not respect Wensleydale all that much for offering for her, sight unseen, on the basis of her dowry, but it was clear that the noble was now smitten. Who wouldn't be? He'd treat her well, lavish his fortune upon her, and in time . . .

In time, he might come to love her as much as Oskar did.

Damn idiotic, to be struck by this epiphany—to finally, *finally* admit it to himself—right as he was transferring her into the care of another man.

Guinevere withdrew her hand from her betrothed's loose grasp. Only then did Wensleydale notice Oskar standing beside her. What was it with these upper-class folk relegating him to the status of shrubbery?

"I do not believe that we have been introduced," Wensleydale hinted.

"Oh, yes, of course." Illiard cleared his throat. "My lord, this is— er—Othello—"

"Oskar," Guinevere and the man formerly known as Othello corrected at the same time.

"Right. Oskar," Illiard mumbled. "He, ah, escorted my daughter over the Amber Road."

"My wagon was attacked by bandits shortly after leaving Rexxentrum," Guinevere elaborated. Swiftly, earnestly. "Oskar rescued me from their clutches and has since then gone out of his way to keep me safe the whole journey to the Coast."

"Then I am in your debt, good sir," Wensleydale said in a solemn tone, extending his hand for Oskar to shake. Oskar got it over with as quickly as possible. "You shall be well compensated. Ask anything of me, and it is yours."

Oskar glanced at Guinevere. He couldn't have helped it any more than he could have helped turning to the warmth of a roaring fire in the depths of winter. There was an ache in his chest that made it difficult to breathe. It was like being underground.

"That won't be necessary," he gritted out in response to Wensleydale's offer.

The lord frowned. "Surely a man of your station must be in need of gold, or a mighty courser—"

"Oskar already has the finest warhorse in Wildemount," Guinevere cut in. "In all of Exandria, as a matter of fact."

Even Oskar knew that it was the height of rudeness to interrupt a noble. Illiard and Betha both looked like they were going to drop into dead faints, but Wensleydale was unperturbed. He shot Guinevere an indulgent grin. "Be that as it may, my dear, he surely requires some reward for his service."

"I really don't," Oskar said curtly. This was the most humiliated he'd ever felt, but he would die before showing it. "As far as I'm concerned, I helped someone who needed my help, and any other traveler would have done the same for me. And that's the end of the matter."

Wensleydale sighed. "In that case, I insist that you come to the engagement ball I'm throwing in Miss Guinevere's honor tomorrow night—and that you avail freely of my estate's amenities until then, and for as long as you desire. I'll have a room made up for you."

Oskar's first instinct was to refuse. He wasn't going to a *ball*. If anyone back home found out, he'd never be able to show his face in the Dustbellows ever again.

But it occurred to him that staying two nights would probably be enough to assess Guinevere's future well-being and find out if Illiard and Betha truly were hiding anything. Then Guinevere turned to him with a beseeching expression that made a mockery of his flimsy attempt to resort to logic to disguise the plain and simple truth that screamed within him.

Namely, that he couldn't bear to say goodbye to her just yet.

"Fine," Oskar heard himself grunt. "I'll stay until the day after tomorrow."

"Wonderful!" said Wensleydale. "I have commissioned none other than the Opal of the Ocean to perform at the ball. It shall be a splendid evening."

There was a long, expectant pause.

Suspicion began to kick in. "You're not going to have me drawn and quartered if I don't bow with gratitude, are you?" Oskar snapped at Wensleydale.

The noble threw back his golden head and let out a booming, urbane laugh. "You're all right, Master Oskar." He clapped Oskar on the shoulder. "You're all right."

CHAPTER THIRTY-FIVE

Guinevere

Guinevere had insisted on changing into more presentable attire because she wanted her parents to see that she'd been well cared for throughout the journey south. She and Oskar might have done unspeakable things to each other in bed—and up against a tree, and in a lake, and one extra-memorable night on the floor of a cave—but he had ensured that she was always fed, and he had always snatched her back from the jaws of peril. She'd put on that new dress out of a desire to make clear that she was none the worse for wear, all thanks to him.

But she should have known that it wouldn't be enough to convince Illiard and Betha.

"Traveling with a complete stranger for days on end!" Illiard paced the floor of the guest bedroom that had been assigned to Guinevere. "You're lucky that his lordship is the amiable sort, girl, no two ways about it!"

"Technically, those guards you sent were strangers, too," Guinevere pointed out. She was seated at the dressing table while her mother tugged a comb through her hair, removing the mats and leaves and gods knew what else.

"That was all very proper and official," Illiard snapped. "They were *hired guards*. Not—not virile young men who undress maidens with their golden eyes!"

Guinevere wanted to argue that *that* was just the way Oskar always looked at people. He had a very intense, broody sort of stare. She was also seized by the very wicked urge to assert that she wasn't exactly a maiden anymore.

How strange—she'd expected to be ridden with guilt once she saw her parents again, and perhaps also upon meeting Wensleydale. But regretting any part of what she and Oskar had done seemed to require an energy that she didn't have. In fact, when her betrothed had made his way toward her in the gardens, all she'd been able to do, her heart in her throat, was offer up a silent prayer to the heavens in gratitude and overwhelming relief that her first time had been with Oskar. Not this man who wanted only her dowry, this man whom she didn't already know and respect and admire.

"I can't imagine the scandal if this gets out." Betha tugged the comb at a stubborn knot of hair, and Guinevere winced. "Lord Wensleydale is too much of a gentleman to say anything, of course, but it's best if you convince that peasant not to overstay his welcome, my dear. High society can be rather unforgiving, you know. And soon *you* will be at the center of it." Guinevere watched a proud smile flit across her mother's reflection in the ornately framed mirror. "My daughter—Lady Wensleydale! How extraordinary!"

"If she doesn't muck it up," said Illiard. "I don't think we can get out of that ruffian attending the ball, as his lordship personally invited him, but it *must* be impressed upon young Oskar that he is not to breathe a word of you two traveling together all by yourselves."

Guinevere watched her reflection roll its eyes. "Well, at least you got his name right, this time."

Illiard and Betha let out identical gasps.

"What's gotten into you, Guinevere?" Betha cried. "Not now, not when we're so close to everything we've ever wanted . . ."

"It's that boy's fault," Illiard growled. "He taught you how to talk back to your parents, eh? That lowborn—"

Guinevere thought about Oskar crying in her arms in a house that had two of everything. She thought about a man who had stayed with the horses in the pouring rain, who had been endearingly attentive as she taught him how to sew. She thought about a dutiful child entering a darkness he feared, just so his mother would be able to eat lunch.

"If he is lowborn, then so are we, Father." She met Illiard's eyes in the mirror. "You and Mother grew up in Yrrosa, after all."

Illiard blanched. Yrrosa was in the Zemni Fields, a ramshackle township mired in crime syndicates and abject poverty. He and Betha didn't like to be reminded of their origins, and Guinevere wondered why she'd waited so long to throw them in his face whenever he embarked on one of his rants.

And, not for the first time since they'd reunited, she wondered if he was lying to her.

The bad dream came back in flashes. The dagger in his hands, the figure over his shoulder. The name that had slipped from her memory upon waking.

She refused to believe that her father had actually stabbed her when she was a child—that was too cruel, even for him—but it occurred to her now that the strange vision might have been a warning from her subconscious.

A warning that she wasn't loved as she ought to have been.

"Who was the man you won the Parure from, Father?" Guinevere asked.

"What?" Illiard was visibly annoyed. "Some minor lord. Cholmondeley, I think it was. Why does it matter?"

That didn't feel right. That wasn't the name she'd forgotten. Before Guinevere could pry, though, Betha came charging to her husband's defense.

"We may have grown up in Yrrosa, but your father got us out," she hissed at Guinevere. "He got out, and he worked himself to the bone so that you would never find yourself in any place like it. I had no idea that we'd raised such an ungrateful child."

The old Guinevere would have cowered and apologized. And there was a part of her for whom this was still the instinct, to slink duly back to her assigned role of obedient daughter in the careful order of things.

But she realized, with some surprise, that she was more than that. She was the Guinevere who'd killed those bandits. Who preferred ale to champagne. Who'd interrupted a mercenary illusionist's spell and survived. She was the Guinevere who summoned the wildfire that Oskar found beautiful. She was the Guinevere who knew the song of the universe. Guinevere of the ravine, Guinevere of the woods, Guinevere of the Amber Road.

She snatched the comb out of her mother's grasp. "I would have liked for the two of you to be happy to see me," she told her parents. "To be glad that I made it through, what with the mercenaries and all. However, if there is nothing to emerge from your mouths but the same brand of criticism that I've endured most of my life, then—I can comb my hair myself." She nodded in cool dismissal at a stricken Illiard, at a fast-paling Betha. "I shall see you later."

Supper that night was by far the grandest meal that Guinevere'd had in weeks. In a dining room lavishly appointed in rich shades of mulberry and gold, amidst damask wallpaper and plush carpets and display cabinets of crystal and porcelain, at a long and glossy mahogany table underneath a blazing brass chandelier—Guinevere, Oskar, Wensleydale, Illiard, and Betha partook of several courses created with the highest artistry by the best chefs gold could hire. They began with raw oysters on the half shell, flecked with sea salt, followed by turtle consommé and then haddock so light and airy that it melted in the mouth. The main course was roast beef, served with gravy and freshly picked vegetables.

It was an enticing array of quality ingredients, of sophisticated flavors bursting upon the tongue. But Guinevere was hard-pressed to enjoy any of it. Oskar was seated directly across from her, looking stiff and uncomfortable in a formal red jacket borrowed from Wensleydale, the seams let out to accommodate his wider shoulders. And all she could think about was that he was leaving her soon.

They filled Wensleydale in on the threat of the Spider's Web. To his credit, he took it in stride that his betrothed's dowry had been rather crassly won in a game of cards years ago and that dangerously armed mercenaries were now trying to get it back. His private army was more than enough to fend off those vagrants, he assured them. There was no safer place for the trunk than his estate.

"I only regret, Master Illiard, that you did not take me into your confidence," he good-naturedly chided. "Had I been aware of the peril, I would have sent an entire battalion to fetch my lovely bride."

Illiard ducked his head and mumbled something about how he'd had no wish to trouble him. Guinevere knew the real reason, though: pride. Her father hadn't wanted to admit to his future son-in-law that he didn't have the means to fund an adequate security escort. He'd gambled with his only child's life, just as he'd gambled for her dowry.

"What is your interest in the Parure, my lord?" Guinevere asked Wensleydale.

Of course, what she really meant was, *What's so valuable about it that someone of your illustrious pedigree is willing to marry a trader's daughter?*

He crooked a smile from where he sat to her left, at the head of the table. "I am a collector of antiquities, Miss Guinevere. When your sire described the Parure to me, I realized that it's a very fine set of great historical significance. It belonged to a lady of House Truscan of the Vale and was lost at some point during the Marrow War."

Ah, Guinevere thought. It all made sense now. The Truscan family was staggeringly influential, a longtime ally of the Dwendalian royal bloodline. Wensleydale would either return their lost treasure to them in order to curry favor or sell it back for an exorbitant sum.

This was to be the rest of her life. Social one-upmanship, political maneuvers, and parlor games. It was what she'd been trained for.

But was it what she wanted?

She looked at Oskar. He was prodding at his beef without much enthusiasm. Earlier, he'd looked contemptuous and bewildered by the myriad spoons and forks and knives, but he'd watched them all carefully to see which utensils were used when. He was making an effort—not to fit in, but to acquiesce to their sensibilities, even if it must have all seemed very silly to him.

Guinevere wasn't quite sure that it didn't seem silly to *her*, too. She'd once held these rules sacred, but she had mostly eaten with her hands from Druvenlode to the Wuyun Gates, and the gods hadn't struck her down or anything like that. So, what was it all for, and to whom did it really matter? She imagined telling Clan Bonecrusher about the existence of a knife that was used only for salad. They'd probably be enraged enough to start a war.

The meal ended with iced oranges and a pristine blancmange. Guinevere begged off from the customary beverages in the parlor, claiming exhaustion. It wasn't even a lie; not only had she and Oskar ridden hard today to make it to Nicodranas before nightfall, but they'd also usually been asleep long before this time while they'd been traveling.

It was . . . awful, to think of it in the past tense. To be brought up short every few minutes by the painful realization that she and Oskar weren't traveling anymore. That soon there would be a goodbye, after which they would never be in the same room again.

Wensleydale kissed the back of Guinevere's hand as she hovered at the threshold of the dining room. "Sweet dreams, Miss Guinevere." He looked deep into her eyes, that ever-present smile dancing at the corners of his lips. "I bid you welcome to Nicodranas. I hope that you will be happy here—that *we* will be happy, together."

She was seized by the urge to cry. She glanced over at Oskar. He was staring down at the floor. Then her gaze swung back to Wensleydale, who was kind and handsome and impeccable in both dress and manner. The sort of man that she had always been expected to marry, that she had dreamed of marrying.

But he wasn't Oskar.

Guinevere didn't, for the life of her, have any idea what it was she said in response to Wensleydale that evening. She fled to her room, where she lay down on a feather tick instead of a lumpy bedroll, and she tossed and turned, astounded by the silence of the indoors, until sleep claimed her at last.

GUINEVERE WOKE UP LATE THE next day, which felt like a luxury in and of itself. There was a staggering moment of disorientation when she opened her eyes expecting the usual canopy of fiery trees but saw, instead, the embroidered flowers on the tapestry hanging over her four-poster bed.

After that, everything came by rote. Tugging at the bellpull to summon the chambermaids, who drew her a hot bath. Slipping into the enormous claw-foot tub, sitting there in the rose-scented water while a servant washed her hair and scrubbed her back. Standing while the same servant dried her off and laced her up into one of the day dresses that Wensleydale had commissioned for his bride. Then drifting downstairs to the salon, to join her mother and a gaggle of Nicodranian ladies who had come to call.

Menagerie Coast nobles draped themselves in brighter colors and more elaborate patterns compared to their Dwendalian counterparts. Aside from that, though, almost everything was the same. Pretty manners, airy voices, politely muted laughter that was as delicate as the clinking of the porcelain teacups, which were held *without* the pinkie finger extended, because that was apparently considered rude here on the other side of the Cyrios Mountains. Guinevere suspected that there were more minute differences in etiquette that she'd have to keep track of.

Despite the innocuous chatter, the guests had clearly come with one purpose in mind: to gawk at Lord Wensleydale's commoner intended. Every question directed to either Guinevere or her mother was subtly steeped in a patronizing edge that sailed right over the latter's head.

How do you not see it? Guinevere wanted to scream at Betha, who was tittering like a schoolgirl at someone's wry, not-that-funny remark. *They're all laughing at us. They know we're buying our way into their world. I will always be treated like an upstart.*

But that didn't matter to her parents. The title was the only thing that mattered.

She saw neither hide nor hair of Oskar the whole day. Wensleydale had taken him and her father around the estate immediately after breakfast, and, once the last of Guinevere's callers had made their exit, the guard that Wensleydale assigned her in view of the Spider's Web threat followed her around wherever she went. He reported to Wensleydale, and she could hardly ask him to let her be alone with another man.

Not that she knew what she was going to say to Oskar if she ever *did* get him alone.

All too soon the dusk descended, and golden lanterns throughout the mansion and its grounds roared to life in preparation for the ball. Guinevere once again submitted herself to the rituals of bathing and drying and powdering, this time with some hair-curling thrown into the mix. It took the combined efforts of three servants to get her into her fiendishly intricate evening gown. As they fiddled with her buttons and her ribbons, she stood at the window, watching one carriage after another roll up the driveway, discharging lords and ladies in jewels and silks, feathers and fur.

"All done, my lady!" chirped the youngest of the servants. The other two lugged the standing full-length mirror over to Guinevere for her inspection.

At first, she could only stare.

The girl in the mirror didn't look at all like she had ever been on the Amber Road. Her hair had been brushed to a radiant sheen, and it spilled down her shoulders in loose waves. Her skin was smooth in the soft light, gleaming with traces of the pearl dust that had been sprinkled into her bathwater. She wore a long-sleeved lilac gown spun from the Menagerie Coast's famed crushed silk, shot through with threads of sparkling silver. The low-cut bodice was cinched tight at the waist and flared out into a voluminous, trailing overskirt that was artfully slashed and gathered up into rosettes in several places, revealing the gauzy layers of embroidered silver tulle beneath.

She didn't look like herself. It was an epiphany that momentarily robbed her of breath. She didn't recognize this stranger in the mirror, who knew nothing about wilderness. She didn't *want* to be this stranger.

Guinevere drifted out of her room in something like a daze. She was barely aware of her parents beaming at her and ushering her off to the west wing of the glittering mansion, every inch of which had been meticulously dusted or polished until it was as sterile and perfect as her life would be from now on. Wensleydale was waiting for her at the top of the staircase in dove-gray formal attire. He did a double take at the sight of her, an appreciative grin spreading across his handsome features.

She should have blushed and preened. She should have been grateful that her future husband was attractive and charming on top of being wealthy and titled. She could have had it so much worse.

But there was more to life than settling for *good enough*. She had watched clouds of mist wreathe craggy peaks and dawn break in gentle golden rivers through an autumnal forest. She had broken bread with goblins and feygiants and gone shopping with gangsters. She had wanted someone so much that it was impossible to breathe, and she'd had him in all sorts of glorious ways, and what she felt for him was stronger than any inferno.

There was a whole world out there, and she had only so recently found it. What a waste, to let go so soon.

Guinevere tucked one hand into the crook of Wensleydale's arm.

"Ready, Miss Guinevere?" asked her would-be husband. His twinkling eyes were blue, not liquid topaz. His elegantly coiffed hair was gold, not a soft, disheveled black. He didn't have tusks.

"As ready as I'll ever be," said Guinevere.

And she fell into step beside him, down the marble staircase, down into her picture-perfect future.

CHAPTER THIRTY-SIX

Oskar

To put it bluntly, Oskar was having the worst day of his life.

He had spent most of it inspecting the mansion and its grounds. With Wensleydale's blessing, he'd briefed Therault, the captain of the guard, on everything he knew about the surviving mercenaries—which wasn't much, and certainly would amount to even less if Bharash and Selene were to call upon reinforcements whom he'd never encountered before.

But the captain had assured Oskar that he and his men were prepared for any eventuality. That, as the security force of one of the richest nobles on the Menagerie Coast, they were old hands at fending off burglars, and what were mercenaries, good sir, but burglars in uniform? It was rather more complicated than that, in Oskar's opinion, but he had to admit that Wensleydale's guards were well armed, knew how to establish and maintain a watchful perimeter, and were in possession of the kind of keen alertness most often found in people who were being paid very, very well to do their job. Several of them also had magical abilities. You couldn't ask for a group better suited to taking on the Spider's Web and their mysterious client, who was, apparently, little more than a sore loser. It couldn't be denied that Guinevere was safer with them than she'd ever be with just Oskar for protection.

And it also couldn't be denied that her betrothed was wealthy on a scale that Oskar couldn't even *begin* to comprehend. The white four-story mansion and its sprawling fields and gardens and gazebos and hedge maze and follies were like a slap to the face of every wretched soul crammed into the Dustbellows tenement where he had grown up. How could a single family have amassed enough land and wealth to last a hundred generations?

How could Oskar even dare *think* of asking Guinevere to give any of it up?

He had entertained the notion in his more unguarded moments—several times during last night's supper, as a matter of fact. He'd fantasized about tearing off the stupid, too-tight formal coat, hefting her over his shoulder, and running from the room.

Let's go, princess, he'd dreamed of saying. *Your parents suck, and your betrothed is a ponce. Let's get the hells out of here.*

Yes, Oskar, she'd replied in the fevered depths of his imagination. *Take me away from all this. Let's be impoverished vagabonds together.*

But even those relatively harmless flights of fancy had died a swift death when Wensleydale and Illiard took him around the estate and he saw for himself just how comfortable Guinevere's life was going to be.

And now he was in a crowded, overly warm ballroom, stuffed into another one of Wensleydale's jackets, worn over his most presentable shirt, which had been starched to within an inch of its life, and a pair of formal trousers that had been purloined from one of the bulkier footmen. He was an impostor lurking within a sea of lords and ladies. He had absolutely no idea what had possessed him to agree to this.

A kindly if somewhat clueless elderly couple had taken Oskar under their velvet-clad wing. The Stannishes were halflings, and Dwendalian—from Zadash, specifically—but they spent the colder months here on the Menagerie Coast, at an estate that had been bequeathed by Lord Stannish's distant cousin in the absence of direct heirs.

There was no damn reason for somebody to have *two* estates, but Oskar kept that thought to himself, lest the horde of nobles tear him limb from limb for such sacrilege.

"Stormfang, eh?" Lord Stannish was peering up at Oskar through a diamond quizzing glass. "Would that be the Trostenwald Stormfangs? Fine old family."

"No," Oskar grunted.

Lord Stannish blinked, looking scandalized. "They're not fine?"

"I'm not one of them," Oskar clarified.

As her husband floundered, Lady Stannish bravely waded in to salvage the situation. "And how do you know Lord Wensleydale and his bride?" she asked Oskar.

Gods, it hurt.

"I'm a friend" was all Oskar said.

"We'd despaired of that boy ever settling down!" boomed Lord Stannish, visibly relieved to have been led back onto solid conversational ground. "But I told my wife—didn't I tell you, Elaine—that he was only waiting for the right one."

"The right woman or the right dowry?" a nearby elven socialite airily remarked to her friends, who all tittered.

Oskar turned to the group, giving their ringleader a cold stare. "Didn't your parents ever teach you that it's rude to eavesdrop?"

The elf's powdered face turned pink. She dropped her gaze from his, and she and her friends shuffled away.

Lady Stannish patted Oskar's elbow. "Good lad," she said softly.

Oskar fidgeted, not knowing how to respond. But it turned out that he didn't have to. The lilting strains of plucked strings cut through the low roar of a hundred different conversations, silencing them with a melody like gold and glass. The Opal of the Ocean had begun playing on her marble dais. She was a beautiful, ruby-skinned infernal, with small pearlescent horns and glossy black hair decorated with chains of the eponymous gemstones. Her slender fingers wove through an ivory harp, and soon her pure, crystal-clear voice soared up into the rafters, singing a melancholy ballad. It wasn't long before a rash of whispers broke out and people were tugging at one another's sleeves. Heads swiveled in the direction of the staircase, and Oskar's automatically swiveled right along with them.

Wensleydale was descending the wide marble steps, and on his arm . . .

On his arm was a goddess.

It was Guinevere as Oskar had never seen her before, a vision in yards and yards of embroidered silk. Her hair cascaded down to her waist in silver waves, and the shimmering lilac hues of her gown brought out the deep violet of her eyes. A small smile graced that amazing face; it was shy, but its sweetness shone through, as her sweetness always would. She was lovely and ethereal, and she belonged in this world of marble pillars and burning chandeliers so utterly, more than she had ever belonged to the wilderness and all its hardships.

More than she had ever belonged to Oskar.

He understood, at last, why he had attended this ball. It was so he could have one more glimpse of her. And now that he had, he also understood, overwhelmingly and irrevocably, that it was time for him to go.

CHAPTER THIRTY-SEVEN

Guinevere

As soon as Wensleydale and Guinevere reached the bottom of the stairs, they were swarmed by well-wishers.

Her betrothed reeled off the introductions with practiced ease. Practiced, too, was the way Guinevere kept her smile in place and her lashes lowered demurely, murmuring the appropriate responses. She lasted ten minutes, by her own count, before she started looking around for Oskar. He'd said he would be here.

Her gaze scoured the ballroom as Wensleydale led her through it. It wasn't as though Oskar was possible to miss. He towered over most people. She knew that she had to believe what her eyes were telling her—that he wasn't in this crowd—but her hope was a stubborn flame sputtering in the wind, rippling, shifting, refusing to be extinguished even as moment after moment passed with no sign of him.

A flute of champagne was deposited into her hand, her fingers automatically curling around its crystalline stem. Perhaps it was Wensleydale who'd given it to her, or perhaps it had been one of the other lords. There was a sameness to all of them—and to the ladies, too. That sameness would come for her as well. Once her novelty had worn off, she'd be indistinguishable from the rest of them, with her impeccable manners and her gowns that were always the height of fashion. One of these days Wensleydale would return north, into the Empire, and he would take her with him, and she'd be on the Amber Road once more—but, if so, then in one carriage out of many, with packed lunches and servants to spread out the picnic blankets, with stopovers at luxury inns in the nice part of town.

Never again Labenda. Never again sitting around a fur trader's campfire pelting someone with turnips. Never again Oskar, listening to her silly dreams of seeing Molaesmyr and summiting the Dunrock.

Guinevere took a sip of champagne. It had a pleasant, slightly tart flavor that vanished almost as soon as it hit her tongue. Someone asked her how she liked it.

"I prefer ale," she absentmindedly remarked.

The people around her broke out into perfectly modulated laughter. Because she was joking, of course. Ladies did not drink ale, or at the very least they didn't like it better than champagne. The future Lady Wensleydale had such a *splendiferous* sense of humor! She cast another glance around the ballroom, feeling lost and alone. Where was Oskar?

At some point the harp music stopped, and, as an orchestra took over, Guinevere was introduced to the Opal of the Ocean. The musician was the first person whom she'd regarded with genuine interest since setting foot in the ballroom. According to the gossip that morning's callers had so eagerly shared, Mia Lavera had been born to a pair of dockside workers. A benevolent patron had nurtured her talents and gotten her to the point where she was in demand at upscale venues throughout the Coast.

Guinevere's callers had so discreetly coughed behind their fluttering hand fans every time they mentioned the Opal's patron. Which meant that, whether it was true or not, the consensus among Nicodranian society was that the Opal had sold her favors to the highest bidder. Guinevere suspected that attitudes here were similar to the

Dwendalian Empire in that most nobles considered it only right that the Opal be compensated for the privilege of her brilliant company, but there would always be those who tittered simply because she'd dared claw her way to the upper crust.

Guinevere searched the infernal's face for a flicker of anything she could claim kinship to—*Hello, my fellow upstart, shall we be friends, down in our muck?* But there was only enigmatic sophistication in those starlit eyes, and Guinevere was hard-pressed to assign blame.

Everyone in this world was surviving the best way they knew how.

"Thank you for sharing the gift of your music with us, Miss Lavera," said Guinevere.

The Opal curtsied. "The pleasure was entirely mine, Miss Guinevere. Although it will be *Lady Wensleydale* soon, yes? Heartiest felicitations."

Guinevere murmured her thanks again before Wensleydale ushered her off to a cluster of his friends. She felt the Opal's gaze linger on the back of her neck a beat too long, but it quickly slipped her mind, because there was another round of introductions to focus on.

Where was Oskar? Why hadn't he come?

At some point, she bent down to help a certain Lady Machemont fix the hem of her gown, which had tangled with the heel of her shoe. When she straightened up, everyone in her immediate circle was staring at her, including Wensleydale. Had she committed an unforgivable social gaffe? With no small amount of apathy, she mentally rifled through all the discourses on etiquette that she'd memorized since she was a child. She didn't think that there'd been anything about how it was anathema to help another lady *not* fall flat on her face . . .

"Why, Miss Guinevere," said Lord Reecca, "that is quite the intriguing necklace you are wearing!"

Her hand flew to her chest, where, yes, the silver-spangled skull of her totem had spilled out from the low-cut bodice. She didn't look at it, but her fingers curved over feather and bone, tracing the thistle petals that a warden of the forest had brought forth.

"It doesn't exactly match your magnificent gown," ventured Lady Portgomery, "but it *is* a rather unique piece, for all that."

Wensleydale recovered smoothly, shooting his friends a sly grin. "It seems I was in error, having provided the gown and not the jewels. I've every faith that my betrothed will provide me with ample opportunity to make up for my oversight."

"As she should!" Lady Machemont declared. Without missing a beat, she turned to Guinevere and said in a stage whisper, "I shall give you the addresses of several renowned jewelers . . ."

More of that droll, decorous laughter, the kind that Guinevere would hear every day throughout a lifetime of balls like this, and brunches and high teas and croquet matches. She didn't say anything as she looked from one set of aristocratic features to the next and the next and the next, still clutching the sparrow skull, digging the tip of her finger into the black earth of its crevice.

Not a single one of these wealthy, privileged people realized that this wasn't just a necklace, when even a ragtag bunch of bandits had known that it was a totem. High society was trapped in a cage of its own making.

Was she really going to lock herself in with them?

No.

The answer stole upon her like a bolt of lightning. It froze her where she stood; it lit her up from within with its stark, undeniable conviction.

This glittering, hollow realm—these insincere, pedigreed people, fabulously out of touch—this monotonous parade of properly regimented days and nights—this was *not* the life she wanted.

Her gaze fell on her parents several feet away, fawning over their conversation partners, drinking to disguise their nerves, oblivious to the thinly veiled contempt that would hound their every move from now on. They looked so small, so harmless. As did everyone else in this room. Her time on the Amber Road had cut them all down to size.

I can go, Guinevere thought. *I can just leave.* It was as simple as that, like unlocking a door she'd had the key to all along. Wensleydale had his historically significant Parure, and her mother and her father had their wits, their gumption, and each other. They were going to be fine.

I can go.

There was nothing stopping her but her own fears.

And she *was* afraid—but she was going to do it anyway. She was going to find Oskar and lay her heart at his feet, and together they would leave all of this behind.

GUINEVERE WAITED UNTIL A FEW of Wensleydale's business part-ners had drifted over to him. "My lord," she said smoothly, "I believe my nose is in dire need of powdering. Please excuse me."

He waved her off with a distracted, indulgent nod, too embroiled in his discussion, too accepting of her ladylike docility to suspect her of any nefarious plans. It would have been insulting, if she'd cared about him one whit.

And that was the thing. She *wanted* to care about someone she was going to marry. She wanted passion, and adventure, and the freedom to just *be*.

That was all within her grasp. She just had to reach for it. She just had to listen to the song of her heart.

Guinevere made her way through the crowd, walking briskly, look-ing straight ahead. Ignoring all those who hailed her and their miffed noises when she didn't stop to chat. She didn't care. She was never going to see any of these people again.

The powder room was mercifully deserted. There was a window over the washbasin, and Guinevere stood on tiptoe to peer outside. No guards that she could spot. She had to do it now, before someone came in.

Her pulse racing a mile a minute, she kicked off her heeled shoes and scrambled on top of the marble counter, prying the window open as far as it would go. Then she tossed her shoes out onto the grass and followed them, hauled herself through the window the way Oskar had taught her how to haul herself over deadfall and rocky slopes. This was the least conspicuous exit from the ballroom; her plan was to search for him on the nearby grounds and, if she wasn't successful, nip back in through the servants' entrance and tear the whole mansion apart looking for him if need be. Her bare feet hit the grass, cool and damp with evening dew. She pulled her shoes back on, and she gathered bunches of her skirts into her hands and lifted them up and ran—at first, with the single-minded purpose of finding Oskar as quickly as possible, then eventually also with the sheer joy of running through the moonlight, unbridled, a lifetime of manacles slipping away.

She ran all along the white alabaster side of the main house, past the gardens and the hedgerows. There were fewer guards than she thought there'd be, and they were all moonlit figures in the distance, their backs to her, looking outward. Then again, the bulk of the security had apparently been concentrated in the ballroom and the hallway where the trunk was located. She would have dashed right past the stables had it not been for the golden light visible through the windows, and within its rays the careful movements of a familiar silhouette that was as dear to her as a homecoming.

Pudding and Vindicator greeted her with soft huffs as she stepped inside, her skirts trailing over dirt and hay. In the glow of a lone lantern, Oskar was in the process of retrieving the horses' saddles from the rack. He paused when he heard Guinevere approach, but he didn't turn around.

"What are you doing here?"

His distant tone set off alarm bells in her head. She belatedly noticed that he was wearing traveling clothes and that his packed rucksack lay at his feet.

"You . . ." She swallowed. "You were just going to leave? Without saying goodbye?"

"I *was* going to," he responded flatly. "But you've caught me. So— goodbye."

Her fists clenched, her nails digging into the skin of her palms. But even that grinding pain was nothing compared to the slow fracture blossoming through her chest. He was as acerbic as he'd been the night they met, yet also less brusque. Less charged. And that was worse than any anger on his part would have been, because it meant that he didn't care anymore.

But it was possible that he was just tired and she was just being overly anxious. She would never know until she asked. She'd come too far to not ask.

"Oskar." His name was a prayer in the shadows. It carried with it all of her hope. Every dream she'd ever had. "Will you take me with you to Boroftkrah? I . . . I want to go with you. There's nothing for me here. I've seen more of the world now, and I should very much like to see the rest. With you by my side."

She waited, hardly daring to breathe. She wished that she could see his face, that he would turn around, but he appeared to be in no hurry to do so. He hung the saddles back on the rack with painstaking deliberation.

"What about your folks?" he asked. "Your betrothed? The life you were trained for?"

She tried to push the words out—tried to give voice to all those realizations she'd had in the ballroom—but they got stuck in her throat, entangling there with her bewilderment at his sudden display of cool, measured practicality. She apparently didn't respond fast enough for his liking, judging from the way his shoulders bunched with tension.

"You're telling me," he continued, "that I traveled in the opposite direction of my mother's last wish—that I crossed from practically one end of the Amber Road to the other—that I risked my life and, yes, my *sanity*, Guinevere—to bring you safely to Nicodranas . . . and you're not even going to *stay* here?"

"I—I hadn't thought of it that way," she stammered.

"Of course not," he scoffed. "People of your class don't ever think about the inconvenience you cause others. It simply doesn't register in your heads."

Oh, gods, she would have given anything for the ground to crack open and swallow her whole. Her skin was crawling with terror and with shame. She remembered the night she'd all but ordered him to rent a room for her, because one gold piece wasn't the luxury for her that it was for him; this was so much worse than that.

Had she truly been such a burden? She'd worked so hard to curb her selfishness, her thoughtlessness. But perhaps she would always be that spoiled girl from the Shimmer Ward.

"I'm so sorry," Guinevere whispered.

Oskar gave a violent jerk, almost like a recoiling. As though those words had burned him. That puzzled her a little, because, yes, she was supposed to stop apologizing for things that weren't her fault, but *this* was. He finally turned around to look at her, and his oakmoss features might as well have been carved in stone, his eyes as hard as topaz.

She trembled as it began to sink in that, after tonight, she would never see this face again. But her hope was stubborn; it lingered, it refused to be smothered, it fanned the weak flames of her last pitiful attempt. "I'm so sorry," she repeated, forcing herself to meet his unforgiving gaze. "I never meant for this to happen—for *you* to happen to me. All my life I was taught to follow the rules, to not want things. But these days that's all I can seem to do. I want the open road. I want to learn how to control my magic. I want to be happy. I want"—a single tear beaded at the corner of her lashes—"I want to be with you."

Oskar's gaze followed the tear as it trailed down her cheek. His jaw clenched. "You and I are novelties to each other," he said, still in that strangely flat tone. "You're a slice of the upper crust that I'll never break into in a million years, no matter how hard I work. And I am something exciting to you, purely because you've never met anyone like me before." He leaned against the wall, shoving his hands into his pockets. "Once all of that wears off—and it *will*—you'll resent me because I took you away from the comforts that you're used to. And I'll resent you because I need someone who knows how to do their fair share, not just make flower crowns and set things on fire."

Guinevere flinched. This wasn't *just* what she'd been afraid of—it was a level of humiliation that she had never imagined possible. All her illusions were shattering left and right. "Why did you stay until tonight, then? You could have left first thing yesterday." She was a stranger to her own ears—defeated yet accusing. But even her accusations were rooted in that ember of stubborn, illogical hope. If she could just stumble upon the right thing to say—the right question to ask—he might give her the answer that she wanted.

A fool's dream, that. As though mere words could unlock a door barred to her.

"I wanted to make sure that you would be safe," said Oskar. "And you will be. There are guards everywhere, and they're more than capable of fighting off the mercenaries. I consider my duty fulfilled in this regard."

There was a part of her that longed to be contrary. To point out that, as a matter of fact, there weren't any guards between the stables and the mansion at all. But she would only sound churlish, and she didn't want him to remember her like that.

Yet she had to try again. One more time.

"I thought we had something." She cringed inwardly as soon as she said it. How weak she sounded. How plaintive.

Oskar shrugged, and she wanted to die. "It was a long trip," he mumbled, looking down at the straw scattered around their feet. "People have needs. You were there and I was there. Let's not pretend it amounted to more than that."

Her tears flowed. She couldn't stop them. He'd said it himself once—that she cried too easily. At the time, she'd thought it was a teasing remark, but he must have meant it with contempt, and now he was clearly counting down the seconds until he was free of her forever.

"It appears that I've misunderstood." Guinevere said this with as much dignity as she could muster through a mess of tears and snot. "I beg your pardon, Oskar. Thank you for—for all that you've done. For taking on the Amber Road with me and seeing me safe to the other side. I wish you good fortune and fair weather on the rest of your travels."

With that, she fled. Her sweet Pudding let out a bewildered whinny upon seeing her go, but she didn't look back. She couldn't. She would throw herself weeping at Oskar's feet otherwise.

The night air was so much colder than Guinevere remembered it being as she made her way back to the mansion. What she had told Oskar still held true even though he would no longer be by her side throughout her next steps. She could not be Lady Wensleydale. She would sneak up to her room and pack what she could carry, and then—

She tripped over something.

Years of dance lessons kicked in once more, and Guinevere righted her balance, narrowly avoiding a fall. She looked around, expecting to find the culprit in the form of a dislodged branch or a poorly placed decorative rock.

But it was a human leg, sticking out of the bushes.

Alarmed, Guinevere hurried over to . . . well, it was a guest, most probably, who'd imbibed too much—

From within the bed of leaves and late-blooming flowers, a dead guard's face stared up at her with open, sightless eyes. His lips were chapped and slightly parted. Specks of ice glittered in his limp hair.

Frost magic. Bharash.

Guinevere was too shocked to scream. She made to run back to the stables, which were about twenty feet away, but another figure had suddenly blocked her path. She almost *did* scream then, clapping her hands over her mouth at the last second when she realized who it was.

"Miss Guinevere?" The Opal of the Ocean squinted at her through curls of smoke emanating from a slim cigar that was pressed between her fingers. "Whatever is the matter? You look like you've seen a ghost."

Guinevere wordlessly pointed to the corpse. The Opal gasped, dropping her cigar, and Guinevere reached out to clutch her arm. "We must get indoors," she said.

But the Opal stayed where she was, resisting Guinevere's tugs. "I have another destination in mind," she said cheerfully.

Guinevere opened her mouth to ask what she meant by that. And that was when she caught the faintest trace of it, on the Opal's breath— the smell of peppermint and buttercups. The smell Guinevere had first encountered wafting from a cauldron behind an alchemist's stall in Druvenlode.

As soon as she noticed it, the disguise potion wore off. Mia Lavera's horns disappeared, her dark hair straightening and her ruby-red skin turning seafoam green. The rounded shape of her eyes shifted into the taper of willow leaves, their irises morphing from silver-black to emerald. All of a sudden, Guinevere was looking not at the Opal of the Ocean, but at the uniya mercenary named Selene.

Selene's arm arced through the air, a dagger flashing in the moonlight. Guinevere felt a burst of pain as the pommel collided with the back of her skull, and then—

Nothing.

CHAPTER THIRTY-EIGHT

Oskar

Oskar spent the first several seconds after Guinevere walked out of his life wondering if it was possible to beat oneself to death.

How he wished he could run after her and beg for forgiveness. Tell her that he hadn't meant any of it, that she was the best thing to ever happen to him.

But he couldn't, because if she threw her lot in with his sorry own, it would be the *worst* thing to ever happen to *her.*

It was better that she hate him. With each harsh word dredged up from some dark part of him that was as unexpectedly cruel as it was desperate, he had been saving her from years of drudgery by his side, from what was certain to be the regret that would consume her. It had been difficult, *torturous,* yet somehow also so very easy, his resigned heart rising to the task with determination. He would do anything for her—even sever all that was sweet and good between them.

But, gods . . . he'd made her cry. Every tear had been a knife raked across his gut. That little flinch of hers—it would haunt him for the rest of his days. And the way she'd apologized, because he'd made her believe it was her fault, because he was scum, like her parents—

Oskar kicked his rucksack. It went flying across the stable, startling the horses.

"Oh, shut up," he growled over the cacophony of disgruntled snorts and pointedly stomped hooves.

The animals fell silent, terrified.

Great. As though he needed *more* reasons to feel guilty.

Oskar dug the back of his hand into his eyes, a futile bid to stem the abrupt sting of tears welling up. He couldn't help but recall the last time he'd allowed himself to cry—in Guinevere's arms, his battered heart turning over with the bittersweet realization that tears were no source of shame. Tears meant that you had lived in the world, that you had been a part of it. Tears meant that you had loved someone.

Tears could even be a victory in their own way, a sign that you hadn't let all the daily struggles—the myriad little uncaring cruelties—get the best of you.

Life could be hard, but *he* didn't have to be. His mother had taught him that. Yet he'd driven Guinevere off with a callousness drawn from years of unending toil.

Ma, Oskar heard himself think, *I fucked up.*

He missed Idun more than ever. It was the memory of her that finally made his hand fall back to his side. That finally let the tears stream freely from his eyes. He would cry in secret for Guinevere; she deserved that much from him, just like his mother had. The two women he'd loved and lost.

Sniffling, Oskar went over to the rucksack. He'd pick it up and be on his way, and Guinevere would go on to live her perfect life and give Wensleydale his perfect blond heirs, and soon Oskar would be a mere footnote in her history. Just something that had happened to her on the Amber Road. It was as it should be.

The rucksack had landed on its side, its top flap loose. He crouched down and shoved the spilled contents back into place. His fingers closed around a length of leather, yanking it free from the tangle of his clothes.

And he stared at the Vigilance Stone dangling from his hand, glowing a bright, pale blue.

Evil intentions.

No more than thirty feet away.

Guinevere had *just* gone outside—

Panic roared within him. He was charging out of the stables before he knew it, running as fast as he could, but, in his state of mind, he felt as though he were running through treacle. *Don't let me be too late,* he prayed to every god he knew. *Please, don't let me be too late.*

It was an inside job.

Only the guards stationed directly along the sides of the mansion and in the hallway where the trunk was located had been killed. The trunk was gone, too, the room where it had been kept covered in blood and torn limbs. It had to be the work of either servants or guests, and, according to the butler, all the servants were accounted for and had been too busy with ball-related tasks to engage in a little light murder, robbery, and kidnapping, anyway.

This begged the question of how the Spider's Web had managed to infiltrate Wensleydale's heavily curated and cross-checked guest list. But, for Oskar, the *how* wasn't important. In terms of his priorities, it paled in comparison to the fact that Guinevere was nowhere to be found, and he was dangerously close to killing her useless parents.

Illiard sagged against the mantelpiece in the drawing room, his head in his hands. Betha was hunched in on herself in an armchair, sobbing noisily into a kerchief.

Wensleydale was . . . also nowhere to be found.

"His lordship apparently departed the ballroom a few minutes before you raised the alarm," Captain Therault was telling Oskar. "It's likely that he and Miss Guinevere were taken together, along with the artifact. The guests are being questioned as we speak."

"Why would the mercenaries also kidnap Wensleydale?" Oskar turned to Illiard. "Did you already give him the key to the trunk?"

"There is no key," Illiard moaned. "Not one you can put into a lock, at any rate. It's—it's magical. A blood spell."

Oskar went very still. "Whose blood?" he snapped, even though he knew the answer deep in his heart, even though he was afraid to hear it confirmed.

There was a knock on the door. Therault excused himself, but Oskar hardly noticed the captain leave the room. All of his attention was focused on Illiard, who was shaking all over. Like a man whose worst fears had been realized.

Like a man, Oskar thought, fuming, who had known that this day might come.

"He found out." Illiard had his back turned to the rest of the room, but a mirror hung over the mantelpiece, and Oskar could see his reflection, white as a sheet, a haunted look in those eyes that were so much like Guinevere's. "He found out, somehow."

"Who found out what?" When Illiard didn't reply, Oskar marched over to him. He grabbed the merchant by his collar and hauled him off his feet, ignoring Betha's alarmed screech. "Listen to me very carefully," he said, knuckles clenching to white around starched fabric. "Your daughter is in danger. I will save her, but in order to do that, I need to know *everything*. I don't care that you're her father—I once promised her that she would never face this world alone as long as I still drew breath, so if you don't tell me what you're hiding, *I will rip it out of you.* Have I made myself clear?"

Illiard's lips parted, but no sound emerged. The last lingering threads of Oskar's patience frayed apart, and he shook the man until the latter's teeth rattled.

"Stop!" Betha wailed. "For gods' sake, Illiard, just tell him!"

Illiard was full-on blubbering now. "I stole it. The trunk. I didn't win it in a card game." He clawed in vain at Oskar's fists, still locked against his throat. "In Yrrosa, there was an arcanist named Accanfal living at the edge of town. He hired me on as a gardener. Paid me a pittance. I could barely make ends meet, and my wife was pregnant."

Something in his gaze begged Oskar to understand, and the truth was that it wasn't difficult to do so. Yrrosa was as much of a shithole as the Dustbellows. Of course he knew to what lengths desperation could drive a man. But there wasn't much room for compassion within him, not when Guinevere had been thrown to the wolves somewhere out there. He tightened his grip on Illiard's collar, a silent command to get on with it.

"One day I was trimming the rosebushes," Illiard continued, "when I heard a scream. Looked up and saw the arcanist flying out of his laboratory window, right over my head. He was on fire. The other servants all ran to help him, but I—I got curious. I snuck into the laboratory and there was the trunk, lying open amidst all the other paraphernalia." He swallowed nervously. "Jewelry like I'd never seen—diadems, necklaces, more—all gold, all studded with gems. All in one trunk. The temptation—too great—"

Oskar belatedly realized that Illiard wasn't pausing for dramatic effect; rather, Oskar's fingers had twisted even more tightly into his collar, cutting off his airway. The man was practically turning purple.

"So you took it and ran." Oskar let go without much ceremony. Illiard collapsed at his feet.

"Yes," the merchant wheezed. "Stole a horse and raced back to town to grab Betha, and we fled."

After he regained his breath, the rest of the sorry tale came spilling out of him. Illiard and Betha had hit the road, selling off pieces from the set here and there, each one fetching enormous sums. Eventually, though, Accanfal had picked up the trail, cornering them in Cyrengreen—and it was only then that they realized that the arcanist had survived the accident. He was the one who'd set the woods ablaze.

And Hammie, the warden of the forest who had saved Illiard and Betha then—who had made the totem for their child, knowing she would need it in her life to come—he'd seen the trunk and the jewelry, and he had revealed what exactly it was that Illiard had stolen.

Oskar tensed up even more as he learned the true nature of the Parure. Of all the deities it could have been connected to, it had to be *her.* The gods had a twisted sense of humor.

"And you still didn't want to give it up, even after finding out what it really was," he said in disgust. "Rather than get rid of it, you hired someone to seal the trunk with your only child's blood."

"It wouldn't have worked with mine or Betha's," Illiard mumbled. "The sealing spell needed to feed off another magic user. It needed *her* magic."

"The same magic that you reviled all her life?" Oskar spat. "You sure didn't have any problem using it for your own purposes, you spineless sack of offal."

The other man gulped, then hurried through the rest of his story as though he hoped that would take some of the heat off him. "We found another arcanist who was willing to do it. A ring from the Parure ensured his service and his silence, but we knew we'd never be able to sell the rest, lest Accanfal track us again. So we headed to Rexxentrum and bought a house in the Shimmer Ward, and we kept Guinevere there with the trunk."

"You *locked her up*, you mean." Oskar wasn't one to kick a man when he was down—in this case, quite literally, on the carpeted floor in a pathetic heap—but he was sorely tempted to do so now. "You made her world small because of your greed. You browbeat every perceived fault out of her because of your ambition. But the plain and simple truth is that she's worth ten of you." He glared at Betha. "And of you."

"Well, it was all for nothing, wasn't it?" sobbed Betha. "Accanfal found us in the end—because of your big mouth, Illiard, you drunken boor—and even him taking her was for nothing, because the blood has to be given *willingly*. That's the condition of the spell."

"Then that's why the Spider's Web took Wensleydale," said Oskar. "Accanfal will make her unseal the trunk in exchange for Wensleydale's life—and she will do it, because that's the kind of person she is. In spite of the two of you." A thought occurred to him. Speaking of Wensleydale . . . "That whole thing about the Parure being a Truscan artifact—that was all bullshit, wasn't it? Wensleydale knows."

Illiard gave a miserable nod. "He didn't want to marry a merchant's daughter. So I said she'd come with a priceless enchanted treasure.

And he and I concocted that cover story. The plan was for him to tell Guinevere the truth—and to get her to unseal the trunk—once they were married."

"You," Oskar said crisply, "are a horrible little man, and I will gut Wensleydale like a fish after I rescue him." He headed to the door, reaching for the knob just as it flew open.

It was Captain Therault with an update. "Two of the guests are missing," he told Oskar. "The Opal of the Ocean and her bodyguard."

Oskar let out a curse. The barest bones of a frantic plan formed in his mind. "We need to watch all the city's exits. Therault, you'll secure the gates. I'll take some of your men down with me to the docks."

The captain saluted. He didn't question the fact that a nameless peasant only tangentially related to his employer was now the one giving the orders. And thank the gods for that, because it was about damn time Oskar caught a break.

CHAPTER THIRTY-NINE

Guinevere

There were four things Guinevere was immediately aware of when she came to.

First was the dull pain at the back of her skull. Second was the teak floorboards she was lying on in the center of a large, mostly bare compartment pervaded by a gentle rocking motion that had her feeling vaguely nauseous.

Third was the fact that she wasn't alone. There was a robed figure some distance away from her, standing in the shadows beyond the sickly yellow illumination of a few oil lanterns. She squinted, trying and failing to make sense of the silhouette, with its dimly lit features that were slightly off for reasons she couldn't pinpoint, the nose that seemed too long and curved and the arms that were too bony and the oddly shaped tufts around the head that surely couldn't be hair.

"You're awake at last." The voice was cold and nasal, with a certain melodious croakiness. It sounded like a sparrow's heartbeat, leaping into the wind.

The Spider's Web had delivered her to this person, to this isolated place she had no idea where. And that brought Guinevere to the fourth thing: she was strangely calm about it.

It was a heavy, blank sort of calm. It tugged at her eyelids. There was a cloudlike timbre to it that drowned out the song of the universe.

"I'm under a spell, aren't I?" she murmured to the wooden floor beneath her cheek.

"A calming one, yes," said the figure. "After all, I could not risk your little friend getting loose." He held something up; it glimmered weakly in the gloom, a chain of silver wrapped around his fist. Her totem.

There was something not quite right about that fist. The palm was too small, the digits too thin. They curved like . . . talons?

"What did you do to the real Mia Lavera? Is she all right?" Guinevere asked this because she needed to know, but her concern for this other woman who'd been endangered on her account was sheathed behind a wall of glass. The calming spell made it difficult to feel much of anything.

"Nicodranas's brightest star is passed out in her own abode. I expect she'll be coming to at any moment," said the figure. "The Zhelezo will probably come knocking to question her on her abrupt disappearance from the ball, but that's hardly my concern."

He stepped into the light. That was when Guinevere realized he was an eisfuura, the first one she had ever seen in the flesh. What she had thought was an overly long nose was in reality an eagle's beak, and the tufts were a frill of brown-and-white feathers around his head. What she had assumed were robes were actually feathers, dangling from his elongated arms like a shaggy pelt.

"Who are you?" she asked.

"My name is Accanfal."

It clicked neatly into place. It fit in her mind, this thing that she had forgotten. This name that she had heard in a dream.

He pointed to something beside her, calling her attention to it for the first time since she woke. It was the pearwood trunk. "And your father stole that from me."

"It's not stealing to win a bet."

Accanfal let out a raucous, cawing laugh. "Is *that* what Illiard told you?"

Guinevere fell silent.

"You don't even know what this treasure is, do you?" Accanfal sneered. "I sailed from my native Marquet to hunt it down. I followed the trail of arcane whispers to the ruins of the elves. And there it was. A trove of enchanted jewelry, each piece brimming with elemental power." He strode over to the trunk and dragged his talons over its lid in what was almost a loving caress. "The Duskmaven's Parure."

The Duskmaven. Yes. Goddess of Death. Matron of Ravens. That explained the magic she'd sensed within when she touched the trunk back in Zadash. She should have brought it up the moment Wensleydale told her all that rot about the set belonging to House Truscan, but she hadn't wanted to cause a stir. Hadn't wanted him to know about her magic.

Now that Accanfal had moved closer to the light, Guinevere noted the jewelry he wore. An emerald ring. An emerald bracelet. A diamond-studded emerald pendant.

"Your father was blinded by his greed," said Accanfal. "He sold these pieces on the black market, never imagining that I would be able to trace them. He also never imagined that I would find the arcanist who sealed the trunk." The eisfuura's pale yellow eyes glinted. "I heard of a man with a ring that could cast lightning magic, and I found him. He didn't know where your family had hidden, but before he died, he told me about his sealing spell. It's a blood rune, Miss Guinevere. Your blood is the key."

The dream of the blade in her father's hands . . . not a dream. A *memory*.

This was why she'd been shut away in Rexxentrum all her life. Until her family's fortunes changed and her father had been forced to play the only card he had left.

Guinevere suddenly badly resented the calming spell. She'd always been afraid of her emotions for as long as she could remember, afraid of their consequences, but at something like *this*—the shock of the revelations, the pain of the betrayal, the anger at the unraveling of all the lies—she should have been able to feel the full scale of them.

"The thing is," said Accanfal, "the blood needs to be given willingly."

A door in the—ceiling?—opened, more light spilling down a ladder that she hadn't been able to make out before. There was another bobbing motion that encompassed the world. It clicked for Guinevere then that she was in the cargo hold of a ship, and it was sailing away from Nicodranas.

Her betrothed came tumbling down in a flash of blond hair and fine clothes, his hands tied behind his back. The person who had unceremoniously tossed him into the hold—Selene—made a more decorous entrance, descending the ladder lithely, still dressed in the Opal of the Ocean's clothes.

"It's difficult to hire competent people when you've spent most of your resources on the trail of a thief for the past twenty years," Accanfal complained to Guinevere, shooting a disparaging glance at Selene. "I was still in Tal'Dorei following a false lead when my spies relayed the news of your betrothal and your dowry, or I would have intercepted you on the Amber Road myself. Fortunately, the Spider's Web *does* have its moments of brilliance."

Selene rolled her eyes. "The sooner you pay up, the sooner my sub-average men and I can be out of your feathers."

"In a minute," snapped Accanfal. "I'll need you to take care of some loose ends after this."

Wensleydale let out a whimper. Accanfal tutted. "I won't *kill* you, my lord. You and Miss Guinevere will be rowed back to shore in plenty of time for a jolly old nightcap while I continue on my way back to Marquet. Assuming that she makes the right decision, that is."

Guinevere slowly got to her feet. The hold tilted precariously—no, it was only her sense of balance that was askew. She'd never been on a ship before.

"What do you say?" Accanfal prodded. "A few drops of your blood, just enough to open the trunk so I can reclaim what's mine. Then you and your betrothed are free to go and have a happy little life together. With my blessing."

"You're utterly mad!" Wensleydale shouted at the arcanist. "Absolutely barking! Taking the Duskmaven's Parure out of the equation, I can't marry a—a *commoner*! That set is the only reason I was willing to sully my illustrious bloodline—" He caught himself with some reluctance. "No offense, Miss Guinevere."

"I will take *some* offense, if you don't mind," Guinevere muttered. She couldn't deny that it hurt to be called that, but . . . didn't it hurt only because she *let* it? She'd met people on the Amber Road more noble in nature than so-called nobility.

Accanfal was clearly taken aback by Wensleydale's outburst. "By the spires of Jrusar." He looked at Guinevere. "This is who you wish to be with?"

"No," she replied with complete honesty.

"Good call," Selene piped up, the expression on her face one of sheer disgust.

A series of thumps sounded overhead. "Tell the crew to cease that racket," Accanfal instructed Selene. Once the mercenary had left, he fixed his piercing gaze on Guinevere once more. "Well, my girl? Your blood for your freedom? A fair exchange, don't you think? Otherwise, I shall have to take you to Marquet with me."

The smart thing to do was agree. But it hadn't been very smart to run away from her own engagement ball, either, and Guinevere found herself oddly reluctant to break her streak. Accanfal was presenting a choice that was no choice at all.

Finish your embroidery, or go to bed without supper.

Master all the table napkin folds by tomorrow, or be locked in your room all week.

Marry a stranger, or be the architect of your family's ruin.

"I don't want to," Guinevere heard herself say.

And that, too, was freedom.

"Don't want to what?" Accanfal cocked his head. "Give up your blood? Or be my captive?"

"Exactly," said Guinevere. "I don't want to do either of those things." She lifted her chin. "I'm done with letting other people make my choices for me."

"Oh, gods," Wensleydale groaned. "We're going to die."

"Maybe *you* will," Guinevere retorted, never taking her gaze off Accanfal. "But if I die, all hope of reclaiming the Duskmaven's Parure dies with me. He can't kill me. He would never dare."

"You're right." Accanfal's talons clenched into a fist, crackling with magic. "I can't kill you. But I can hurt you. I can make it so that you would be so desperate for relief from your pain that you'd do anything. I have all the time in the world to do that."

"*Over my fucking corpse!*" came a deep bellow from above, and Oskar dropped into the cargo hold, kicked Wensleydale in the stomach, then took a running leap at Accanfal and tackled him to the floor.

CHAPTER FORTY

Oskar

Oskar was admittedly startled when Selene popped out of the ship's hatch in the clothes that the Opal of the Ocean had been wearing—but not so startled that it could override the instinct stamped into every drop of blood in his body to get to Guinevere as soon as possible.

He swung first, his sword already dripping with the blood of Accanfal's hapless crew. Oskar had taken ten men with him in his frantic race to the docks, where they'd spied one ship leaving port—a trimasted wooden barkentine with Marquesian sails. They'd rowed out to it, and Oskar had lost seven men battling the crew and the remaining three in taking down Bharash, the dragonblood.

Now there was only Selene left to tangle with on the upper decks. Oskar's blade landed in the intersection of her two daggers, swiftly produced from the folds of her formal skirts, but he had taken her by surprise as well, her stance unsteady, her grip loose. In the tussle that followed, he didn't relinquish his advantage, didn't give her any opportunity to switch from purely defensive maneuvers; he rained blow after blow upon her, forcing her backward across the ship. He had to save Guinevere. He might already be too late.

At last, Selene collided with the railing, and she stumbled. With another powerful slash, Oskar knocked one dagger out of her hand. The mercenary lunged at him with her remaining blade, grazing his cheek, but he caught her by the elbow—and pushed her overboard.

The distant splash of a body hitting the water barely registered as Oskar turned and ran for the hatch. He flung open the door, and he was barreling down into the cargo hold—into a world of shadows and flickering light—and he was brawling like a man possessed. And he *was*—by fury. He was running high on it and the adrenaline it produced, insulating him from the burn of frostbite on his right arm and the dagger wound on his cheek. Accanfal's hollow bones cracked under the onslaught of his fists.

But fighting an eisfuura was trickier than fighting most other humanoids. The anatomy wasn't where it should have been. The feathers were slippery. It wasn't long before Accanfal tore his right arm free, and there was a flash as the emerald ring on one talon took on an unnatural luminescence, colliding with Oskar's shoulder . . .

Oskar hissed as a million bolts of static shot through his body, prying his veins apart like burning knives. He didn't *want* to collapse— not when Guinevere was still in danger—but he did, laid out on his back on the floor, curling in on himself as the lightning wreaked its havoc on his system. Through the dark haze of pain, he saw Accanfal's blurred form tower over him, more emeralds glowing around his wrist. He reached for his sword, but the nerves on his hand were deadened, refusing to cooperate, and a dozen knives fashioned from pure ice came barreling toward him.

Oskar somehow managed to roll away from the initial attack, the knives sinking into the floorboards after him in a glittering trail. But his luck was quick to run out. Another flash of frost, and then—

It was the chill he felt first. Followed by the pain. He tried to move, but there was resistance, something tearing. He went still.

As the clamor in his head died down, he became aware of the spear of ice in his chest. It had shot straight through and into the teak underneath, pinning him to the floor.

He braced himself for Guinevere's screams, knowing that the sound would cut much deeper than any weapon could, but the only person carrying on was Wensleydale, and Oskar certainly didn't care about *him*. Guinevere was silent. He craned his neck and looked at her for the first time since he'd entered the cargo hold.

There was an unearthly blankness on her face, but she was pale, her violet eyes fixed on him, her lips moving soundlessly.

"No help there, my friend," said Accanfal. He waggled Guinevere's totem at Oskar. "Gently bred misses brought up in the Shimmer Ward don't know how to fight. Not without their elementals."

Oskar ignored him. *It's all right,* he tried to tell the woman he loved. The woman he had hurt beyond measure. The woman he couldn't save now. *It's all right. I'm sorry.*

But the words refused to come. His mouth was also not cooperating. Nothing was working as it should have been. The bracelet on Accanfal's wrist blazed with eldritch light once more, and a new knife crystallized out of thin air, the tip of the blade poised directly over Oskar's forehead.

"Stop." Guinevere's voice was barely above a whisper, but it echoed through every chamber of his heart.

Accanfal arched a downy brow. "Oh, so *now* you're ready to negotiate."

"Yes." Guinevere was still speaking softly, but Oskar knew her well enough by now to recognize the steel behind it. "If I open the trunk, you'll heal Oskar with your magic. Then you'll let him and me go. Those are my only terms." A dismayed cry rose up from Wensleydale, and she sighed. "Oh, all right. His lordship, too."

"Done," Accanfal said at once. "The Duskmaven's Parure includes a scepter of healing. But, from the looks of your sweetheart, there's no more time to waste, eh?"

Guinevere stumbled over to the trunk and stretched her arm above it, pulling back the lilac-and-silver sleeve of her bedraggled gown. With a flick of Accanfal's wrist, the knife that had been hovering over

Oskar was sent zipping in Guinevere's direction. It sliced cleanly across the length of her arm, leaving a streak of bright red blood in its wake.

Oskar was powerless to do anything but watch. He watched the blood drip in scarlet beads from copper skin, landing on the lid of the trunk. He watched the pearwood respond at once, an assortment of runes forming across its surface in swirls of molten silver. There was a noise like the grinding of celestial gears, followed by a sharp *click*—and the lid popped open.

And there they were.

Nestled amidst folds of red velvet, the golden ornaments took what little lantern light there was in the cargo hold and magnified it a thousand times over. They shone like fire—a crown, a scepter, earrings, brooches, and several rings, all adorned with dark emeralds in various cuts and sizes.

Oskar was actually sort of glad that he was on the brink of death at that very moment. Otherwise, he would have broken out into a cold sweat at the realization that he and Guinevere had blithely carted several fortunes' worth of gold and gemstones around Wildemount. Gods, the number of times they'd left the trunk unattended while they f—

"Finally," breathed Accanfal. He went to the trunk while Guinevere ran to Oskar and knelt by his side.

"You came after me," she murmured. Her hair hung around him like curtains of moonlight. His vision was darkening at the borders, but he forced himself to stay conscious, memorizing every inch of her face. That amazing face. He could have asked for no better last sight.

"Oskar. Hang on. We'll heal you. You'll be okay." She squeezed his hand. "The scepter?" she called out to Accanfal over her shoulder.

"About that . . ." The eisfuura had donned the crown. He sauntered over to them, twirling the scepter in his talons.

Suddenly his free hand lashed out, the claws tangling into Guinevere's hair. He yanked her toward him, still on her knees. Another wave of murderous rage swept through Oskar, but this time it was maddeningly impotent. He couldn't do anything. He couldn't move.

She needed him, but he was dying.

"I've decided," Accanfal snarled, looking into Guinevere's eyes as she struggled in vain, "that I'm not quite willing to let bygones be bygones. Your father stole what was mine. It's unfair that you and your two swains have to die for his sins, but what better vengeance than to ensure he never sees his daughter again?"

"I hate to break it to you," Guinevere spat, brimming with defiance, "but he doesn't love me that much." She paused, then added, sounding rather annoyed, "Also, you shouldn't monologue so much, because it gives people time to plan how to fight back."

And, with a surprising burst of strength, she lurched forward, her fingers closing around her totem as it dangled from Accanfal's wrist.

CHAPTER FORTY-ONE

Guinevere

Some things were gifts, some things were to be learned, and some things were both.

No one's first arrow hit its mark, but a boy who trained every day with the blades he forged could come to know their heft and arc, and grow up to be a man who might take on a dozen and live.

The ear for melody was a gift, but the voice had to practice so that it could bend with ease. Social graces were learned, so that a girl born to common thieves could hold her own in a ballroom full of the finest pedigrees.

There were some for whom magic was a gift, and the only thing left to do was understand how to control it. And there were some for whom magic was the product of years of careful study to produce a single flame.

Fear was a natural state, neither gift nor curse. But everyone possessed the ability to overcome it. It was just a matter of when and how.

Teinidh, Guinevere begged, there in the darkness, through the haze of the calming spell. *Teinidh, wake up.*

Her fingertips brushed against the soil of her totem.

And magic stirred in the deep of her soul.

My sister.

A voice like smoke. Eyes like embers, opening. The gift she hadn't wanted, the curse she had borne all these years—as much a part of her as her too-soft heart and her eagerness to please.

The connection was faint but *there.* Guinevere held on to it, forcing it open. The wildfire burned low in her core.

Teinidh shimmered in the dark, bound not by Guinevere's fear but by the ghostly shackles of Accanfal's calming spell. But that's not exactly right, is it? she mused. Perhaps we were sisters of a sort, once. *And now?*

Guinevere listened to the voice in the inferno. She listened to the beating of her heart, and to the currents of her magic. She heard what Teinidh was trying to say—what Teinidh had been trying to tell her all along.

To live in this world is to change, said the wildfire spirit. To live in your world is to become you. To hide from me is to hide from yourself. One blazing wrist strained against the manacle that tethered it to the shadows. Give me your fury. Make me the instrument of your vengeance. Give me your fear. We will not die on water. Give me something.

I can't. Accanfal's spell was too strong.

Yet Teinidh was resolute, pressing against her mind. Get us out of here. Give me something.

And Guinevere knew only what she had learned on the Amber Road—that fire could destroy, but it could also be used to cast light in the dark, to give warmth in the cold, to protect from evil. And she could think only of Oskar, and how Exandria would be a worse place without him in it, and how he had to go to Boroftkrah because he'd promised his mother.

I can't be angry, she told Teinidh. *I can't be afraid. But I—we—will save him. We have to save him, because I love him, and if you don't come now, I will never forgive you.*

Teinidh smirked. *Good enough.*

It was Guinevere who reached out first. Her hand moved through air and darkness, through soul and being. She pressed her palm to Teinidh's burning heart.

The white shackles disintegrated, each shard scattering like snow, only to be melted into nothingness by the same heat that poured into Guinevere's veins. The flames engulfed her, and she welcomed them, because to live in the world was to want to save it.

No matter what.

In the cargo hold of the arcanist's ship, the wildfire spirit burst into existence beside Guinevere. Teinidh wrapped her smoldering arms around Accanfal, who screamed as he was reduced to cinders in the red-gold embrace. First the feathers, up in smoke, then the pink flesh beneath, then the hollow bones. A death of seconds, inches from Guinevere's face. Teinidh released what was left of him and made to sweep around the hold in a victorious dance of carnage, but Guinevere held her back, with a cool assurance she had not known she possessed. Teinidh was her magic, her darkness, her worst fears and her most wicked impulses magnified; she was *her*, and she was *not* going to let Oskar burn. She tightened the tether until the spirit's charred lips twisted into a pout and she grumbled, *Fine, have it your way.*

You mean our *way*, Guinevere corrected.

Teinidh laughed and vanished.

What fire there was had already snagged on the floorboards. Guinevere had to move fast, if there was to be any hope of saving Oskar. She hurriedly slipped her totem over her head and snatched up the scepter from where it lay in a heap of Accanfal's ashes. It was too hot to touch, but she didn't care; magic surged through her, a song soft and sharp all at once, like sunbeams falling on lace, like clean sheets and salt air. The ring of lightning had also been left unscathed, and she shook off a few specks of Accanfal before slipping it on, just in case. She turned to Oskar—Teinidh's heat had melted the ice spear, leaving

Guinevere with an unobstructed view of the hole in his chest, his tunic wet with blood and water. His skin was gray at the edges, and those golden eyes were already at half-mast.

She listened to the song that only she could hear, letting it guide her next steps. She aimed the scepter at Oskar's wound, and the emerald that crowned it glowed a bright green. There was the sound of wings, the skein of fate respooling, and then—

—the hole in Oskar's chest closed up, oakmoss skin knitting over red to form a puckered scar.

He jerked, his breath returning to him in a stuttered gasp. He bolted upright, normal color fully returned to his face. Guinevere felt tears of joy and relief prickle at the corners of her lashes, and she waited, her entire being aglow, for him to hug her, for him to whisper sweet words of comfort and gratitude . . .

"*Why are you still here?*" Oskar roared, a vein throbbing at his temple. "You daft woman, the ship is *on fire!*"

He scooped Guinevere up before she could respond, tossing her over his shoulder. The scepter slid from her grasp as he broke into a run, barely pausing to bring his sword down over the ropes that bound Wensleydale's wrists. The cargo hold was fast filling up with smoke, and Oskar and Wensleydale shot up the ladder with flames licking at their heels.

The inferno chased them across the ship's deck, devouring hull and masts and barrels and rigging. Oskar hurled Guinevere into one of the dinghies hanging off the edge, then clambered in after her.

"Hold on tight," he said.

"How?" she muttered from where she'd landed face down on the floor of the small vessel, her derriere sticking up. "You *threw* me—"

Oskar's sword slashed through the air, severing the ropes, and then she was screaming as they fell. The calming spell had apparently worn off with Accanfal's demise, and one unladylike expletive after another burst from her lips all throughout the sharp drop.

The boat landed in the ocean with an almighty splash. Guinevere struggled upright, completely drenched, spitting out salt and soot.

Oskar wasted no time in grabbing the oars, and soon he was paddling them away from the burning ship.

Even as she shivered—even as she did her best to wring water out of her hair and her hopelessly ruined gown—a strange calm settled in, one that had nothing to do with magic. It was over, in more ways than one. The night's disaster had wrapped up; the mystery of the trunk had come to a close. Her betrothal was nullified—in her eyes, at least, and *that* was the only opinion that mattered—and her relationship with her parents was never going to be the same again, and that was for the best. Her journey had ended, and the start of a new one lay on the horizon.

But there was something about the issue of her betrothal that was nagging at her . . .

"Oskar!" She turned to him sharply. "We forgot all about Lord W—"

A spray of water shot up beside the boat. A hulking form reared its head from the depths, tangled up in seaweed, teeth glinting in the moonlight.

Startled out of her wits, reacting purely on instinct, Guinevere punched it.

"Argh! How dare you!"

She relaxed. "You gave me quite a fright, my lord."

"And you," Wensleydale panted, slinging one arm over the gunwale while his free hand clutched at his injury, "gave me a broken nose."

"Adds character," Oskar piped up, with rather more cheer than the situation called for.

Wensleydale sniffed. "Help me on board, Miss Guinevere."

The thing was, she really would have. She was, in fact, reaching over to do just that. But then he added, in the kind of aristocratic mumble that was meant to carry, "Since the manservant is busy rowing."

And that was when Guinevere drove the final nail into the coffin of her old life and pushed Fitzalbert, Lord Wensleydale, back into the water.

CHAPTER FORTY-TWO

Oskar

Oskar switched course, steering the dinghy toward the golden orb of a remote lighthouse at the western tip of Nicodranas's coastline rather than the main port, where Wensleydale's guards and the Zhelezo were sure to have congregated by now. It was a longer trip back to shore this way, but he would gladly row to the Rime Plains so that it could be just him and Guinevere for a little while longer.

"Will he be all right, do you think?" she asked, peering at a distant point over his shoulder—no doubt at Wensleydale, whom they'd left furiously treading water.

Oskar didn't care, but Guinevere had asked him an earnest question, and so he answered earnestly. Only for her. Only ever for her. "A rescue ship's bound to come for him soon. And he's got plenty of debris to cling to."

"You may have a point." Her gaze shifted, and now her eyes reflected the dead arcanist's ship burning upon the ocean, splintering apart bit by bit.

"I'm sorry your former betrothed turned out to be a prick," he said.

"*Now* who's apologizing for things that aren't their fault?" There was a playful warmth to her tone that he didn't deserve. There were so many things he wanted to tell her. How proud he was that she'd learned how to control her magic in the cargo hold. How struck by grief he was because of everything he'd said to her in the stables. He still wasn't sure how he was going to live with himself for that.

"I suppose you want me to take you back to your folks," he said gruffly.

"Yes, but only so I can grab my things."

He was mystified. "Where are you going?"

"I don't know." She shrugged. "Anywhere I want, I guess."

He rowed them in silence for several long minutes, still absorbing this information. But Guinevere was never one to let silence be.

"I was always going to run away," she said. She leaned against the hull, idly trailing her fingers in the water. "Even before that bit of bother with Accanfal. Even if you weren't going to let me go with you. What I told you about wanting the open road—that still holds true. You were right, I'm fairly useless, but I can learn—"

"Stop," he croaked. The oars stilled in his hands as the inside of his chest fractured anew. "I didn't mean that. I didn't mean any of it. I thought you were planning to throw your life away because of me. At the time, Wensleydale seemed like a decent sort who would give you everything I couldn't. You're so damn stubborn that I knew I had to be deliberately cruel." The words caught in his throat. "But it killed me to say those things, Gwen. You asked why I didn't leave immediately after dropping you off, and I told you some bullshit about checking the estate's security. The truth is that I wanted one more night around you. I would have done anything for even just one more *second*. I'm sorry. You'll never know how sorry I am."

She ducked her head, hiding her expression from view as his words sank in.

Then she flicked water at his face.

He blinked at her through a stinging haze of ocean, salt on his lips.

"You're going to have to work very hard to earn my forgiveness,

Oskar," Guinevere said peevishly. She was glaring daggers at him in the moonlight, and it was the most magnificent sight he'd ever been privileged to witness. "You really hurt my feelings, you know."

He bit back a shout of relieved laughter. The dinghy rocked as he threw himself into a kneeling position in front of her, burying his face in her midsection, his fingers digging into her embroidered skirts.

"You will be nicer to people we meet on the road," Guinevere instructed.

Oskar kissed her stomach. "Yes."

She threaded her fingers through his hair. "I will make flower crowns when I'm bored, and you shall wear them without complaint."

"Yes." He leaned into her touch, his eyes closed with pleasure, what felt suspiciously like tears of relief trickling from the corners. But he was fine with that. Tears, laughter, joy, sorrow—there would be all of that and more with Guinevere in the years to come.

"When we visit your mother's clan in Boroftkrah," she said, "you and I will embark on several expeditions through the wilderness. Perhaps even see the elven ruins."

"Well, I don't know exactly how safe it will be—" Oskar started to protest, but she cleared her throat, and he immediately changed his tune. "Yes."

"All right, then," she said primly.

He grinned up at her. At this woman who had so daintily thrown a wrench into all his plans and made a home of his heart. "I love you," he said.

Some of her bravado wore off, silver moonbeams and the residual glow from the now distant inferno playing on the blush that gilded the apples of her cheeks. "Oh, Oskar." Her eyes filled with starlight. "I love you, too."

CHAPTER FORTY-THREE

Guinevere

It was near dawn by the time Oskar and Guinevere returned to the estate—on foot, because Oskar had left the Wensleydale horse he'd borrowed at the docks. There was a lot of carrying on as Illiard and Betha tried to stop them from packing up Guinevere's effects, and then from retrieving their own horses from the mews.

"You can't leave us like this, Guinevere!" Betha screeched as Oskar helped Guinevere up onto Vindicator's back. "We have no other prospects—"

"I will not stay with family who would have sacrificed me for their own ambitions, and I will not marry a man who considers me beneath him," Guinevere said firmly, leaning back against Oskar after he'd climbed onto the saddle behind her. "You may explain that to his lordship once he returns from his swim."

"You *owe* us!" Illiard snapped. "You lost the wagon and my oxen and most of our wares, and you bartered away everything else—" He grabbed Vindicator's reins to stop them from leaving.

"Damn." Oskar let out a low whistle. "You shouldn't have done that."

Right on cue, the stallion lowered his great black head and sank his large incisors into Illiard's shoulder.

As her father staggered back, his screams rending the air, Guinevere took off the ring of lightning and tossed it in her mother's direction. Betha was too slow to catch it, and it fell to the ground in a flash of gold and emerald.

"There," said Guinevere. "That's all that remains of the Duskmaven's Parure. The other pieces must be at the bottom of the ocean by now. So it should be quite valuable, because it is the last. More than enough repayment, I think."

Betha was too busy scrabbling through the grass to respond. Illiard soon joined her in her search, blood dripping from his shoulder. Guinevere couldn't deny that, as far as farewells went, this one hurt. But she had to stop asking people for more than what they were willing to give.

"Ready?" Oskar asked her quietly.

"Whenever you are," Guinevere replied.

He coaxed Vindicator into a brisk trot, Pudding following happily, and the four of them left it all behind.

THEY TOOK THE MEANDERING ROUTE back to the Wuyun Gates, skirting around the edges of civilization. It was a nice day, and they were in no rush.

When they reached a field of wildflowers, Guinevere tugged at Oskar's sleeve. "We should probably change."

He was, after all, still in his blood-soaked, soot-stained, salt water–crusted clothes, and her evening gown was faring no better, which had earned them no small number of confounded stares as they'd made their way out of Nicodranas.

Oskar looked around. "Here?"

"Why not?" Guinevere loftily challenged. "I can do whatever I want now."

"That doesn't bode well for my future peace of mind," he grumbled.

But he dismounted and then assisted her down without further question. He tethered the horses to a couple of nearby stumps, and, when he'd straightened up from the task, another one of those rare grins was fighting for its freedom against the stern line of his mouth. She was rather looking forward to spending the rest of her days cajoling more smiles out of him.

He grabbed her without warning. The world tilted, and she shrieked as he lifted her with ease despite the heavy gown, one hand tucked under her knees, the other pressed to her spine.

"Oskar!" she cried. "What are you doing?"

"You wanted to change, yes?" He leered at her. "I'm going to help you out of those clothes."

Guinevere laughed, loud and unladylike and joyous, looping her arms around his neck. He carried her through the field of wildflowers and laid her down in the long grass and the blooms like jewels. He stretched out on top of her, covering her with his broad body, kissing his way down her neck. She hummed, low in her throat, reveling in the feel of him.

Oskar paused as his wandering fingers ventured to the back of her gown and found the first complicated clasp. He lifted his head with a scowl, oakmoss brow knitting. "This might take a while."

"It doesn't matter," Guinevere said. The road was long, yet it would always lead back to him. "We have all the time in the world."

His topaz eyes softened. She tugged at the collar of his shirt, drawing him down to her. They were both smiling when their lips met, there beneath the blue sky, amidst the rolling, sun-drenched fields. A gentle breeze blew in from the ocean, and it sounded like a song of forever.

ACKNOWLEDGMENTS

As a huge fan of Critical Role since the Vox Machina days, I still can't believe I got the opportunity to write this book. My unending gratitude to the cast—Matthew Mercer, Laura Bailey, Travis Willingham, Sam Riegel, Marisha Ray, Ashley Johnson, Taliesin Jaffe, and Liam O'Brien—and the crew—Dani Carr, Shaunette DeTie, Niki Chi, Darcy Ross, and Gary Thomas—for trusting me with Oskar and Guinevere's story.

Every book is a team effort, and this is no different. *Tusk Love* would never have been possible without the hard work of the wonderful people over at Penguin Random House—namely, Sarah Peed, Lydia Estrada, Elizabeth Schaefer, Erin Korenko, Jocelyn Kiker, Laura Dragonette, Alexis Flynn, Susan Seeman, Ella Laytham, David Stevenson, Lauren Ealy, and Annie Lowell. Thank you all!

ABOUT THE AUTHOR

THEA GUANZON is the *New York Times* and internationally best-selling author of the Hurricane Wars series. She holds a bachelor of arts in international studies, with a specialization in international politics and peace studies. Aside from being a writer, she is an avid traveler, an enthusiastic fangirl, a dungeon master, and an iced coffee junkie. Born and raised in the Philippines, she currently resides in Metro Manila.

theaguanzon.com
X: @theagwrites
Instagram: @theagwrites

ABOUT THE TYPE

This book was set in Garamond, a typeface originally designed by the Parisian type cutter Claude Garamond (c. 1500–61). This version of Garamond was modeled on a 1592 specimen sheet from the Egenolff-Berner foundry, which was produced from types assumed to have been brought to Frankfurt by the punch cutter Jacques Sabon (c. 1520–80).

Claude Garamond's distinguished romans and italics first appeared in *Opera Ciceronis* in 1543–44. The Garamond types are clear, open, and elegant.